When Eric opened the door of the idling police car, the musty smell of blood rushed out at him. His body tensed. On the passenger's seat, on the seatbelt, on the front dash and the floorboard, was smeared blood.

At first, Eric did not realize what he was looking at. He stood there, one hand on the car door, the other dangling at his side, as his mind processed the image before him. His heart froze in his chest, his ears filled with the roar of the engine.

A police officer slumped in the driver's seat with his throat cut open; blood dripped down his blue uniform like a red bib. Every few seconds, his lips twitched and he gurgled, as if he were trying to speak. The cop's eyes fixed on Eric with a primitive desperation.

He was alive.

But he was also dying fast.

Blood pooling on the officer's lap, that sick coppery odor everywhere, Eric stuck his head further into the car. He didn't know what to do, but he had to do something. He couldn't let the guy sit there and die.

The stench of death roiled in his nostrils. He could almost taste it on his tongue, almost feel the energy draining from the cop's body. The engine sounded even louder now, like the deep growl of some prehistoric beast.

As he leaned into the car, moonlight glinted off something in the passenger's seat. Eric inspected the glimmer and spotted a curved knife, which he had overlooked in his excitement. It extended six inches long with a black handle.

Staring at it, a vision flashed in his mind of himself snatching up the blade and finishing the police officer off. An impulse as strong as any Alcoholic faced gripped him. He almost reached for the knife, the same image of himself slashing the policeman's throat flickering in his head.

Why was he feeling this way? He jerked his hand outside of the car, as if his limb would take on a mind of its own and grab the knife against his will.

In a rare moment of clarity, under that bleeding moon, Eric looked at the policeman and admitted something to himself for the first time in his life. It was the same, familiar feeling he had resisted all his life. He spoke the confession out loud to the dying cop: "I want to kill."

PAST LIVES

by Christopher Kokoski

a BlackWyrm book
Louisville, Kentucky

PAST LIVES

A BlackWyrm Book
BlackWyrm Publishing
10307 Chimney Ridge Ct, Louisville, KY 40299

Printed in the United States of America.

ISBN: 978-1-61318-109-6
LCCN: 2011932191

Cover design by Dave Mattingly

First edition: July 2011

My wife is my biggest supporter and greatest fan,
the love of my life,
and without her none of this would be possible.
Thank you, sweetheart.

Note to readers in Louisville, KY: Geography and street names may have been altered to fit the author's purpose. The hope is that you will be so consumed with the story that you won't even notice!

PROLOGUE

Five minutes before she was assaulted, Rosalie Parker toddled into the chilly, shadow-laden parking garage on 5th Street in Louisville, Kentucky, lugging three plastic bags full of milk, bread and chocolate. *Lots of chocolate.*

With each step she grunted, silently cursing her husband for making her go shopping. For insisting it was good for her health. The gall! "I'm pregnant," she mouthed bitterly to the shadows. "I need my rest."

Dirty fluorescent light poured from the ceiling every ten cars or so, shimmering across the vacant hulls of lifeless machinery, coalescing into strange, urine-yellow pools. The only sounds were the clopping of her shoes against the cement floor, the crinkle of the plastic bags and the soft hum of an air vent moaning in the background. She never heard the attacker.

As she side-stepped a puddle of urine-light, as she passed under a vent, Rosalie tilted her head back to bath in the cool rush, letting the air tousle her short brown curls. She rubbed the bulge under her dress, speaking to her unborn child: "One day you'll get to feel the wind in your face, too."

She had no way of knowing that her words were a terrible kind of false prophesy.

Plastic bags stinging her fingers, she continued to her Rav 4. Everything hurt right now – her feet, her legs, her shoulders. Men had it easy. Shaking her head, she sat the bags down and fished in her pocket for the keys, found them and pressed the automatic button to unlock the trunk.

Heaving the plastic bags into the back of her vehicle, Rosalie decided this was the last time she would go shopping until the baby arrived. Her husband could get off his lazy butt and help out around the house. It would be good for his health.

She snickered at her inside joke and had only partially closed the trunk when something heavy smashed into the back of her head. Her skull cracked. Her vision blurred and for a confused moment the parking garage shattered into a brilliant circus of colors. Crying out, she toppled forward, ramming the bumper of her Rav 4 with her belly.

"My baby," she screamed.

She was hit again, this time on the back of her neck. Pain and shock and fear flooded her body. Rosalie planted her hands on the bumper, shoved herself onto her feet. All she could think about was the life in her womb. The precious, innocent life.

Anger flared through her like a madly blazing torch. She balled her hands into fists and turned to protect herself and her baby. But it was too late. Something metal and solid hammered the side of her head. The young mother crumpled to the cement floor of the parking garage, blood pooling around her head. She felt it rushing out, and with it, her life.

As she laid there, body twisted at an awkward angle, cheek flattened against the cold, filthy floor, someone kneeled next to her. Rosalie tried to speak.

"Shh," the stranger said. "It will all be over soon."

Please God, Rosalie prayed. *Save my baby.*

CHAPTER 1

Darkness.

Pain.

Eric Shooter felt the blow against his face, light but painful. His head lolled to the right.

Another slap. What's going on? Where am I?

"Hey, man, you awake? Buddy, you awake?"

Eric lifted his head, tried to open his eyes. Blinked. Some of the darkness receded, but not all. The blurred image of a man wavered over him like a phantom.

"You awake?"

"Ungh."

Someone slapped him twice again. His head lolled back and forth, his thoughts disjointed and slow, unable to lock onto details that might help him respond appropriately to his present circumstance. The ghost morphed into a somewhat humanoid figure.

"You awake?" the specter asked.

Eric blinked and more of the darkness receded. "What? What's happening?"

A stocky man with a moustache bent over him. "I'm Detective James Wolfe. You're in the hospital. You passed out. We have a dead pregnant woman over there. I'm taking you downtown. Capeesh?"

There was no time to respond, no time for questions or for clearing his mind. Eric barely had time to change clothes before being whisked out of the hospital and packed into the back of a police cruiser. Twenty minutes later, he was stashed away in a small "interview" room at the Louisville Metro Police Department in downtown Louisville, KY. He'd seen enough movies to know that the window-sized mirrors meant this conversation was anything but private.

Detective James Wolfe lumbered around the steel table on which he had just laid four photographs of a woman. Eric turned away from the images and fought the urge to puke. It was too late.

He didn't think he'd ever rid his mind from those cruel, bloody pictures.

"Look at them," Wolfe said, grabbing Eric's face and twisting it back to the pictures. "You did it. So look at it."

Eric shoved his metal chair back – *screeeeech* – and wrenched his head out of Wolfe's hands. "I didn't kill her."

Wolfe laughed. "You were the only one there."

"I was passed out." Eric shrugged his shoulders, sighed. "I've already told you that."

He'd been over this same story nine or ten times. What more did this guy want?

"You could have made yourself pass out after you bashed her brains in."

Standing up, Eric glanced at the only door out of the cramped room, his hope against hope that was really no hope at all. "Yeah, that was my brilliant escape plan. I guess you figured it all out," he said mockingly. "I didn't do anything and I want to go home."

"Sit down. You're not going anywhere."

Eric glanced at the detective, easily twice his weight, and at the other officer leaning against the wall – with his weasel-thin face and blank expression he was more decoration than backup. There was no way he could get past the burly detective, so he sat back down, folded his hands on the table and forced himself to take a second, longer look at the pictures.

"Again, I don't know who killed this lady, but I didn't. Again, I was passed out. Again, I don't know why. I don't know what you want me to say, but that's the truth and no matter how many times or how many ways you ask, the truth isn't going to change."

Detective Wolfe stared at him for a long moment, the sides of his mouth curving upward in a half grin. "That was a good speech, but I know you did it, son. I just haven't proved it yet. But you killed that woman in the wrong city. *My city.*"

Eric closed his eyes, shaking his head. This was insane. He was innocent. But how could he prove it? He willed him mind to think. There had to be a way. There was always a way.

When Eric opened his eyes, Wolfe was tugging at his brown mustache. He wore black slacks, a white dress shirt and a black and white checkered tie. For some reason, his face looked familiar.

"There's got to be something that proves I didn't do it. Video, fingerprints, something." Scenes from *CSI* and *Law and Order* flashed through his mind. Eric watched the detective for any hint of support or encouragement. He didn't see any.

The detective plopped down in the metal chair across the table from him. At first he remained silent, brooding, fixing him with the dark, beady eyes of his canine namesake. The way he compulsively tugged at his moustache reminded Eric of some sheriff from the old West. Except he looked more like a linebacker than a sheriff.

"I'm having the body checked for fingerprints. And I've already seen the video. You're not on it."

Eric beamed, spirits suddenly up. "Then there's no proof that I was even involved. So I'm off the hook."

Wolfe shook his head. "Not so fast, Sparky." His brown eyes never left Eric's green ones. "You were the only one there. That makes you the prime suspect or the only witness. Either way, I can keep you as long as I want."

"But I didn't see anything. The last thing I remember is climbing out of my car."

"Doesn't matter."

Eric slung his hands up in the air. "Doesn't matter?"

"When you consider one thing," Wolfe added, raising a single finger.

Eric laid his hands back on the table, fingers almost touching the photos of the dead woman. He leaned forward. "And that would be?"

Wolfe reached into his back pocket, where most guys kept a wallet, and retrieved a white envelope; out of it, he brought a photograph, which he placed next to the others.

Eric stared at the new picture, his jaw dropping. He blinked, not believing his own eyes. How could that be? It didn't make any sense.

The photo showed a close up of the woman's stomach, her dress thrown back, exposing naked flesh. On her belly, in large, jagged letters, was carved a single word.

Eric.

CHAPTER 2

Reeling with mixed emotions of fear and confusion, Eric waited in the interrogation room for a technician to return with a polygraph instrument.

Eric stared at his hands, shook his head. Why would his name be carved on the stomach of a dead woman? Why was he passed out? He had no answers. He agreed to a polygraph exam only because he knew he was innocent; and he would prove it, one way or another.

Anger flared up his spine. Why was this happening to him? What would his parents think? Or his coworkers?

When the door to the interrogation room swung open, a man in a dress shirt and red tie marched in holding a large black bag. He placed the bag on the table, unzipped it, and took out a laptop computer and a tangle of black wires.

"That doesn't look like the machines on the movies," Eric said, wriggling in the steel chair.

The technician raised one bushy eyebrow. "Nervous?"

"Wouldn't you be if you were accused of murder?"

The man shrugged his shoulders. "Never happened to me."

Eric watched as the man, who had not introduced himself, strapped a blood pressure cuff around his right bicep. Then two rubber tubes around his chest and abdomen. He called them pneumographs. Lastly, the technician attached fingerplates to two fingers on Eric's left hand.

"So how does this work?" Eric asked.

Hooking the laptop up to a small metal box and to a plug in the wall, the technician said, "I'll ask you questions and you'll answer them truthfully or I'll know you're lying."

Eric frowned. He had no way of knowing if the man was telling the truth; his only experience with lie detectors came from cop shows on T.V. or the movies.

When the technician finished setting up the equipment, he sat down across from Eric on another steel chair. Eric stared at the table where the pictures of the murdered woman had been and tried not to see her carved belly in his head.

"Okay," the man said, "I'm Officer Graham. I'm going to ask you a few questions. No biting your tongue, lips, or cheeks. Got it?"

Eric fidgeted in his chair. "Why not?"

"It'll mess up the test. And take off your shoes."

"My shoes?"

"Did I mumble?"

"Why?"

"In case you have any tacks inside them."

"Tacks... in my shoes?" What was with these people?

Officer Graham nodded, and when Eric had removed his shoes, said, "Let's get started. Here's the first question: Is your name Eric Shooter?"

"Yes."

Eric glanced at the wall-length mirror which dominated the left wall and wondered if Detective Wolfe was standing behind it, watching.

"Are you 24 years old?"

"Correct."

Officer Graham looked at the screen, nodded, and then went on to the next question.

"Do you work for The Courier-Journal Newspaper?"

"Yes."

"In telemarketing?"

"It's called Outbound Sales now, but yes."

"Have you ever lied about anything in your life?"

Eric paused. "Yes. I'm sure I have, but..."

"A simple yes or no is fine."

Eric nodded. "Yes."

"Were you at the 5th Street parking garage last night around 9:30 PM?"

"Yes." Eric twisted in his chair. His head itched.

"Have you ever stolen anything in your life?"

Eric paused, considered how to answer the question, and then said, "Yes."

"Did you kill Rosalie Parker?"

"No." This time there was no hesitation.

Eric noticed that Officer Graham leaned toward the monitor when he responded, and took a longer time to move onto another question.

"Did you pass out in the parking garage?"

"Yes."

"Before or after you killed Rosalie?"

Eric glared at the officer. "I didn't kill her."

Officer Graham nodded and almost imperceptibly glanced at the wall-length mirror. "Did you see a woman in the parking garage?"

"I didn't see anyone."

Another long pause, then, "Did you make yourself pass out?"

"No. I don't know why I passed out."

Officer Graham drummed his fingers on the steel table. "This will be the last question using the polygraph."

"Shoot."

Officer Graham raised an eyebrow.

"By that I mean go ahead."

"Uh-huh. Have you ever killed anyone?"

The image of Rosalie's sunken skull, of her mangled right ear, and of his name etched into her pregnant abdomen flashed through his head. His fingers felt sweaty, his mouth dry. In his chest, his heart doubled its regular pace.

"No," he answered.

Watching the screen, the technician's fingers stopped in the middle of drumming. His eyes widened. "You're lying."

CHAPTER 3

The interrogation lasted another three hours, Detective Wolfe firing off questions in machine-gun fashion, one after another, while the other officer continued to lean passively against the wall. Eric answered the questions the best that he could, which usually meant not really answering them at all. He was passed out and remembered nothing about the apparent homicide.

At the exact moment when, exhausted to the brink of insanity, Eric seriously considered confessing to the entire bloody crime, Wolfe finally sighed and stood up. "Stay put," he said. "I'll be right back." Twenty minutes later he returned. "Okay, the semi-good news is that the polygraph test indicated that you might have been passed out the whole time like you said."

Eric leaped to his feet. "I've been trying to tell you that all day."

Detective Wolfe raised a hand in a not-so-fast gesture. "But that doesn't mean you're free and clear. The polygraph also indicated that you might have killed someone in the past. Even if it hadn't, you might know more about what happened during the crime than you think. I'm ordering some more tests done. Officer Jones here will take you home. In the morning you have an appointment with a Dr. Samantha Jones, hypnotherapist."

"Hypnosis?" Eric asked, stunned. "Is this a joke?"

"No," Wolfe said. "And if you don't cooperate fully, I'll charge you with interfering with a criminal investigation."

Eric looked to the other officer, expecting him to grin, slap his hip and say, "Gotcha." But the man simply averted his eyes.

Shaking his head, Eric said, "I'll cooperate. I'll just need to call my work and straighten it out with them."

At his apartment in New Albany, IN, Eric took a deep breath and dialed the Courier-Journal. His boss, Mr. Sanchez, picked up on the third ring. Did the man ever leave work? Eric gave him a quick summary of the circumstances, stuttering in his nervousness. He left out the part about the hypnotism. "So, what's going to happen to my job?"

Silence.

"Mr. Sanchez?"

"Yes, um, look, Eric, I'll okay the absence so long as you provide proof of your cooperation with the police. Of course, depending on how long the investigation lasts your position can not be guaranteed upon your return." It sounded like he was reading from a piece of paper.

"Are you serious? I'm one of the top Outbound Sales reps."

"Sorry, Eric, I'm just following company policy."

Eric hung up and stomped around his apartment until he calmed down. Not only was he accused of murder, he might also lose his job. This was tuning out to be one piece of good news after another.

And the appointment tomorrow baffled him. What could a hypnotherapist reveal about the case? Eric knew little about hypnosis, except for a guy that performed at his high school during his junior year. That hypnotist snapped his fingers and ten people seated in a semi-circle behind him slumped in their chairs.

As Eric locked his apartment door, he pictured the prom queen squawking like a baboon while two of his other classmates swatted imaginary spiders off their heads. He went to his bedroom and flicked on the light.

Undressing, he piled his boot cut jeans and blue tee shirt next to the mattress on the floor, killed the lights, and lay down. When he closed his eyes, he saw the dead woman in his mind.

Shivering, he jumped up, turned the light back on and checked the front door. Locked. After he poured himself a cup of white grape juice, he checked the lock again.

Out of the corner of his eye, he swore he saw the dead lady standing on his porch, her blood-drained hands pressed against the glass door. Eric ran to his bedroom and slammed the door behind him. This time, when he lay down on his mattress, he kept the lights on.

Since he couldn't sleep, he sipped the glass of white grape juice and thought about the last two days. Shopping in downtown Louisville. Packing his bags in the backseat of his Nissan Sentra, climbing into his car. Why did he get back out? As much as he wracked his brain, he just could not remember now. But he had gotten out, that much was fact. And then he fainted. He woke up in University Hospital but Detective Wolfe convinced the doctors to transfer him to the police station, where he was interrogated about a murder, and took a polygraph test. Tomorrow he would be hypnotized. The whole thing seemed like a dream, something that might happen in a movie, but not in real life. *Not to him.*

He thought about calling his parents, but decided against it at the last moment. What would he say? Hey, Mom, how's the factory treating ya? Really, that's good. Pa still drinking like a fish? Oh, by the way, I'm the lead suspect in a murder case. Yeah, and it gets even better: the woman I supposedly killed was pregnant.

He placed his glass down on the floor beside the mattress, pulled his blanket tighter around his body, and turned toward the wall.

Five hours later, when Eric finally fell asleep, his dreams were haunted by memories of a past he could not remember, of Rosalie's pale, dead fingers reaching out for him in the dark, and of the secret he feared would be revealed in the morning.

Detective James Wolfe parked his car behind Molly Malone's, an Irish Pub on Bardstown Road in Louisville. When he was sure nobody was watching him, he got out, locked the car, and slipped inside through the open back door.

Thirty minutes earlier, in the middle of a conversation with Chief of Police John Baxter, his informant had called on his cell phone.

"I've got some juicy info for you," the familiar troll-like voice told him.

"Where?"

"Molly Malone's."

"Thirty minutes," James said.

James cut the meeting short with Chief Baxter, something he was happy to do, and hurried to Bardstown Road. With no fingerprints on the body, or in the crime scene for that matter, no video of the crime, no hair fibers or any other trace evidence, and the only witness passed out at the crime scene, he was in no mood to discuss the case.

He entered Molloy Malone's, welcoming the cool air thrust at him by the vents in the ceiling. All the sounds of a bar at noon assaulted him at once – the droll of two wall-mounted televisions suspended over the U-shaped bar, the tinkling of silverware, and the chatter of bored waitresses leaning against the wall, gossiping.

The nearly vacant pub made easy work of spotting Brandon. He perched at a corner booth, head buried in a menu, sipping a bottle of Bud light. A cigarette burned in a handcrafted clay ashtray in the middle of the table. James crossed the bar and sat down.

Brandon kept his head bowed but rolled his eyes up to look at his guest. Under a greasy spit of black hair, his eyes shimmered blue-gray. He wore a black suit, like he always did. James guessed he had a closet full – all identical.

James, himself, dressed in a casual green polo and khakis. He bridged his arms on the table. "So what do you have for me?"

Brandon took a chug of his Bud Light and seemed to ignore the foamy drops left on his mouth. For a guy who wore suits every day, he was pretty much a slob.

He cut right to the chase. "I heard something about the guy that killed your wife and kid."

James' pulse jumped. He leaned over the table and would not have been more interested in a cure for cancer. The moments of silence – because they were certainly only moments – stretched out like an eternity before Brandon answered.

"But before I tell you..." His trollish voice trailed off. He lifted his head, grinned.

James, frowning, took five twenties out of his wallet. He curled his upper lip, thinking of all the sordid ways the scrawny guy would blow the money. Laying the cash on the table, but not releasing his tight grip, he waited for his informant to speak.

"I've doubled my price," Brandon said quickly, then jerked back as if Wolfe might strike him.

"What?" James gripped his stack of twenties in his hand and pounded the table. "You're crazy."

The bartender and two waitresses glanced over at them. James bit his bottom lip, settling on his cushioned bench seat, his heart a live wire in his chest. He wanted to reach over and pound Brandon's face. In his mind, he did worse. Much worse.

Brandon puffed at his cigarette. "I'm only crazy to let you rip me off. You'd pay triple to find the guy who murdered your wife. I should make you pay even more than that because she was pregnant."

In an instant, he was there. Kneeling on the bathroom floor where he found his wife, hands wet with her blood as he rocked her lifeless body back and forth, back and forth...

James felt tears brim at the corner of his eyes, but he refused to cry in front of this weasel.

"This is what's going to happen," he said, voice lowered to a growling whisper. "Tell me what you know or I'll rip your teeth out."

Brandon's smile faded. He leaned back in his seat, clearly shaken by the threat. "Okay, Okay. Whatever."

James glared at him.

"I said okay. Good grief. Okay, so this guy I met told me he did time with your guy. They called your guy, The Russian, because he sort of looked like that guy off Rocky. You know the guy, right? He says he'd talk to you."

"What does he want?"

"You to help him with a parole hearing."

"What's his name?"

Brandon slid a business card across the table. It was flipped upside down and had a name and address scribbled on it. James threw the stack of twenties in Brandon's face and snatched the business card off the table as he bolted for the back door.

CHAPTER 4

Eric arrived at 300 Emery Road in the backseat of a gray police cruiser, his first time in a cop car in years – the last time resulting from a misunderstanding between himself, a couple of bottle rockets and a drunken clown. As soon as the vehicle parked against the curb, he thanked the driver and hopped out.

As he ambled up to the two story house, with its low slanted roof, brick chimney, and English cottage décor, Eric couldn't help but feel like he was in a fairytale about to meet a witch. However, the slim-bodied brunette that answered the door was nothing like the scraggly wart-nosed legends. She wore a red dress and matching red-heels, extended her hand and introduced herself.

"Dr. Samantha Jones. You must be Eric. Come on in."

Nodding, Eric followed her into the house, closed the door behind him, noticing that the police officer was still at the curb, staring at him. The door shut with a soft *thud*.

Samantha led him into a large living room, furnished with deep brown rugs and a matching over-sized living room set. Paintings, mostly of couples strolling down city streets, huddled together under big umbrellas, smiling and trying to avoid the rain adorned most of the walls. On the wall behind the couch, three dark walnut plaques displayed a degree in Hypnotherapy, and membership in the National Society of Clinical Hypnotherapists and the American Society of Clinical Hypnosis.

"If you want anything to drink, I have some bottled water in the fridge. If not, we'll get started," Dr. Jones said, settling into one of the chairs.

Eric shook his head and chose the sofa, into which he immediately sunk three inches. It had to be the most comfortable couch on which he'd ever sat. With the lights in the room turned low, the smell of incense wafting in the cool air, and his troubled sleep last night, at least maybe he would get a good nap out of this experience.

Dr. Jones crossed her legs. "Have you ever been to a hypnotherapist?"

"No," Eric said. He hesitated, then added: "And I thought you should know up front that I really don't believe in it."

Dr. Jones raised her eyebrows. "Then why are you here?"

Eric thought about the dead woman with his named scratched into her stomach. "I'd let you sprinkle fairy dust on me if it would get the detective off my back."

"James isn't all that bad. This case is just really important to him." Dr. Jones tilted her head, spilling some of her brown hair over her face. "Anyway, I'm all out of fairy dust."

Eric found himself laughing and wondering why she wasted such charm on this New Age nonsense.

"You know," she said, "Hypnosis is used by dentists, doctors and therapists every day to help clients relieve stress, lose weight or stop smoking. In fact, people are hypnotized several times a day without ever realizing it."

Eric was half listening as he read the titles of books on her bookshelf – Eriksonian Hypnosis, Edgar Cayce, Induction Techniques. None of them rang any bells.

As Dr. Jones explained in detail how their session would go, Eric looked at her blue eyes and her plump lips and her long legs.

"Hypnosis is really just a heightened state of awareness," he heard her say.

It certainly was so far, he thought, as he stared at her mouth. She should be a model or on commercials. Not hiding in this dark house with her magic mumbo-jumbo.

"Are you okay?"

Eric blinked twice. "What?"

"I said, are you okay?"

"Peachy."

"Okay, then let's begin. I want you to close your eyes and imagine a relaxing place, like the beach. Feel the breeze roll over your skin, smell the salt water in the air, enjoy the warm sun on your skin. Hear the slow, monotonous roll of the waves."

Warmth floated up from his feet, quickly dispersing to the rest of his body.

"You slip deeper and deeper into a state of complete relaxation..."

Eric breathed deeply. He did feel relaxed. But he wasn't hypnotized. No way would he bounce around like a baboon on command.

"It's not working," he mumbled, as Dr. Jones led him down a mental set of stairs. When he got to the bottom, his chin slumped to his chest.

He was in trance and the questions began.

CHAPTER 5

Detective James Wolfe sat across from the prisoner, who wore a prison-issued orange jump suit and slouched in his chair. Freddie Williams was two days late for a shave, his expression hardened by years behind bars.

Resting his forearms on the steel table, James glanced at the security guard leaning against the wall, puffing away at a cigarette, not looking in their direction.

"I'm told you have information for me."

"I'm told you can help me with parole."

"Maybe. Depends on what you got."

The prisoner nodded.

"What can you tell me about my wife's murderer?"

Freddie raised his eyebrows, chewed on his bottom lip. "You don't beat around the bush do you?"

"I don't have the time."

"I have all the time in the world." He looked up at the ceiling, as if planning a way to fly out of here. "Man, what I wouldn't give to *not* have time."

James held in a lecture about making different decisions, about personal responsibility and getting what you deserve. "If you tell me what you know, maybe you can have no time again."

Freddie lowered his gaze from the ceiling. "Sure, man. I get it."

"What do you know, Freddie?"

"The Russian, the one who killed your wife, and I..." he paused, as if searching for the right words. "We became friends."

"Nice friend."

Freddie snorted. "Yeah, well, he and I, we been the same places, if you know what I mean."

If he meant *prison*, then James knew.

"How do I know you won't just leave me in here after I tell you?"

"You don't. But it's the best chance you've got."

Freddie nodded. He leaned forward, whispering, as if the prison bugged the visitation room. The result of too many drugs,

James thought. Too many years looking over his shoulder for boogey men. Except, his boogey men were real and everywhere.

"The Russian is in the Mid-West. He's driving a 1985 green Volkswagen Van. You can't miss it."

"How do you know?"

"I just know."

"How?"

"Why does it matter?"

"It matters."

For a moment, they just stared at each other. Freddie shrugged his shoulders. "Whatever, man. The Russian's brother. Aleksei. I've known him since he was a kid. He told me."

James recognized the name. Big dope dealer on the East Coast. Samantha and he had been instrumental in putting some of his lackeys behind bars a few years ago. That line of questioning would need to be pursued. But not now.

"How does he contact you?"

"Who?"

"The brother. How does he get in touch with you? This is a prison, not the Hilton."

Freddie snorted. "I'd almost forgot."

"So how? Phone? Letters? What?"

"Phone. Only the phone."

Which probably meant letters, too, James thought. "When does he call? Morning? Night?"

"Night. Well, late afternoon."

"Who patches him through?"

"Come on man, I can't tell you everything."

James grabbed Freddie by the palm, bent back his wrist until the pain was evident in the prisoner's face. "You'll tell me or you'll never even see a parole board."

"Okay. Okay," Freddie said, voice pinched. "One of the guards."

"Who?"

"I don't know."

James applied pressure to Freddie's wrist. The prisoner bit his bottom lip until it bled. James eased up. "I really don't know, man. He's tall, Puerto Rican I think."

"Why would a guard help you?"

"I don't know," Freddie said, massaging his wrist. James believed him. Those as low as Freddie on the totem pole generally knew only what was absolutely necessary and little else.

Switching gears, James said, "You told me the guy was in the

Mid-West. What part of the Mid-West?"

Freddie glanced down at his wrist, an unconscious gesture, but James picked up on it. "The Mid-West was all he said."

James wrote all the information down on a note pad he'd brought with him. Then looked back up. "What else?"

Freddie shook his head. "Nothin' else. That's all I got. For now."

The detective narrowed his brow, leaned towards the prisoner in what he hoped was a very threatening gesture, and spoke softly. "My wife. My child. I don't care about anything when it gets in the way of finding the man who murdered them. If you have any other information..."

"I don't have nothin'."

"If he contacts you again..."

"I'll let you know."

CHAPTER 6

Fifteen minutes later, after asking a batch of basic questions, after several more trance deepening exercises, Samantha finally asked about the case.

"Eric, do you remember going to Fourth Street Live on Saturday night?"

"Yes," Eric said, glazed eyes peering into another world.

Samantha glanced down at her notebook, where she had scribbled a list of questions. "Why did you go to Fourth Street?"

"To shop," Eric said. "And eat."

"Do you remember leaving?" Samantha slipped a photograph of the murdered woman while she was alive and smiling out of her notebook. She wondered if Eric had killed her.

"Yes, I remember leaving."

"Can you tell me what happened when you left?"

"I walked out into the parking garage with my bags. Then I got in the car, closed the door, and..."

Samantha looked up at Eric, whose face wrinkled and eyebrows narrowed. "And then what, Eric?"

"And then... I got out of my car."

"Why did you get out of your car?"

Eric stared into nothingness, searching his mind for the right memories. "I... don't remember."

Samantha sat up straighter in her chair, uncrossed her legs, and leaned forward. "Do you remember anything – something you heard or felt?"

His face twisted once again in the struggle to remember. Eric shook his head.

"Something's blocking your memory. Do you know what that something is?"

When Eric remained silent for a moment, Samantha thought he either did not know or could not remember. Yet, she must discover what was blocking Eric's memory so she could move past it.

"Yes, something in my past."

Shocked, Samantha blinked and stared at him. "In your childhood, Eric? Something in your childhood?"

"No."

"But you said it was in your past. Are you sure it's not something in your childhood?"

Eric said, "I'm sure."

Samantha's body tingled with adrenaline. Leaning further towards him, perched on the edge of her oversized-chair, she could think of only one solution: something had happened to Eric in the first stages of his life, maybe even the first few months. Something that affected him even twenty-four years later.

"Did it happen to you when you were very little? When you were just born?"

Her heart thundered in her chest as she awaited his answer. Could this be a breakthrough?

"No," Eric said, deflating her hopes.

Samantha sat back in her chair, breathing slowly and deeply. "If it's not in your childhood and not when you were just born, then when did it happen?"

Eric's face suddenly changed form. She could not describe it in any other way. It just... transformed. Not in a magical way. More like he was an actor switching from one role to another. His chin jutted out, his cheekbones lifted, his eyelids fluttered. And when he answered, he grinned.

"Before that," he said.

Samantha choked. "Before that? Before *what*?"

Eric was still grinning when he answered: "Before I was born."

CHAPTER 7

After alerting police stations across the Mid-West about the green VW van, Detective James Wolfe drove to his three-story house in the Highlands, the one his wife had picked out after they got married.

Unlocking his front door, James walked inside and relocked the door behind him. Even in the Highlands, danger loomed around each beautiful spruce or behind every new Porsche. Wealth, reputation and power didn't protect you from the crazies anymore. If it ever did.

Although his stomach grumbled, James avoided the kitchen and headed directly to the den, a spacious, darkly decorated area of the otherwise bright and cheerful house. Second Empire style, the house emanated an almost spooky reaction from most visitors, who predictably oohed and aahed over the square-shaped roofs, wide eaves, balconies and bay windows. On the far side of the den, James opened the back door to the thrilled cries of his two Pit Bulls, Napoleon and Caesar.

The two dogs scrambled up to the house, leaping at him, covering his hands and arms with excited licks. "Down boys," James said, laughing. "You two are supposed to be vicious attack dogs."

Napoleon and Caesar danced around him, tongues dangling out of their mouths. James rubbed their heads and scratched behind their ears and told them how great they were the entire time. They, in turn, raised their heads toward his hands, each fighting for his undivided attention.

"Let's go get you some grub," he said.

Napoleon and Caesar rushed for the kitchen, almost knocking James down, yelping in approval of their master's genius.

Smiling, James followed them into the kitchen, dumped dog food into two large red dog bowls, each imprinted with the respective canine's name. Napoleon and Caesar dove for the delicious feast. James leaned against the sink, watching.

On the windowsill, above the sink, stood a picture of his wife, seven-months pregnant and loving it. In the photo she was making a funny face at the camera, complete with crossed eyes and protruded tongue. Distracted by his pets, he had – for a little while, at least – forgotten about the criminals, about the case without any leads, and about the revenge he so desperately craved. Now all three things crashed back over him like pit bulls; and this time, he was knocked down.

Where would he go now on the current murder case? He had to solve it quickly. He needed time to focus on his wife's case. Maybe the hypnotherapy would reveal something. He sure hoped so.

He looked back at the photo on the sink and thought about the last day he was with his wife: the two of them chatting about nothing in particular over a couple of Starbucks' Caramel Lattes – well, his was a real latte; she, being pregnant, just pretended her Green Tea Lemonade contained caffeine. Picking up the picture, he pressed it against his burly chest. Contrary to what the singers and poets all promised, time had not healed his wounds. Not even close.

Someone had to pay. Pay hard.

Speaking to the picture through teeth gritted in anger, as if his wife could hear him, and he thought maybe she did, he said, "I'll catch the man who killed you and our son. No matter what I have to do. I promise."

CHAPTER 8

"Reincarnation?"

Eric paced the brown carpet in the living room, holding his head with both hands, feeling dizzy and confused and sick. When he reached the end of the carpet, he spun on his heels and treaded back across.

"It's not unheard of—" Dr. Jones started to say.

"Not unheard of?" Eric stopped and stared at her like she had just sprouted wings. His hands dropped to his sides. "It's reincarnation."

Dr. Jones sat in her over-sized chair, legs uncrossed, hands in her lap. "I know it's confusing."

"Confusing? It's not confusing. It's ridiculous!" Eric marched the length of the brown carpet, pivoted, and strolled to the opposite side. A dense, suffocating heat smothered his entire body. In his chest, his heart thumped a double-time cadence to his march across the carpet.

The house was quiet and cool and cozy. After the hypnotherapy session, the doctor had turned on brighter lights, chasing the surviving shadows into the corners of the living room.

"There are many intriguing stories of people who claim to be reincarnated. There are thousands of people who believe in it. It's a world-wide phenomenon."

Eric said nothing, only continued pacing the carpet, back and forth, back and forth.

"There was just a story in the news a few months ago about a guy in Europe, Germany I think. Anyway, he woke up from a year-long coma and could inexplicably speak perfect Japanese, even though he'd never taken a class or visited Japan in his life. Doctors can't explain it."

Eric didn't slow his monotonous, animal-like movements across her living room. The wheels were spinning in his head, and he felt like a volcano about to erupt.

"Let's talk about it," Dr. Jones said. She brushed a few strands of brown hair from her face.

"I'm sorry," Eric finally said, "But I can't do this. I don't believe in this."

He ended his walk, stuffed his hands in his pockets, and looked at the carpet. This was crazy. It didn't make sense. It ended now.

Dr. Jones stood up, came to him, and placed a gentle hand on his arm. A shiver shot though his body, confusing him even more. Forcing the shiver away, Eric glanced at her hand on his arm, both wanting to pull away from her and to enjoy her touch.

"I felt the same way when I first learned about it," she said. "But once I understood it better, reincarnation made sense."

Biting his lip, he stepped away from her. "I don't want to understand it. I just want to prove my innocence."

Eric edged towards the hallway that led to the front door. He could ask the police officer for a ride back home and then he would call Detective Wolfe and tell him he was through. It was over. He had played nice with the nut job hypnotist. It just wasn't his bag of beans.

She took hold of his arm, and her hand slipped down to his wrist as he turned back towards her. "But I think it *will* prove your innocence, Eric."

In her eyes, Eric read honesty and determination and hope. Three traits he rarely encountered these days. He didn't need a polygraph test to know that she truly wanted to help him. But why?

Not knowing why, wondering if he was crazy, he let her lead him back to the couch, where they both sat down. She let go of his wrist.

"I think it's more than that," Dr. Jones said. "I think it's the key to everything you ever wanted to know about yourself."

As Eric finished his second cup of hot tea, Samantha peered through her blinds at the patrol car parked across the street from her house. Earlier in the day, James had told her about the dope dealer and the Puerto Rican guard who was MIA. He had insisted on the extra security. As she wondered what might be out there in the dark, Eric coughed and she caught herself jumping.

Turning away from the blinds, Samantha said, "Okay, let's get started with tonight's session." She put him into a trance again. This time, with Eric's consent, he went under more quickly. And deeper. She waited to begin her investigation until his breathing slowed, his muscles relaxed, and his eyes rolled upward, leaving only the whites visible.

One of the common misconceptions about hypnosis, she knew,

was that it is a form of meditation or sleep, requiring closed eyes; but although the term Hypnosis comes from the Greek word, *Hypnos*, which literally means sleep, hypnosis does not require relaxation, and can be done with eyes wide open.

"I want you to go back in time, back to when you were a child, age five or six. You are yourself as a young child now."

"I am a child now," Eric droned like a robot.

Although dating clients went against her policies of a therapist-client relationship, she couldn't help but notice how handsome he looked slumped in her couch. Hint of a beard on his chin. Clear green eyes the color of emeralds. The way the collar of his shirt hung low she had a clear view of his neckline, and of a tiny mole between his neck and collarbone.

Could he really be a cold-blooded killer? He had shown no propensity toward lying, and she knew that most people, without intervention, acted normally under hypnosis.

"Now I want you to go further back, to when you were a baby. You go back now."

"I go back," Eric repeated.

The dim light splashing over his face, the gentle curve of his chin, the baby-like complexion... she shook her head. Ok, she thought, I've been attracted to several of my clients and I've always resisted my impulses. Now was not the time to break that track record.

She could still think he was handsome. No harm in window-shopping.

"Further back to when you were just born, further back."

"Further back," Eric said.

Samantha glanced around the dark living room. Too many shadows looked oddly shaped, warning signs of monsters lurking near. She wondered if she had locked the door.

Wanting to pick up the phone to make sure she still heard a dial tone, that no one had cut the wires before breaking in and hacking her to pieces, she silently berated herself for being paranoid.

"Now, I want you to go back into the womb, keep going back, further and further."

"Into the womb," Eric mumbled.

"Good," Samantha said. She was glad Eric didn't know this was her first time doing a past life regression.

In hypnotherapy school she had studied it and believed in it, but she got into this practice to help people overcome fears, lose weight and deal with pain. Not to introduce them to their former lives. Like all areas of hypnosis, regression was often shrouded in controversy because of the fear of false or created memories. She would have to be very careful.

It was time.

"Now I want you to go even further back, back to before you were born, way back to who you were before you were born."

CHAPTER 9

The call came to Detective James Wolfe at three O'clock in the morning. Still bleary-eyed from sleep, rubbing his face with one hand, he answered the phone. He recognized the voice at once: Chief of Police, John Baxter.

"Wolfe, sorry to call you so early..."

"No problem. What happened?"

"There's been another murder. Same MO as the person who nixed the pregnant woman in the parking lot. Looks like we have a serial killer on our hands."

"Where?" James asked.

"1023 Allison Lane."

"On my way."

James dressed quickly in the dark: blue jeans and a Sigma Chi Fraternity shirt he still kept from his college days. Five minutes later, he pulled out of his driveway in his Saab, and sped out of the Highlands, towards Allison Lane.

He heard the crime scene before he saw it: sirens shrieked against the otherwise quiet night, rattling through a neighborhood not known for homicide. But in his years as a detective, James had learned that no one was safe, not anywhere.

Parking his car, he strolled past a few police officers pressing back a growing crowd of onlookers. Yellow crime scene tape stretched across the street and surrounded a single-story house: gray brick with a tiled roof, trimmed front yard vacant of foliage. James headed towards it.

At the front door, a Medical Examiner greeted him. He had a flat nose that hooked over a small, feminine mouth.

"This way, Detective. It's ghastly."

"That's a compliment coming from you," James said as he followed the white-coated and latex-gloved man into the back bedroom.

Every light in the house seemed to be turned on. James heard soft chatting, so he guessed only the essential professionals had been called out this early in the morning. He noted that Chief

Baxter was absent.

In the bedroom, spread out on a king-sized bed, two women lay naked and butchered. Both were pregnant. James covered his nose and mouth with one hand. His heart felt like it had dropped into his stomach.

Pointing at the bodies, he said, "Were they here when you found them?"

"Yes," the Medical Examiner said, nodding his head. "And that's where they were killed, too, in case you were going to ask. Strange, huh?"

"Thanks. And—"

The Medical Examiner cut in. "They both died from blunt objects to the back of the head." Then, darting his eyes from the bodies to the detective: "Their skin was flayed open after they were dead."

James looked at the dead women. From their ankles to their thighs, and from their wrists to their shoulders, both women's skin was slit and muscle rolled back, exposing the bone.

"What about—"

"Someone carved a name on both abdomens. Same one as before. Eric."

"Ti—"

"Time of death is 11:00 P.M., last night."

James wanted to slug the guy, but controlled himself. "I'd appreciate if you didn't interrupt me again."

"Sorry." The Medical Examiner huffed, shot him a not-nice look, and walked off. "Don't ask me for any more information, then," he said as he left.

I never got a chance to ask anyway, James thought. "Wait," he said.

The medical examiner spun around, same sour expression on his face, hands on his hips. "What?"

You mean you don't know already? James wanted to say, but restrained himself. Instead, he asked, "Any trace evidence?"

"Yes, there was actually some and if you weren't so rude to me earlier, I might have told you what it was right away. But you messed that all up, now didn't you? I'm tempted to make you read about it with everyone else in my official report. Unfortunately that's illegal. But I can make you wait." He peered at his wrist watch and feigned surprise. "Oh dear. Would you look at the time? I'll be right back."

With that, the Medical Examiner whirled back around with the dramatic flourish of an actor, and vanished into another area of the house.

James hardly noticed. There was trace evidence. A crack in the case. Which meant he was one step closer to closing it and moving back to his family's murder. He almost dropped his cell phone in a frenzy to call the Forensic Investigation Unit of the Louisville Metro Police Department. Wait? Don't be ridiculous. He had ways around moody Medical Examiners.

Trace Evidence.

When someone picked up on the other line, James was nearly salivating. He had to know what they found.

CHAPTER 10

The sudden transformation shook Samantha like an earthquake. Regressing to a past life, Eric's face contorted as it had during their last hypnotherapy session – just as fast, just as frightening, dredging up forgotten memories of Dr. Jekyll and Mr. Hyde.

Taking a deep, cleansing breath to compose herself, Samantha continued the session. This was it. A real past life regression. Her whole body trembled with child-like electricity, as if conducting a regression transported her back to a younger, more vital self, too.

"Can you tell me who you are?" she asked, hands together, fingers entwined to keep them from shaking. A smile extended across Eric's face that, although it felt warm in the dark living room, made her shudder.

"I am many people, Samantha," Eric said. "Many names." It was Eric, but it sounded different. Eric's voice was deeper. The voice that answered her was almost snake-like. The voice of Hannibal Lector.

Samantha swiveled her gaze around the room, sensing something not quite right. Goose bumps popped up on her arms and legs, the back of her neck tingling as if touched by an unseen hand. Half-raised out of her seat, ears absorbing the softest, whispered noises in her house, body tingling on high alert, she stuffed the urge to check if the police officer remained outside. *Stop it. You're not going to screw this up.*

"What do you mean, you are many people?" she asked, voice balanced and controlled.

Eric answered in that same slithering voice: "I have been many people. I have lived many lives. To which one do you refer?"

Samantha contemplated the man sitting on her couch. A moment ago, she thought she knew him, at least something about him. Now she felt lost.

"You mean reincarnation? You have been reincarnated many times?" Her eyes wide and her heart racing, she listened. *This is it,* she thought. *Here it comes.*

"You're a fast one, aren't you, Samantha?"

Stung by the comment, but unrelenting, Samantha asked, "How many lives have you lived?" This was incredible. *Incredible.*

"Hundreds."

"How do you know that?" Samantha perched her elbows on her knees.

"How do you know you are alive? How do you know that thinking exists? How do you know that while you sleep soundly and comfortably at night that somewhere out there a black terror lurks, watching and waiting? You just know."

For a moment, all she could do was sit and stare at him, like the climate in her living room had suddenly shifted and frozen her to her chair. Scrambling for her notebook because she forgot what to ask next, she held it in front of her and read the questions.

The case. Caught up in the excitement of the moment, she forgot the objective of this session: to find out why Eric could not remember the murder of Rosalie Parker.

Hundreds of lives.

She picked a question at random. "In your life before becoming Eric, who were you?" She was hoping to discover some clue to break into Eric's memory. First, however, she would have to deal with whatever blocked it.

"Much like your intelligence, your question is flawed. I am always the same person."

Samantha frowned. Rubbed her goose-pimpled arms with her hands. "You are always Eric?"

"No. You are too dumb to grasp such a high concept, which is remarkably clear."

"Then tell me what you mean and stop beating around the bush," Samantha snapped back. This voice, whoever it was, was nothing like Eric.

Appearing drugged and buried in the couch, Eric said, "I am always the same person. The same soul. Only the names and the bodily shells change. But, in time, I always become the same thing."

Samantha felt like grabbing him by his shoulders and shaking him. But that would not be fair to Eric. "And what is that?"

When Eric's head rose, Samantha gasped because it seemed like the dark presence inside of him was looking directly at her, peering through space and time with cold, intelligent eyes, that same child-molester's smile etched on his face.

"I always kill people."

CHAPTER 11

Standing on Allison Avenue outside the gray-brick house, next to an ambulance, Detective James Wolf held his cell phone to his ear and listened to the forensic specialist.

"We found a strand of hair. We're running DNA tests now." The voice was of a young woman, professional and cool. It reminded him of his wife when they first met.

"When will you know something?" James spoke into the cell phone.

A strand of hair. Could it really be? Could the same killer who left no evidence at the first crime scene have bungled up this time? Like Thomas sticking his finger into the wounds of Jesus, he would have to see to believe.

Seventeen years of experience taught James that criminals, especially violent ones, always screwed up. It was just a matter of time. Sometimes you had to wait them out because, sooner or later, every one of them left a clue that ultimately convicted them. But he could not help but doubt. The killer they stalked was good, as experienced in killing as James was in investigating. That much he knew without a second opinion.

He did not hear the police cars backing out and leaving; he did not see the ambulance driver stride behind him and climb inside the emergency vehicle. All of his senses concentrated on the silence of the cell phone.

When the woman spoke again, her words rushed forth like the voice of God, minus the blinding spotlight and chorus of singing angels. "Because of the urgency of this case, we are pushing it through faster than normal. We'll have the owner of the hair identified tomorrow morning."

James had to physically keep himself from jumping. "Thanks. See you in the morning." Then he hung up.

CHAPTER 12

When he emerged from the hypnotic trance, the first thing Eric noticed was Dr. Jones's unusual expression – her pale, stiff face drained of all color, widened eyes and slackened jaw reflecting the image of someone who had just seen a ghost waft through the living room.

"What's wrong?"

Dr. Jones said nothing. Just sat there hugging herself, furiously trying to rub the goose bumps from her arms.

She was scared. Terrified. Of me? Of something she learned?

"What happened?" he asked again when she did not answer. Now he felt goose bumps forming on *his* arms.

Finally, shaking her head as if coming out of her own trance, still rubbing her arms, she said, "Sorry, it's just... it's incredible."

Eric sat up even straighter, which was difficult in a couch that seemed determined to swallow him whole. "Tell me."

Pausing again before she spoke, she stood up, looking once again the part of the professional therapist. No longer shaken. No longer scared.

"Don't get upset," she said.

"What happened?" He was upset. How could he not be, how could anyone not be, after a comment like that? Eric joined her, standing on the carpet.

Dr. Jones reached out and touched his arm with her left hand. "You should probably sit down."

"No. Just tell me. What did I say?"

Dr. Jones avoided his eyes, turning her head towards the dim lamp beside the couch, a shadow falling across her face. When he touched her arm, she shivered. *What could be this bad? What could she have found out?*

"Dr. Jones?"

As if her name activated her voice, she turned back towards him. "You have been... reincarnated many times. Hundreds of times."

"What? Are you kidding?"

"No." Her eyes sparkled in the darkened room. He smelled the faint remainder of perfume drifting off her body, something light, sweet.

"There's something else, isn't there?"

Dr. Jones nodded.

"Tell me," he said softly.

This time she shook her head, shaking loose strands of hair into her face. She tucked them behind her ear. His heart jack hammered against his rib cage, not only because of the stunning revelation of his reincarnation, but also because of something else, too. Something he was not ready to admit to himself just yet.

"Tell me," he repeated, and Dr. Jones seemed to force the words out.

"You said you were a serial killer, Eric."

Eric flinched, retreating a step. "What? But I'm not." In his chest, his heart drummed madly for another reason now. "I'm not a serial killer."

"I know," she said, moving towards him. "In your past life."

Eric shook his head as she told him. No. No. NO. "I agreed to do this because you said it would prove my innocence. Now you're telling me that I'm a serial killer. In a past life?"

Dr. Jones, coming closer to him: "In all your past lives."

"What does that mean?" He kept stepping back, shaking his head in perpetual defiance. His whole body felt hot now, full of sharp, mind-numbing adrenaline.

"You said you were a serial killer in every life. That you always became one." Although Eric thought the look in her eyes and on her face was one of concern, not judgment or disgust, he stepped away from her again. He turned towards the hallway.

"Don't go," she pleaded, touching his arm.

He pulled away from her, looking over his shoulder. "Why not? You're not safe with me. I might fall on the floor, thrash around, and turn into a monster."

"I didn't mean it that way." Once again, Dr. Jones advanced towards him.

Not able to stand the look on her face, Eric left her standing in the middle of the living room and stormed down the hallway, out the front door.

CHAPTER 13

Under a blood-red half moon, Eric staggered down the front steps of Dr. Jones' house, swept up by a flood of emotions, dropped on his knees in the front yard and covered his face with his hands.

Warm night air embraced his chilled skin. Eric inhaled the scents of grass and tulips and the coppery hint of approaching rain. Only the sound of chittering insects and the idling police car across the street accompanied the silence. Lights blinked like watchful eyes in the windows of a few neighboring houses.

But Eric would not have cared if he were in the Sahara desert, with nothing but the dry, endless desert for company. His body shook. His eyes teared up, but he rubbed them clean before they wet his face. Kneeling in the front yard, his lungs pumped air in and out, in and out, like an uncontrollable machine.

Disjointed thoughts tumbled through his mind: reincarnation, hundreds of past lives. He became a killer in each one? What did that mean, that he would become one in this life? As much as he denied it, the feelings and memories of his past haunted him.

Had he not suffered enough? All his life, he had felt different. Out of place. And those urges. Urges to break things, to hurt them. The question that he'd asked thousands of times once again found life on his lips. He spoke it into the night air, a prophet expecting an answer from some unearthly power. "Why me?"

Why him? Why had he fought those feelings to hurt people? He had promised himself that he wouldn't harm another person, but secretly those urges crouched inside him, waiting, growing, until one day...

Eric forced himself to stand up. Staring at the sky that did not answer his question, that never answered, he spoke to it anyway. "I'm in control of myself. I choose." It was a phrase one of his counselors had taught him, something to say to himself when those urges tempted him to stray outside the boundaries of normal behavior. Eric guessed it helped. A little. Not enough.

Glancing back at Dr. Jones' house, he sighed. He could not go back in there. The house no longer offered hope or peace, only pain and embarrassment.

He turned his attention to the police car. As he studied it, he noted that all the windows were fogged. Strange, Eric thought, isn't the point of police protection to watch the surroundings for anything suspicious? The guy in the car couldn't see anything but a wall of whiteness.

Wandering out of the front yard, crossing the street, Eric approached the police cruiser. The closer he got, the more worried he became. By the time he arrived at the vehicle, he had convinced himself that something was wrong. Very wrong. Why else were the windows fogged? Why hadn't the police officer cleared them?

Eric took hold of the passenger's side door handle and, with a wary slowness, opened the car door.

CHAPTER 14

Samantha stooped on a barstool in her kitchen, heartbeat thudding as she nursed the frozen margarita she had prepared for herself, recounting the hypnotherapy session, and trying not to cry. She was successful at all but the last objective and fresh, salty tears flowed down her cheeks, onto her neck.

Never before had she experienced anything so fascinating. She felt like she did the first day of hypnotherapy school, six years ago. Or the first time she helped James crack a big case. Or how she would feel if she had three of four more of these margaritas.

Sneaking another sip, Samantha whispered, "Hundreds." Hundreds of lifetimes, centuries of experiences. The thought boggled her mind. And in every life Eric became a killer.

That brought her to the obvious, more practical question: "Was he a killer, now?" She didn't think so. There was no evidence and he had passed the polygraph test. And agreed to hypnotherapy. Only an insane guilty person would agree to all those things. Only an innocent person would pass all with flying colors. Still...

Her thoughts ran in circles. Was he innocent? Didn't he just confess to killing people? Sure, it was in a past life; but, she was not certain that mattered. Something deep inside of her, some ancient remnant of her caveman brain, whispered a silent warning that it did not.

Maybe he is schizophrenic or possessed by the devil, she wondered. Once you accepted past life regression, wasn't anything possible?

CHAPTER 15

When Eric opened the door of the idling police car, the musty smell of blood rushed out at him. His body tensed. On the passenger's seat, on the seatbelt, on the front dash and the floorboard, was smeared blood.

At first, Eric did not realize what he was looking at. He stood there, one hand on the car door, the other dangling at his side, as his mind processed the image before him. His heart froze in his chest, his ears filled with the roar of the engine.

A police officer slumped in the driver's seat with his throat cut open; blood dripped down his blue uniform like a red bib. Every few seconds, his lips twitched and he gurgled, as if he were trying to speak. The cop's eyes fixed on Eric with a primitive desperation.

He was alive.

But he was also dying fast.

Blood pooling on the officer's lap, that sick coppery odor everywhere, Eric stuck his head further into the car. He didn't know what to do, but he had to do something. He couldn't let the guy sit there and die.

The stench of death roiled in his nostrils. He could almost taste it on his tongue, almost feel the energy draining from the cop's body. The engine sounded even louder now, like the deep growl of some prehistoric beast.

As he leaned into the car, moonlight glinted off something in the passenger's seat. Eric inspected the glimmer and spotted a curved knife, which he had overlooked in his excitement. It extended six inches long with a black handle.

Staring at it, a vision flashed in his mind of himself snatching up the blade and finishing the police officer off. An impulse as strong as any Alcoholic faced gripped him. He almost reached for the knife, the same image of himself slashing the policeman's throat flickering in his head.

Why was he feeling this way? He jerked his hand outside of the car, as if his limb would take on a mind of its own and grab the knife against his will.

In a rare moment of clarity, under that bleeding moon, Eric looked at the policeman and admitted something to himself for the first time in his life. It was the same, familiar feeling he had resisted all his life. He spoke the confession out loud to the dying cop: "I want to kill."

As cool relief flooded Eric's body, the police officer's eyes grew wide, and he coughed up a wad of blood, which splattered wet and shiny against the windshield and the steering wheel. Too late for me to do anything for him, Eric thought. He needs an ambulance.

Retreating out of the car, Eric glimpsed something from the corner of his eye. He half-expected to see the dead corpse of the butchered pregnant woman clawing for him out of the shadows.

Four cars to the left, standing under the thick shade of a spruce, he could swear he saw someone in dark clothes. Whoever it was, if it was someone, they were not moving. Eric squinted into the darkness. *Is that a person?*

Inside the police car, the officer hacked again. Eric thought he might be dead, but when he checked, the officer was still breathing. A thought seeped into his mind that made him wish he had not turned his back to look in the car: *The killer could still be close.*

Snapping his head around, certain that the figure in the shadows would be behind him with another knife raised and read to gut him, he saw only the deserted street. Panicked, he dared not search the night for more dangers; instead, he left the car door open and fled back towards Dr. Jones' house.

CHAPTER 16

Sprinting across the street, the front yard, and up the front steps of Dr. Jones' house, Eric feared he'd be shot in the back and die right there on the porch. *What had he seen in the shadows?*

He ripped open the front door and flung himself inside before a second realization stunned him: the killer could have slipped in the house while he was outside.

Gulping air that now seemed too heavy, too dry, Eric stood in the entrance, not sure what to do next. Should he go back outside to find help for the police officer? Or should he search the house for Dr. Jones?

Outside, the cop made a gurgling noise, and, to Eric, it sounded like he vomited. *I have to find Dr. Jones. She is the only one who can help me discover my past.*

Surprised by the number of insights gained tonight, yet realizing that the present, not the past, demanded his attention, Eric closed and locked the front door. He couldn't risk the killer sneaking up behind him. Which way to go first?

"Dr. Jones," he called out, hoping for a response that would indicate the correct direction. But the house remained as quiet and as still as a crypt. Slowly, he inched down the front hall, trying to look in every direction at once.

He felt like those soldiers he'd read about who led their squads, probing the ground for mines, their whole bodies tensed, as they pushed their eyes and ears to their limits. One mistake meant certain death.

Nothing much in the front hall, just a long red carpet, a wall mirror, and pictures of Dr. Jones and her family on both walls. Eric glanced at the pictures as he passed through the hall, into the living room.

Two pictures showed her alone and smiling. The other four were of family members, some with Dr. Jones in them, a few without. They looked like lovely memories, a lovely life.

Eric peered into the black hole of the living room. *Had it been this dark in here earlier?* Once again, he called out, "Dr. Jones." No response. He moved onto the brown rug, listening for sounds of struggle. Sounds of anything.

Footsteps behind him.

Spinning around, he gazed into the empty hallway. Maybe it was his own beating heart that he heard. Eric wiped the sweat off his face with the back of one hand, then crossed to the other side of the living room and peeked into the kitchen.

It was darker than the living room. After a few moments, he made out a table, a bar, and a few barstools. The living room wall blocked the rest. He moved out of the familiar living room, into the unknown rest of the house.

With each passing second, worry twisted fresh knots in his gut. Would he find Dr. Jones with her neck ripped open? With his name scratched on her lifeless belly?

He shrugged off those thoughts. The policeman outside needed him. Dr. Jones needed him. And the killer might be in this very house. There was no time to think. It was a time for action.

Searching the kitchen quickly, Eric started to backtrack through the living room; then fished through several drawers until he found the knives. Grimacing at the clatter he made, he chose a long, thin blade. It looked sharp enough.

His hands trembling, he went back to the hallway. The front door remained closed. Continuing to the end of the hall, which only took ten steps, he came to a choice between a door and a set of stairs.

No time to think.

Eric tore open the door. A closet. Full of coats and boxes. A vacuum. He took a few steps up the stairs and paused to listen. He didn't hear anything and wondered if that was good or bad. No time to think.

Halfway up the staircase, he stopped to listen again; once again, he heard nothing. He kept going, and at the top of the stairs stood in a small open area surrounded by three doors.

Opening the middle door, he found a bathroom. Even in the dark, he could see the pink, fluffy rug and toilet seat, and identical pink shower curtain. It contained all the regular amenities overflowing women's sink counters all over the world.

No time to think.

The door on the left opened to another closet, this one a bit bigger than the one downstairs. It was stuffed with clothes. Only one more door to check.

Eric readjusted his grip on the knife and moved to the last

door, the one on the right. He listened. Did he hear something? Heart thundering in his ears, hands trembling, his mind promising certain death, he reached for the door handle.

CHAPTER 17

The door opened to a spacious bedroom dominated almost completely by a California King-sized bed, the linens of which were bright pink. Chests squeezed into the slivers of space around the bed overflowed with socks and shirts and undergarments.

Eric entered the room, his knife raised in front of him like a medieval warrior sneaking into a dragon's den. A lamp perched on a bedside end table splayed curdled, yellow light over the room. He didn't see Dr. Jones anywhere.

About to check the window on the far side of the room in case her dead body hung from the roof, a door that he suspected was another closet burst open and Dr. Jones stepped out in a long nightshirt and nothing else.

She screamed.

Eric fumbled with the knife, dropped it, and bent over to retrieve it before he figured out why she was screaming. He stood up without the knife.

"I'm sorry. I'm not here to hurt you."

Dr. Jones darted back into the bathroom and slammed the door.

"I'm sorry," Eric repeated, walking toward the closed door, careful not to step on the sharp blade of the knife. "I thought you were in trouble."

He waited there breathing fast for a few minutes before the door opened again. Dr. Jones stood in the doorway, this time with jeans on. Her brown hair was tussled, and even though she wasn't wearing makeup, Eric thought she looked amazing.

"I'm sorry," he said again.

"You can't just barge into my bedroom with a knife." Dr. Jones slipped past him and stood in front of the window.

"I know," Eric said between breaths, "But I thought... I thought something had happened."

"Like what?" Dr. Jones sat down on the windowsill, a lip large enough for an adult to sleep on, pulling her knees up to her chest. Eric took a step towards her. "I thought you might be dead."

"Dead?" She raised her eyebrows. Her face muscles tightened, stretching the skin over her jawbone.

Eric stepped closer to her again, remembering why he had barged into her house and into her bedroom. "The cop outside. He'd dead. Murdered."

Dr. Jones jumped to her feet. "Murdered. What do you mean?" She looked out the window as if she could see through the blinding darkness.

"His throat was cut open," Eric said.

Dr. Jones turned back towards him, glancing down at the knife on the floor. Eric followed her gaze. "I didn't do it," he said.

She nodded, but didn't relax. Flitting past him, she crossed the bedroom and disappeared through the bedroom door without saying a word. Eric went after her and found her in the living room, picking up the phone. She looked at him and then said, "Lock the doors."

Eric did a thorough search, finding and locking each door, returned to the living room, and then left again to check all the windows. As he soldiered through the house, he heard Dr. Jones talking excitedly into the phone, telling someone about the dead cop and the killer that could still be on the loose. He wondered if she had also mentioned that he was in her house and could be the killer, himself.

Finished with his sentry duties, Eric sagged into the leather couch, which he now thought of as partly his own. Dr. Jones hung up the phone and, instead of sitting in her usual chair, took a place at the end of the same couch. Tucking her bare feet under her butt, she wrapped her arms around herself. "James is on the way. Tell me what happened."

Eric explained how he went outside, discovered the dead cop, and thought he saw someone in the shadows. He left out the part about him confessing his desire to kill and the images of him slashing the cop's throat.

"Oh my goodness," She said. "I'm glad you're okay."

"Me, too." Eric leaned back in the couch and stared up at the ceiling. He was thinking about the argument that they had earlier. "Dr. Jones—"

"Call me Samantha," she interjected.

"Ok. Samantha, I'm sorry... for earlier."

She engrossed herself in the same white spot on the ceiling. "You don't have to go through any more hypnotherapy. I completely understand. It must seem so weird to you."

Eric turned his body to face her on the couch. "No, I want to keep doing it."

Samantha appeared stunned. Looking over at him, she said, "What changed your mind?"

"I know this sounds strange, but it feels right. I don't know how to explain it. I've dealt with these... feelings all my life. Nothing helps."

"And you think you are finally getting somewhere?"

"Yes," Eric said, wondering how she could read him so well after only knowing him for a few days. "I'm getting answers. Strange answers. But answers."

"Don't tell me you're starting to believe in this crap." Samantha poked him in the arm and laughed. Eric found himself laughing, too. Laughing out the fear and the confusion. Laughing out the past.

Five minutes later, sirens screeched outside and twin car lights shot golden beams through the living room windows. Detective Wolfe had arrived.

CHAPTER 18

After the ambulance sped away with the cadaver, after giving their statements to the police, and after everyone left, Eric, Detective Wolfe and Samantha huddled in the kitchen to discuss the case.

"Finally, some proof that I'm innocent," Eric said, gulping down sweet iced-tea Samantha had made for them.

"We'll see." Wolfe tugged at his mustache, looked at Eric and grinned. "But we do have a hair."

Samantha and Eric exchanged looks.

"What is it?" Wolfe said. "You two are driving me crazy."

"You were already crazy," Samantha said, sliding a glass of iced tea in front of James. "Don't blame that on us."

"Out with it. I feel like the third-wheel." Wolfe glanced back and forth between Eric and Samantha. Eric spoke up.

"We found out something," he said.

"What?"

"That I've been reincarnated."

Detective Wolfe raised one eyebrow at Samantha. "What did you do to this poor boy?"

"I plead the fifth," Samantha answered, pouring herself a glass of tea. She refilled Eric's half-empty glass, said, "It's true. He's been alive many times before."

"Have you found out anything about the case?" Wolfe sipped his glass of tea, eyeing both them with obvious skepticism.

"I don't remember the murder, but I think we're close to finding out why," Eric said.

"That's comforting. Meanwhile, some psycho is writing your name on dead pregnant women all over Louisville."

"There's been more?" Samantha asked.

Wolfe stabbed a finger at Eric. "Two more and both with your name on them. Both murders occurred while you were under police watch, so you're clear for now. Someone is obviously infatuated with you. We should know who our killer is tomorrow. Then we'll figure out how you're involved. I haven't let you off the hook yet.

And I want you to continue hypnotherapy, as a precaution."

"Here?" Samantha placed the jug of fresh tea in the center of the table and sat down. "Is it safe?"

Wolfe nodded. "I think it is. We'll bring a few more warm bodies to watch the place, and besides, we should have the guy tomorrow, anyway. Just lock up and use common sense."

"There goes my plan to wander the streets alone tonight," Samantha said, snapping her fingers. They all laughed.

"You two are meeting tomorrow then?"

"Tomorrow," Samantha said.

"Tomorrow," Eric agreed.

CHAPTER 19

The following morning Detective James Wolfe pulled up at the Louisville Metro Police Department to find out the identity of the serial killer. Even at 7:00 a.m., the police department buzzed with activity, packed full of officers drinking steaming cups of coffee and mingling over stacks of procrastinated paperwork.

James walked next door to the forensic office, where he hoped all the mysteries of this case would start to unravel. The door stood closed so James knocked. A few seconds later, a middle-aged woman wearing a white lab coat over a dark suit opened the door. With her short blond hair, steady gaze, and firm handshake, she presented the perfect picture of the modern working woman. Ambitious. Smart. Sexy.

"We've identified the owner of the hair," she said, leading him into the lab full of polished steel and lab equipment that might double for torture devices. Like most detectives, James knew a little about forensics, but it certainly wasn't his specialty.

"I want to know everything." James wriggled his nose. The room smelled of chemicals, the names of which he probably couldn't pronounce. It wasn't a hospital, but it *felt* like a hospital.

The lab technician stopped in front of a small desk shoved into the corner, an antique next to all the modern technology. She plucked a file off the desk and tugged a few pieces of papers out of it. James checked his watch. Shuffled his feet.

"Here we are," the woman said, scanning the report. "The name is Richard Beck. Age: 32. Brown hair and eyes. Height 5'11. 175 pounds. Male, of course."

Furiously taking notes, James looked up when she stopped talking. "Does he match the profile?"

"Yes. Perfectly, actually. He's a white male, in his 30's. Changes jobs every few months, and has a history of violence against women. One arrest. He did six months in prison for that, and got out because of some loophole in the system."

Which one? James wondered silently, scribbling a few notes. "Address?"

"1403 Minglin Street, Louisville, KY. I'm guessing I don't need to give you the zip code."

"I think I can manage." James wrote the address down, checked his watch again, and then thanked the forensic lab technician. This had already taken too long.

He left the forensic office and headed to talk to Chief Baxter. He had a serial killer to catch.

CHAPTER 20

As Detective James Wolfe barged into Chief Baxter's office, Samantha put Eric in a hypnotic trance. He went almost immediately, sunk into his favorite place on her couch, head up, shoulders slouched, eyes open and focused.

"I want you to revert back through time to your past life," she said, leading him through another past life regression. "I want to talk to the person I spoke with before."

"Before," Eric repeated. Samantha could tell from the dark rings under his eyes that he had slept as little as she had. Stubble darkened his chin and neck. He wore blue jeans and a wrinkled blue-and-white UK basketball tee shirt. *Poor misguided soul,* she thought. *Every enlightened person cheered for U of L.*

After more prodding to regress into a past life, Eric's face and voice changed once again.

"Am I talking to the person I spoke with before?" Samantha punched the record button on the small, black recorder she had fished out of one of her storage boxes earlier. A red light on the recorder blinked.

"It is as you say, Samantha." The voice was eerie and cold, and Samantha was glad she had rescheduled her other appointments to hold this session during the day.

"I want to know more about you and your other lives. Can you tell me?"

"For you, anything."

"So you are a charmer. A ladies man?"

"You have no idea," the voice said.

"Are you always a man? Or do you sometimes reincarnate as a woman?"

"Shut up. Never ask me a question like that again."

Samantha drew back, shocked by the sudden outburst. Was this safe? "I... I'm sorry."

"You should be. But you are a woman and I guess I can't blame you anymore than those retards they lock in hospitals."

Not knowing how to respond, she said nothing. Just gawked,

mulling over his words. Teachers at her hypnotherapy school told stories of people going berserk under hypnosis, defying commands, attacking people. Could that happen here? Anything was possible.

"Why do you hate women so much?" she finally asked. Feeling more in control when leading the conversation with questions, Samantha regained her composure and checked to make sure the red light was still on. It was.

"You are mistaken. I love women. I love to watch them, especially at night when they sleep and don't know I'm there. I creep into their rooms and sit beside them for hours, counting their breaths."

A shiver ran down Samantha's spine. Like Alice falling down the rabbit's hole, things just get stranger and stranger. This was groundbreaking hypnosis, though, and she was as thrilled as she was frightened.

"You stalk women?" Samantha asked.

"I love them," the voice snapped. "Watching them, touching them, feeling them. Do you like to be touched, Samantha?"

"We are talking about you," she said, straightening her gray skirt.

"And I'm talking about you."

"I won't answer the question. Let's move on."

"You've been touched many times, haven't you?"

"I'm going to end this session."

"No. Wait. What's the next question?"

Samantha tugged at her skirt again, looked at her notebook full of questions, at the black recorder watching them with its one red eye. She didn't like the way she felt, like she was in a room full of rapists.

Samantha chose a question. "Why do you kill people?"

"Why does Mozart write music or Shakespeare plays?"

"You're comparing art with murder?"

"Yes, they are both compulsions, are they not? I could just as easily ask you why eagles fly or sharks hunt."

The tape recorder clicked to let her know that one side was full. Samantha took the tape out, turned it over, and placed it back in the recorder. She pushed the record button and the red light blinked again.

"So you are born with the desire to kill?"

"Everyone is; they just hide it. Society teaches them to walk a straight line, to blindly follow the rules, and punishes them if they don't."

"I believe that's called 'civilization,'" Samantha said.

"It's brainwashing. One big, world-wide cult. And everyone drinks their cool aid. You're a member of it, but I can free you."

"How can you free me?"

"Come closer and I'll show you."

"I don't think so." Samantha imagined Eric leaping off the couch and dragging her to the carpet by her neck. She shook off the thought.

"Are you scared?" he asked.

"No."

"You should be."

CHAPTER 21

"How many times have I told you not to barge in here like this?" Chief of Police John Baxter slapped his desk hard – *thwap* – and pushed back his black, leather chair.

"I have the name and address of the serial killer," James said, ignoring the Chief's comment, and dropping his notes on the desk. He stood because there were no other chairs; the chief hated long meetings so he made everyone stand.

"You do? Thank God. The media's been hounding me all day. They want statements, statements, statements." The Chief examined the notes, nodded, and said, "Looks good. How soon can we bring him in?"

"Give me a team and I'll go get him today."

"I want this guy locked and sealed, this case closed. We can't afford more bad publicity after that police shooting incident." Chief Baxter stood up, his large frame hiding the waist high file cabinets behind him. Other cabinets, identical in every way, lined all four walls. He drummed his fingers on the desk.

James checked his watch. "About my team..."

"I was thinking," Chief Baxter said. James mentally shook his head. Whenever the Chief started thinking, bad things were bound to happen. Meanwhile, time was ticking away. "I believe I'll join you."

"What? I don't think that's a good idea," James said.

"It's a great idea. It'll be good publicity for the department. All around." Chief Baxter grinned at his marketing savvy. His eyes looked glazed over, like he was visualizing something.

"It could be dangerous."

"Remember, I wasn't always Chief," he said, shuffling paper around on his desk. "I started as a beat cop just like the rest of them."

Spare me the misery, James thought and looked at his watch again. A serial killer was on the loose and he was worried about publicity.

"Okay," James agreed, against his better reason. "We'll go

together. But let's go soon." After all, Chief Baxter was still the boss.

"Just give me a second to call the media. I want everyone there." Peering down at his coffee-stained shirt, he appeared alarmed. "And I'll have to change. Can't be televised in this."

James rolled his eyes. Tugged at his mustache. Checked his watch again. "I'll gather a team. We leave in an hour."

CHAPTER 22

"I enjoy the hunt almost as much as I delight in the killing," Eric said, buried in Samantha's couch, her lamp throwing plaque-colored light across his face.

In the living room, cool air kissed Samantha's skin. Perched on her chair, which usually made her feel confident and professional and in charge, she trembled with the unadulterated giddiness of a child.

"In all my lives I learn to relish the choosing of my victims, of watching them, sometimes for days. Learning their routines: when and where they go, and for how long."

Beside Samantha the black tape recorder whirred; the red light blinked.

"After I watch them for awhile, I decide when and where and how I will murder them. In the beginning I was sloppy, attacking people with blind abandon. That was fun, but immature. Later, I learned to control myself, take the time to plan. I also figure out how I will escape. I take the utmost precautions."

"I bet," Samantha responded, while again imagining Eric scrambling off the couch and pressing his thumbs into her larynx, strangling her to death. Instead, Eric, who was not Eric now, but someone – or something – else jabbered on about his murders.

"I love standing in the shadows, watching them come. Knowing that they don't know what's going to happen. Unaware that they are taking their last steps, their last breathes. I am filled with intense thrills."

Listening to his story, Samantha was swept back into the world where he lived and breathed and waited in the shadows. Was he waiting now? Toying with her until, at last, he would step out of the darkness to take her life?

"I love looking into their eyes when they see me. When they see the blade or pipe or rope in my hand. Their eyes register it first, even while their minds struggle to grasp reality and their feet keep moving."

Eric's hands suddenly curved at the wrists like the clawed

talons of an eagle. Samantha jerked back in her chair, her neck tingling, her hands clasped in her lap.

"I beat them and cut them. Bathe in their blood. It is what I am born to do. It is what I am. What I always become."

The tape recorder whirred. The red light blinked.

"Always?" she whispered.

He grinned and said nothing.

CHAPTER 23

Blocking mid-day traffic for miles, police cruisers and news vans, radars attached to their roofs and names imprinted in gigantic colored letters on each side, rolled across Louisville like a funeral procession.

They were on their way to catch the killer.

James Wolfe led the pack with an unmarked green Subaru. The Chief rode with him, constantly combing the few strands of gray-brown hairs nature had spared him.

"Hey," James said, wiping a thick layer of sweat from his forehead. "I know the air conditioner bothers your allergies, so can we crack the windows a bit?"

The Chief touched his hair. "It's only a few minutes away."

James mopped more sweat from his face as he tried to ignore the smell of week old meat rising from the car. The strangled-cat cries of a country music singer blared on the radio. Something about drinking and trucks. Then again, weren't they *all* about drinking and trucks?

When they arrived at Minglin Street, the police cruisers fell back, letting James drive past the target address and park a few houses down.

In his rearview mirror, he noticed a police car and one of the news vans, WHAS-11, pass the street and keep going. Probably circling around the block.

"Okay," Chief Baxter said, checking himself in the mirror one last time. "A team will surround the perimeter of the house. You'll go in, make sure he's in there. Then, I'll come in and make the arrest. Sound good?"

James bit his bottom lip. "Sounds like good publicity."

"That's the spirit." The Chief slapped him on the shoulder.

Do it again and I'll run your face through the windshield, James thought. Any publicity is good publicity, right?

"Did you say something?" The Chief asked.

James realized he had been mumbling. "No. Let's get on with it."

Climbing out of the car, he waved the other police officers over. With a series of hand signals, he told them to initiate the plan already explained at headquarters.

Performing moves they had rehearsed a hundred times, the officers lined up, split into two flanks and paced towards the house.

Across the street, two black teenagers in white A-shirts and sagging sweat pants washed a brown Lincoln Continental. One scrubbed the hood with a sponge, dripping soap bubbles on the driveway, while the other followed with a hose. They watched the two lines of police officers tread through the front yard and begin surrounding their neighbor's house.

They also watched WAVE-3 news reporters set up their complicated-looking equipment.

On the opposite side of the street, WHAS-11 news appeared and idled at the curb behind a police cruiser. The driver of the news van nodded at James.

Could the serial killer live in this neighborhood? James strolled along the sidewalk. Broken beer bottles, food wrappers and cigarette butts crowded the gutters.

At the front door of the target house, he pulled out his badge and gun, which he rapped against the door. "Police. Open up."

Nothing.

He knocked on the door with the gun again, louder this time.

Still no response.

"Police. This is your last chance to open the door or I'm coming in the old fashioned way." He waited for a few seconds, glanced over his shoulder at the Chief, who remained in the car. He shook his head.

When Chief Baxter gestured for him to enter the house, Wolfe stepped back, took a deep breath and kicked the door.

Crunch.

The door swung inward and Wolfe followed it, juiced up on adrenaline and yelling.

CHAPTER 24

"Who are you? What are your names?" Samantha asked, hoping to uncover more information, any information that could help Eric.

Hands bent at the wrists, fingers hooked into claws, Eric said, "I have been so many people, possessed so many names." Even in the amber-fire of lamplight and the mid-day sun, his face appeared to darken.

"I am John Lugers, a farmer. Oh, how I liked pretty little girls, the younger the better, with yellow ribbons in their hair. I grabbed them on their way home after school and took them into the barn. Introduced them to a side of the world they've never known. When I finished with them, I cracked their tiny skulls with a hammer and buried them in a field."

A sudden chill seized Samantha, its arctic fingers playing up and down her spine like a concert piano.

"I am Robert Thornton," Eric continued, "Drowned four wives before they caught on to me. Nasty whores deserved it. Tore off the nose of one of the prison guards with a smuggled wrench. The other inmates loved it."

When it did not seem that Eric would keep talking, Samantha egged him on: "Who else? What were your other lives?" The more he revealed, the better possibility she would discover something helpful.

"Charlie Manderline. I loved being him. I led women down into the cellar of my church, where I cut them, inch by inch, with gummy shards of glass until they bled from every pore. On Sunday mornings, when I preached, I'd get so excited thinking about the women I kept down there."

"Anyone else? Do you remember anyone else?"

"Jesse Garfield, Blake Rumdrummer, Frank Ferretta, Bobby Temple, Danny Spurs." Eric rattled them off as if he were reading a list. "I remember them all," he said.

"And in all of them you killed?" Samantha checked the recorder to ensure it was still working.

"Yes, I murdered and raped and chopped up body parts. I did what I was born to do, what we're all born to do, but most forget. Unlike the average person, I don't deny my natural urges."

"The urge to kill and rape and cut up people?"

"No, the urge for power. Control. Domination."

Leaning back, letting everything Eric had told her play through her mind, Samantha stared at the recorder as if it would tell her what to do next. "The names you've given me. Those are the only ones that you will share?" She finally said, frowning. She didn't recognize even one of them.

"There is one more," Eric said, straitening his spine, glazed eyes suddenly clear. "A name I think you'll be very familiar with."

CHAPTER 25

Holding his SIG Model P-229 pistol in front of him, thinking, *Catch the killer, catch the killer, catch the killer, catch the killer,* James burst into the silent house. The door opened to a small living room in which blankets and video games and clothes sprawled on tan carpet like drunken college kids.

The living room was empty of murderers. James moved into the hallway, which ran left and right.

Going left, he entered the kitchen. He glanced out the sliding glass door at several police officers crouched in the backyard, guns drawn. He nodded at them. Looked over his shoulder. He didn't want someone to creep up behind him.

No lunatics with shotguns and itchy fingers appeared. Instead, two officers shuffled into the hallway, looked at James and hurried in the opposite direction, toward what he suspected were bedrooms.

He turned back to the kitchen. Animal magnets held lists of scribbled phone numbers and pizza coupons to the refrigerator. Gnats buzzed in circles of insectile delight over a blue bowl of brown goo. Unless the serial killer was also a contortionist able to twist his body into a pretzel and pack himself into a cabinet, the kitchen was clear, too.

Deciding he preferred the smell of the Subaru to the one rising from the sink, he reached for a door that must lead to the garage, based on its location. From deeper in the house, he heard the other two officers yell, "Clear. Clear."

Flipping open the door, James stepped inside, directing his gun to the corners first, then behind the door.

The garage was full of the usual junk – tools rusty from months of disuse, grass-stained lawn mower, weed-eater, trashcan, large freezer, but no vehicle. As he expected, the owner of this fine establishment had evacuated the premises.

With nothing blocking the middle of the garage, James walked back and forth. Something kept pulling his eyes to the freezer. By the look of it, you could stash a body inside.

"You might have to saw off a limb or two, but a body would probably fit," he said out loud to the empty garage. The echo of his voice made him shiver.

Approaching the freezer, he cupped the lid with one hand, tugging it upwards, finding it unlocked. Raising it slowly, it sighed, blowing cold mist over his hand.

He lifted the lid higher, aiming the gun as if there were a frozen corpse confined to the freezer, somehow reanimated and waiting for him to lean close enough for it to grab him and drag him inside.

Of course, the freezer was empty. It contained neatly packaged deer meat, not human heads.

Going to the wall, leaving the freezer open, watching white mist curl up into the dark, James punched the button to the automatic garage door opener. The steel door rumbled upward.

James grinned. The two camera crews outside were probably going crazy, zeroing in on the slowly revealed garage. Who or what would step out?

Once the garage door fully retracted, he strolled out into the driveway. The sunlight blinded him; cupping his hand, he lifted it above his eyes, throwing a shadow over his face. When he saw the cameras pointed in his direction, he waved.

The two other police officers that had gone into the house with him stood in the lawn. One held an orange cat in his arms. "Only suspect we found," one of them said.

James crossed the lawn and treaded down the sidewalk to where the Chief still sat in his car. How does he stand the smell?

With the window down, Chief Baxter said, "Any clue where he is or how to find him?"

"Afraid not."

Poking his head out of the window at the WHAS-11 set up, the Chief sighed and drooped his shoulders. "I hate to waste the publicity."

And my time, Wolfe thought. But he said, "I know," while trying to look empathetic.

As Chief Baxter struggled out of the vehicle, Wolfe turned and stared into the garage. He half heard the Chief deliver the bad news to the other officers.

Something in the back of his mind nagged at him. Usually, it was a small detail overlooked or a connection unrealized. In the past, these details had saved the case. He learned to trust these instincts. But what did he miss?

Standing beside the green Subaru, he blocked out the Chief's media interview and mentally retraced his time in the house. Kicked open the door. Living room. Clothes. Video games. Down the hallway. Left. The kitchen. Glass door. Back yard. Smelly sink. Bowl of brown goo. Refrigerator. Photos. List of numbers. Garage. Freezer.

Wait.

Passed it.

The list of numbers.

Checking to see if anyone was looking, finding that they were all paying attention to the Chief, Wolfe slipped back up the driveway into the garage, into the house.

CHAPTER 26

"They called me Jack the Ripper."

Samantha gasped. It had to be a lie. But why would he lie? Her heart pulsed erratically in her chest, and her throat felt like a clogged pipe.

Eric sat on the couch, silent, as if he knew his revelation paralyzed her. Then, in the same raspy voice, said, "I used so many disguises, fooled so many people. I enjoyed tearing those prostitutes apart."

Unable to stop herself, overcome by the need to discover, reined in by curiosity, Samantha said, "Tell me more."

"I thought you'd want to know. Inside of you, now you see, there is a craving for the sinful. I will give you a buffet of pleasure, then. Those Unfortunates, they never saw it coming. Out of the shadows of the Whitechapel District I snatched them like jewelry off the dead. I cut them, but I was no doctor. I was overcome by inspiration, but I was no artist. I stabbed them over and over and over. Sometimes, I took part of them home with me."

Samantha sat transfixed, unable to move, much less ask another question. Afraid that even a breath would shatter the dream of this confession, the most astounding revelations since Edward Cayce, she bit down fiercely on her bottom lip.

"I wrote letters to the police," Eric said. "Changed my handwriting, used different hands, all sorts of nasty tricks to frustrate them. I was never caught. It was a most beautiful life."

Beside her, the recorder clicked to a stop. What do I do? I can't stop the session. What if he never comes back to this? Where's more tape? Up in the bedroom. No time to get it.

Fumbling out of her trance like a drugged teenager out of an all night rave, Samantha straitened her skirt; it had ridden to an unprofessional height on her thigh. She blew out the pent up air in her lungs. Blinking, she looked at her notebook of questions. Where do I go from here? She couldn't remember the last time she had looked at them. None of those listed made sense at this point and there were no smooth transitions to reach them.

Laying the notebook aside, Samantha cleared her throat. "Did you always get away?"

"Sometimes I got away."

"So you were caught."

"Sometimes. Sometimes I was killed."

Wishing she were still recording the conversation, frowning at the tape recorder, she picked up the notebook again. She could at least take notes, and one of the questions would make sense here, after all. "And you did all this alone?" she asked.

"The murders?"

"Yes."

"No."

Samantha once again fumbled, nearly losing the notepad. A clawing heat spread from her face to her neck to her body. "You weren't alone?"

"I was never alone."

CHAPTER 27

Through the dark garage, past the freezer, back into the house. James stopped in the kitchen only long enough to snatch the list of numbers and a few of the photos off the refrigerator. He didn't look at them until he was outside, sitting alone in the smelly green car.

Making sure no one was watching, he searched the photos. Although different faces dotted the pictures, the same man grinned back at him from several of them. Gotcha. Next, he read each typed name and number carefully. Unlike the rest of the killer's house, the list was organized, so he found what he was looking for quickly: a scribbled *My Cell* followed by a phone number. Must be new.

He had the killer's contact information.

Digging his own cell phone out of his pocket, flipping it open, James dialed the number on the list. After two rings, someone answered. "Hello?"

"Richard, what's up? Where are you?" James said.

"Waterfront Park. Who is this?"

James hung up.

CHAPTER 28

Out of the trance, Eric stood up, stretched and asked what happened. Samantha decided to let him listen to the recorded tape over a glass of wine.

"Normally I wouldn't drink with my clients," she explained, taking a bottle of Chianti out of a wine rack on the kitchen counter, scooping up two glass goblets and placing them on the table.

"Normally your patients don't claim to be reincarnated serial killers."

"True."

Samantha filled both goblets with purple wine, dark as blood, and then returned the Italian wine to the wine rack. Settling into a chair at the table next to Eric, she covered his hand with hers. "This could be disturbing."

"I know."

"If you want to get something to eat afterward, or just get out, we could go."

"You don't normally eat dinner with your clients either, do you?"

She squeezed his hand and then let it go. "No. But I think it would be a good idea for both of us to get out."

"Me, too."

"And after listening to this tape," Samantha added, "I think we'll have plenty to talk about."

Eric sipped his goblet of wine. Samantha turned on the tape recorder. Tiny gears turned inside and after a few seconds, they heard Eric's voice.

"I am John Lugers, a farmer. Oh, how I liked pretty little girls..."

CHAPTER 29

Winding through the traffic-clogged streets of Louisville at rush hour, James Wolfe negotiated the lime-green Subaru like a stunt driver. Around him, thrusting into the sky, corporate buildings loomed like gigantic gray waves about to crest and pound the wearied travelers below.

Fifteen minutes later, passing by the Humana building, James parked the car; he stepped out in front of the Kentucky Center for the Arts, and blinking in the sunlight, left the car unlocked as he pushed through a throng of secretaries waiting to cross the street.

He hoped the killer was still there.

Treading up the small hill that led to the Waterfront Park, James examined every person in eyesight. Two young men sporting Sigma Chi Fraternity tee shirts lounged on stone benches. An old lady with blue hair hobbled down the hill, assisted by a younger-looking woman in a military uniform.

From the right, he heard the thunder-rush of fountains. A moment later, he saw water shoot into the air, arc, then spray the laughing children playing beneath it. He passed under the historical arch and over the plaques on the pavilion memorializing Louisville's past as a popular river port.

Right now, history did not interest him – not the arch, the plaques or the statue of the famous explorer, George Rogers Clark. He was fully engaged in the present.

Glancing left and right, James searched for the killer, whose face flashed like a vivid photograph in Wolfe's head.

No sight of him.

He shrugged off the doomsday voice in his mind that said the killer had fled, that all was lost, the same voice that haunted him his whole career.

He must think like the killer. Where would he be?

Angling toward the Great Lawn, where thousands gathered every April to drink beer, eat greasy food and watch fireworks burst colors across the sky during Thunder Over Louisville, he kept an eye on his surroundings. A couple strolled hand in hand.

Three old men with cameras snapped pictures of the Ohio River. A skinny mop-haired kid bicycled by, singing, "Smells Like Teen Spirit," by Nirvana.

Was he still here?

Every person or group that he passed increased his doubt. The doomsday voice mocked him: "The killer is gone. You've missed him. He's escaped to kill again because you couldn't find him." No wonder there's such a high suicide rate among detectives.

James walked faster. On his left sailboats, their white sails flapping like tongues, dotted the Ohio River.

Checking faces, seeing no one he recognized, fighting the voice in his head, James jog-walked the rest of the way to the Great Lawn, where several families lounged on blankets. A young boy guided a yellow kite across the sky.

Was he here? Would he catch the criminal? Or would it be too late?

All three of these questions were answered when, across the field, a man stepped from behind two blondes. The killer.

James jogged across the field, past the kite-wielding kid. "Police," he announced. The criminal and the two women stared at him. He closed the gap quickly, stopped, and gulped air. He trained as an endurance runner – at least he used to – not a sprinter.

"Police," he repeated. Walking up to the criminal, who wore a green tee shirt, baggy khakis and tan Timberlands, he retrieved his wallet from his back pocket and flashed his badge. "You're under arrest."

The killer looked back and forth between the two girls – both blonde and probably anorexic – and the detective.

James traded his badge for a set of handcuffs. "Richard Beck, you are under arrest for murder. You have the right to remain silent—"

"Screw you," the dark-haired man said, kicking out with one boot, catching the detective in the shin. James quickly discovered that the Timberlands were steel-toed.

Richard spun and darted up a staircase of layered stone slabs. James followed, dragging slightly from his aching shin, up the stairs, down a gravel-floored pavilion, into the street. A jeep swerved out the way, jumped the sidewalk and narrowly jerked back on the street before ramming a series of newspaper racks.

James heard the driver lay on the horn as he trailed the perpetrator into an alleyway and watched him crash through the side door of one of the buildings. Taking out his gun, he limped toward the door.

CHAPTER 30

Samantha and Eric arrived at Buckhead Mountain Grill in Jeffersonville, Indiana at six o'clock. After a short wait, a pretty hostess led them to a table outside on the expansive wooden deck overlooking the Ohio River. If this were a date, it would have been perfect. Except for the lingering dread that pulled at Eric's gut.

Settling into their chairs, they ordered drinks – a coke for him, a sweet iced-tea for her.

"You were right," Eric said, enjoying the breeze on his face. It made the sun almost bearable.

"About what?"

"It *is* good to get out."

Staring blankly at the Ohio, she said, "I didn't think you were ever going to speak after listening to the tape."

"You were also right about that. The tape gives us lots to talk about."

The waitress, a middle-aged woman with frizzled black hair and a double chin, delivered their drinks and took their orders. Samantha ordered the Durango chicken salad; Eric chose the rib eye. When the waitress left, they continued their conversation.

"There's something I've been thinking about," Eric said, swirling the ice in his glass of coke with a straw. "On the tape I say that I always become a serial killer. That means, unless I figure out a way to stop the cycle, I'll eventually become one, too."

For a moment, after Eric verbalized the truth both of them knew but had not previously discussed, neither spoke. Instead, they looked across the Ohio River at the Louisville skyline.

Eric frowned when he saw the bright yellow kite, the kid running beneath it care-free and happy. It reminded him of his imprisonment. He felt like the kite, tossed about by the winds of fate, yanked along by the cruel string of destiny.

"Dozens of lives are at stake," he said.

"More than that." Samantha shifted her eyes from the skyline, the Riverfront and the Ohio River to Eric. "If the cycle continues uninterrupted, you'll keep becoming a serial killer in every life, not just this one."

Eric absorbed her words, the truth of them slowly sinking in. Although it could have been his imagination, he thought fear flashed in her eyes. Without realizing it, his hand froze on the straw – he was no longer stirring his drink. "You're right," he said. "Dozens of lives aren't at stake... hundreds are."

CHAPTER 31

Detective James Wolfe exploded through the door, shin burning, gun raised and trained in front of him. His heart raced along at a steady gallop.

The door revealed a long hallway. James hurried down it, wishing he had more time, knowing he should be more careful. Curled and disintegrating, posters hung from the walls like bad memories: a clown offering a lollipop, a half-naked girl shaking her hips and batting her eyes, dance club advertisements.

The hallway stretched on twenty more feet, then twenty more. Moving fast through the dirty yellow light, the stench of trash spoiling the air, James wondered: *how long is the darn thing?*

He had the insane idea that the hallway would never end, only get longer and longer, darker and fouler, a never-ending tunnel in which he was trapped forever under the mad eyes of clowns and strippers.

Even with his bruised shin, James was going too fast; he never saw it coming.

From a doorway further down the hall, the killer stepped out and fired two shots. One of the bullets barely missed his head. It smashed into the wall beside him. The other bullet zipped close to his waist, but missed him, too.

The killer disappeared through the door.

Thank God he's not a professional, James thought, hobbling after the criminal, body shaking with adrenaline, breath ragged. Or I'd be dead.

As happy as he was to be alive and not spasming on the floor with two brand-spanking new holes in his body, the situation confused him. Wasn't the serial killer a professional? He murdered three women that they knew about – probably more that they didn't. The only evidence he left at either crime scene: a single strand of hair. If he was so good, so careful, so uncatchable, why hadn't he been able to shoot him down? In the dark, standing still, he certainly had the advantage. It didn't add up.

Advancing through the doorway, checking in all directions,

James found himself in a large room. Shadows clung to the walls and ceiling like droves of bats.

Maybe the killer wasn't good with guns. None of the victims died from gun wounds. The three women were killed with blunt objects to the head, their stomachs ripped apart by something sharp and personal.

James didn't see the gunman. The room was mostly empty, occupied only by half a dozen stacks of pallets partly covered by black plastic tarps. The killer had to be in here somewhere.

Back against the wall so that he only had three directions – left, right and straight – to worry about, James closed in on one of the pallets.

CHAPTER 32

"I think we're very close," Samantha said, smothering her salad with honey mustard dressing. "At the end of the session you said that you were never alone."

"I have a partner," Eric said. It was part question, part statement.

"Yes. I think that's the key."

"You do?"

"Sure. If you have a partner in every life, you'd have to have one in this one, too. If we can find out who that person is, maybe we can answer some of our questions."

Eric cut his 12-oz medium-rare steak into bite-sized chunks. Samantha turned her fork into a salad kabob: chicken, lettuce and tomato on one utensil. After both took a few bites, after the double chinned waitress returned to refill their drinks, Eric spoke up.

"Well, you know all about me, but I know next to nothing about you."

Samantha forked another salad kabob. "What do you want to know?"

"Well, for starters, how did you ever end up as a hypnotherapist?"

"You say it like it's not a noble pursuit."

"I'm sure your parents are very proud."

"I usually don't tell my clients about myself," she said, sipping her iced-tea. "But since you used to be Jack the Ripper, I guess you can keep a secret pretty well."

"Funny."

"I thought so."

As Samantha told him about her past, her childhood, and how she met Wolfe and first became interested in hypnotherapy, Eric glanced across the Ohio River. The young boy pulled his yellow kite down from the bruise-colored sky. Somewhere on his side of the river sirens pierced the afternoon.

CHAPTER 33

James found only dust and cobwebs behind the first stack of pallets. Not the killer. He inched along the wall to the next stack, surveying all directions, the pain in his shin dulling to a bearable throb. The second stack of pallets also revealed nothing. James stopped and listened.

He heard breathing.

Somewhere close.

Scanning the massive room, examining every stack of tarp-covered pallets, every corner where the gunman might hide in the shadows, James fixed on the last stack of pallets. The killer has to be behind it, he thought. With some hesitation, he left the relative protection of the wall.

Halfway across the room, he scratched the floor with his shoe. If the gunman stood behind the pallet, there was no way he missed the noise.

James paused, hoped the ensuing silence would convince the killer that the noise was a fluke, that he wasn't close and standing out in the open. He slowed his breathing as much as possible. A lump formed in his throat.

It didn't work.

Jumping from behind the stack of pallets, the gunman bolted across the room. James positioned himself to shoot, locking his gun on the fleeing suspect. He wanted to take the guy alive, but he'd take what he could get. "Police. Halt."

Almost at a door on the other side of the room, Richard must have realized his precarious situation. In a bizarre ballet-like motion, he twisted around and raised his weapon.

Before he could get off a shot, James jerked back on the trigger on his own gun, the bullet tearing through the air at blinding speed, then striking the killer's shoulder, flinging him backward onto the floor. Richard Beck dropped his gun.

Racing over to him, James pointed his pistol at the wounded criminal.

He had the killer.

CHAPTER 34

On the other side of the Ohio River, Samantha reached across the table and squeezed Eric's hand. A pulse of electricity shot through her. Wow, she thought, what the heck was that about? She smiled.

When she looked up, a beautiful blond woman was piercing her with steely blue eyes. The woman mouthed something while sliding her index finger across her neck in a slicing motion. *Oh my God, did she just say what I thought she said?*

"What is it?" Eric asked.

"That woman. I think she just threatened my life."

"What woman?" Eric whirled in his seat, but the woman was gone. He stood up. "She was just there." She shuddered. "Can we just leave?"

As Eric hunted down the waitress, Samantha sat listening to police sirens blare across the river.

Now, as Eric padded across the wooden planks of the deck towards her, he heard the shriek of sirens from the other side of the river. When he reached the table, he said, "I never would have pegged you as an old Western movie buff or fan of 70's music."

"I guess you can never tell about people."

He thought about that for a moment, nodded.

As they gathered their things and stood up to leave, she said, "You know, these discoveries we're making could alter the way the world views the mind – even the way the world views life itself."

He didn't know about that; but he did know she fascinated him just as much. And it had nothing to do with past lives.

"Come on, let's go."

On the way out of the restaurant, Eric was suddenly overcome by a heavy, dark pall. He looked around, feeling the itch of someone watching him. From somewhere in the parking lot he heard the loud snarl of an engine, and then silver Nissan 350Z with its windows down tore onto the street, the driver a woman, blonde hair waving madly in the wind.

CHAPTER 35

Detective James Wolfe ushered the handcuffed criminal down the endless tunnel, toward the door that led to the outside.

"I've been shot. I need medical attention," the killer whined, shuffling in front of him.

"Shut up and keep walking."

"I'm bleeding. Look at me, I'm bleeding."

"I told you to shut up," James said, "Or the only place you'll need to go is the morgue."

The criminal slumped his shoulders, hung his head, sighing loudly like a scolded child.

Before they reached the end of the tunnel, two police officers scrambled in, guns drawn. Behind them, Chief Baxter stepped into the tunnel, red blotches streaking up his face, neck and ears.

"Thank God," the criminal said, shooting James a glance over his shoulder. "This guy threatened to kill me—"

Wolfe stabbed the barrel of his pistol into the man's shoulder blades, silencing him.

"Chief, good to see you." James holstered his gun. The killer would have to be crazy to try anything with two guns trained at his head.

"Don't give me that crap," the Chief said, stopping behind the two officers and breathing heavily. "You deliberately lied. And for what? To get all the glory for yourself, that's what."

Wolfe thought fast. "I had a hunch. There was no time to tell anyone. If I'd waited, I might've missed the window of opportunity."

"There are rules for a reason, James."

Keeping the officers between himself and the handcuffed killer, the Chief shook one angry finger, like a mother at a misbehaving child. "One of the officers saw you sneak off in your car and followed you. When you started chasing the guy, he put in a call to me." The red streaks on his face branched out like a fast-acting tumor. "You knew what this meant to the force."

Wolfe sighed. He would never understand how the Chief

thought. His priorities were as out of whack as the criminal handcuffed and bleeding in front of him. "You can escort the perp out if you want."

"Of course I can. It's the best thing for our community. They want to see the police chief taking care of business, cleaning up and all that."

Chief Baxter ordered the two officers to move the criminal to the doorway, where they were to pull back, allowing the Chief to walk out with him.

James followed them out of the building, where the officers stepped to the side. James waited and watched from the alley.

On the street, reporters from local news stations rushed forward like the offensive line of a football team. Cameras clicked and flashed, followed by a barrage of questions: "Is this the serial killer?" "Did you find any bodies in the building?" "Who caught the serial killer?"

The Chief smiled all the way to the police car, where another officer stuffed the criminal in the backseat. James watched the cruiser pull away, headed towards University Hospital, where the serial killer would receive the medical attention he demanded, and by law was his right. He wondered how many of the serial killer's victim's pled uselessly for those same rights.

By tomorrow, they would have DNA evidence linking him to the murders. After that, a criminal trial, sure to be long and drawn out.

Somehow that didn't satisfy James. Although he wanted to get back to his personal case involving his wife, as he walked back to his car, avoiding the crowds by blending in with the wide-eyed spectators, he thought about the fiber of hair. The ease with which he had tracked the killer to River Front Park. The wild run across the large shipping and receiving room. Twenty years of hunting down bad guys (and occasionally, bad girls, too) provided him an education in criminal behavior unmatched by any class or workshop; he knew the difference between a professional and an amateur.

The person who murdered the three pregnant women without leaving any trace evidence, except a single fiber of hair, was unquestionably a professional. The man whose house he had just raided, whose cell phone he had called, who he had chased into a building and shot in the shoulder was an amateur.

CHAPTER 36

Samantha picked up the phone on the second ring. She was in the middle of preparing for her next session with Eric. As she said, "Hello," she stared at the stack of blank audiotapes on the table next to her chair.

"Samantha, it's James."

"Hey, how are you?" She wondered if he could tell she was smiling.

"Not good. Bad news."

"Tell me."

"Did you catch the news?"

"Yeah, you got the bad guy. What's the bad news? Chief get a book deal?"

James laughed, but it sounded forced. A pause, then: "He's not the guy."

Her smile faded. "Are you sure?"

"Positive. His alibi is solid and he passed a polygraph exam like a seasoned FBI agent."

"What about the fiber of hair?" Samantha nervously twisted the black phone cord in and out between her fingers.

"Matches, but it was probably planted. Not our guy."

"What do we do now?"

On the other side of the line, James sighed. "I'm meeting with the Chief today. I'll call you afterward."

"Okay, goodbye, James. "

"Goodbye."

The line went dead, the silence hovering like a bad omen.

Arriving at her house at exactly 3:00 P.M., Eric rang the doorbell and waited, sweating in the sun. He heard footsteps clattering toward him. Samantha opened the door, releasing a pent-up breath of cool air from the house.

"James called," she said, letting him step inside. Instantly enveloped in the rush of air-conditioning, he blinked and adjusted his eyes to the darker interior of the house.

Samantha, closing the front door behind them: "He arrested

the wrong guy. The serial killer's still on the loose."

Eric wiped beads of sweat from his forehead with the sleeve of his blue tee shirt. He also wore khaki shorts and Nike sneakers. "The media's going to eat that up," he said, imagining the Newspaper headline: *Police Arrest Wrong Man,* and the inevitable calls to the customer service department about the article from angry relatives of the officers involved. When call volume was high, he sometimes helped out in that department. He breathed a silent sigh of relief that it would not be *him* taking those calls.

"I know."

"Then we better get started. We don't need two serial killers out there."

Samantha stared at him, the unsettling meaning of his words flooding her face. She nodded. "True."

They moved into the living room, Samantha taking her chair; Eric, the couch.

"I went to the library, today," Eric said. "Read up on hypnotism. Pretty fascinating stuff. I think this is the first time I'm actually looking forward to one of our sessions."

After preparing the tape recorder, Samantha clicked it on. Gears whirred. The light blinked red.

"Okay, close your eyes." Samantha led him into a trance, Eric recognizing the words and images she used, the subtle sentence structures, from the books he studied at the library. Ten minutes later, he was deep in trance, so deep and so relaxed...

As soon as he lapsed, Samantha started firing off questions, ready for anything. "Last time we spoke, you said that you never murdered alone. Who is with you?"

CHAPTER 37

Something about his voice reminded Samantha of the dead phone line she heard after talking to James.

"Who is with you?" Samantha repeated.

Eric's glassy-eyed stare turned in her direction. "You would like to know, wouldn't you, Samantha?"

"Yes, I do."

"Well, I won't tell you."

"Why not?"

"Because," Eric said, drawing out the end of each word. "I have something superior to convey."

Samantha glanced at the tape recorder. It was still on. The tape allowed for sixty minutes of recording on each side and their session had only run fifteen minutes so far. "And that would be?" she asked, raising one trimmed eyebrow. Her heart pattered in her chest.

"Did you like it?"

"Did I like what?"

Eric's body bowed forward, hands hooked at the wrists. "Did you like it when he grabbed you by the throat?"

"What? Who?" Her body temperature jumped up about ten degrees.

"When he choked you until your face turned white and you thrashed around on his bed..."

In her chest her heart rammed against her ribcage. Flustered, she tapped her pen against her notebook. Tap, tap, tap. How could he know? He couldn't possibly...

"When he pulled down your pants and forced himself on you and you couldn't scream because you couldn't breathe..."

Samantha dropped her pen. She gripped both arms of her chair, her back rigid, her notebook in her lap. "You can't know this. I didn't tell you."

On the couch, Eric grinned. His body shook as if an alien squirmed inside, growing tired of its earthly shell. "You liked being raped, didn't you, you whore?"

"Shut up."

"Whore."

Standing up, her own body trembling, notebook toppling out of her lap onto the carpet, Samantha ordered him to stop.

"Whore, whore, whore," Eric taunted, spittle flying from his mouth.

"This session is over. When I snap my fingers, you will awake." Samantha's voice shook and she found it difficult to continue. Her throat felt clogged.

"No, wait," Eric pled from the couch.

"You are slowly awakening. You will awake fully when I snap my fingers."

"I apologize. That was uncalled for."

Tears flowing over her cheeks, legs wobbly and weak, Samantha raised her hand, touching her middle finger to her thumb. *Snap.*

Eric's body stopped shaking. His hands uncurled and his eyes were clear again. He took one look at her and, alarmed, said, "What's wrong?"

She tossed her head back and forth. "Leave. Just... leave," she said, turning from him and fleeing upstairs, where she shut and locked her bedroom door. Her crying became weeping; her fear, terror; her anger, hate. Collapsing on her bed, she curled herself into a ball. And remembered the night she was raped.

CHAPTER 38

"I looked like a fool," Chief Baxter said, making a short pace, back and forth, behind his "L"-shaped cherry desk. His head didn't sit atop his neck – it slouched there. A vein slashed itself across his forehead like a scar, blue and swollen.

"There's no way either of us could have known." James sat on the other side of the desk in a stiff, wooden chair he borrowed from the hallway, thinking *Prisons have more comfortable furniture.* The small office smelled of paper and was decorated with every memento of praise the Chief ever received in his life. Glossy black plaques hung on the walls. Paperweights, nameplates and miniature trophy cups had taken the top of his desk hostage.

"We should have known," Chief Baxter said, stopping at the edge of his desk, which was crowded with manila folders, pens and paperclips. Underneath it all, a thin pane of glass separated the chaos from a large desk calendar, covered in illegible scribbles. "The media made me out to be a buffoon. Every channel I turned to, all I heard was, 'big public mess,' 'chief arrests wrong man' or 'chief outdoes himself with recent screw up.' How am I supposed to run a respectable force?"

James, sensing he should say nothing, obliged his wiser instincts. Best to let the Chief get his feelings out.

Clamoring back to his black, leather chair – which oddly reminded James of the Captain's chair on Star Trek – the Chief sighed. It looked like bad acting. "This case is crucial to how the public views us. So far, all they've seen is us bumble around and come up with nothing. Now with this publicity crisis…" Trailing off, Chief Baxter shook his massive head.

"What are you getting at?"

The Chief looked up at him. "We must close this case soon. The media is having a field day. The city is terrified with a serial killer on the loose. And who can blame them."

"Chief, we're going to catch this guy."

Staring down at his mess of a desk, breathing heavily and cocking his head to add to the dramatic effect, Chief Baxter shrugged his shoulders. "I know you want to. Heck, we all want to. Yet, wanting to isn't enough."

"Am I missing something, Chief?"

"James, I'm taking you off the case."

"What? You can't."

"You haven't accomplished anything. No leads. No evidence. No nothing."

"I'll get him. I'll get this guy. You have to keep me on the case. You know how much this it means to me."

"Three women are dead, James," the Chief said, shrugging his shoulders again, releasing one of those flatulent-like sighs. "I know you have a personal connection here, with what happened with your wife and all, but time is of the essence here. Nobody is blaming you."

James stood up, pushing back his chair. "This is my case. I just need time. I will catch this guy."

"This is a sensitive matter."

"No disrespect, sir, but I want this case. I deserve it."

Even as the words escaped his lips, he wondered about the irony of trying to ditch this case for the last few days, and now here he was fighting to keep it.

"I don't know."

"Well I do. Keep me on. I'll crack this case."

Chief Baxter stood up. Now they stared at each other across the crowded, unkempt desk. The sounds of rustling paper and clacking keyboards provided a fitting soundtrack to their conversation.

"I'm the best detective you've got," James said.

Unable to meet his eyes, the Chief slouched and nodded. "Okay."

Then he surprised James with a firm stare. "But you only have six days. That's the best I can do."

"That's not enough time, and you know it."

"Six days. If you don't have a good lead by then, you're off the case."

CHAPTER 39

Eric hesitated in the middle of Samantha's living room, wondering if he should go upstairs to check on her or leave, when he heard a car pull into the driveway.

He started for the door, but then heard footsteps on the stairs. Samantha padded past him wearing the same clothes, but they were wrinkled now. Her hair, however, was ruffled, her face mottled and tear-stained. Eric followed her to the door.

As she grasped the doorknob and pulled open the door, he felt an almost overwhelming urge to wrap his arms around her, to wipe the tears from her red cheeks.

Detective James Wolfe stood on the porch in gray slacks, a white dress shirt and an asphalt gray tie. "What's wrong?" he said.

She let him in as Eric backed out of the way, feeling awkward and uncomfortable. They all went to the kitchen and sat at the table. Once they were all seated, Samantha said, "I can't do this anymore. I can't do this case."

"Why? What happened?" Wolfe asked, glaring at Eric. Eric had seen kinder eyes in pit bulls.

Holding up the black tape recorder he had been clutching since Samantha locked herself in her bedroom, Eric placed it on the table. Samantha looked at the recorder as if it were an alien, something black and sticky, straight out of a Stephen King novel.

"Is this okay?" he asked her, his finger touching the ON button. She nodded. Detective Wolfe shifted his gaze from her to him, and then back to her.

Turning on the tape recorder, Eric settled back in his chair, letting them listen to the entire session, which he had played for himself earlier while Samantha was upstairs. Because she forgot to turn off the recorder when she ended the hypnotherapy session, it lapsed into white noise.

When Eric turned it off, Samantha was crying again. Wolfe held her hand, gently rubbing her knuckles.

Sniffling, she said, "I'm sorry. I just can't do this."

Wolfe reached over, tucked her hair behind one ear like a

father might his daughter, and kissed her forehead. "The rape happened four years ago," he explained to Eric. "I worked the case. That's how we met."

Eric nodded, unsure of what to say.

Wolfe left his chair to retrieve a box of Kleenex from the kitchen cabinet. He brought them to Samantha, who tugged a single tissue out of the box to clean her face.

When Wolfe returned to his seat, he spoke to both of them. "I met with the Chief earlier. He's not happy about the publicity he's getting."

"I bet," Eric said, remembering the news he'd watched earlier that morning before heading to the library.

Dabbing at her face, Samantha said, "What did he say?"

"He wants to take me off the case."

"He can't do that," she said, dropping the hand grasping the tissue to the table.

"He's not," Wolfe tugged at his mustache. "For now."

"What does that mean?"

"He gave us six days."

Samantha shook her head. "Six days isn't enough time."

"It has to be."

The three of them sat in silence for a few moments, a bright orange sun pouring a river of fire through the kitchen windows.

Eric spoke first: "I'll do whatever I have to do. I know I'm not a detective, but somehow I'm connected to this psycho out there. And if I know about Samantha's rape, maybe I know other things, too." He thought he saw appreciation in Wolfe's face. Both he and the detective looked at Samantha.

"I understand if you can't help," he said to her.

"No." She straitened herself in her chair, lifted her chin. "I'm in this as much as the two of you."

"I could find another hypnotherapist."

Samantha shook her head, dabbing the last of her tears away. "No, James. They would have to study all my notes, establish rapport. The first day or two would be wasted on back peddling. It has to be me."

In Samantha's kitchen, under the dwindling sunlight, they forged a pact three strong. Detective Wolfe explained his plans. "First, I'll interview the families, neighbors and friends of the murdered victims again. Then I'll have a forensic team re-comb the crime scenes. And if that doesn't work, I'll visit a few of the more seedy areas of town to see if anyone has heard someone bragging about the murders."

"And we'll continue hypnotherapy, find out what we can," Eric said.

Wolfe looked at them. "Can we meet each night to discuss any progress?"

They both nodded.

Eric stood up and stretched. "If we're going to do all that, I'm going to need a good night's sleep."

"Six days," he heard Wolfe call out as he closed the front door and walked to his car.

CHAPTER 40

James slouched as he shuffled up to Samantha's front door. He frowned all the way to the kitchen table, where Eric sat inhaling a Coke. Samantha and Eric both waited for him to speak.

"Nothing," he said and recounted the day's fruitless events.

Nothing had come of a day's work. Not that this was uncommon. A detective's job was often long and hard and thankless, nothing like the glamorized versions on television. Cases stretched on and on, and more often than he would like to admit, were interrupted by new, fresh ones.

This particular case seemed to be playing out like the worst one of his career – his family's murder. Both cases were still open, with zero leads, zero clues. Both involved grisly murders of pregnant women. Both killers remained free to kill again. Although he considered a connection, so far nothing but coincidences linked the two.

"Tomorrow forensics will re-check the police cruiser, and then the other crime scene with the murdered couple. But the scenes weren't sealed, so no one expects to find anything new or helpful."

"We didn't get anywhere either," Samantha explained, setting a Mountain Dew in front of the detective. Samantha popped open one for herself, too. It fizzled as she sat down.

James bent the aluminum tab on his soda can, opening it with a loud *POP*.

"Eric wouldn't cooperate again… under hypnosis," she added at the end, blushing. "All he wanted to talk about was my rape."

Wolfe sipped his drink. One day down and we've got nothing. Five days to go.

"I did say something," Eric said. "At the very end."

"Let's hear it." Wolfe grabbed the black tape recorder and turned it on. The three of them listened to the session, Eric antagonizing Samantha in that raspy, sometimes shuddery voice from the grave.

At the end of the recording, as Samantha threatened to cut off the session, as she began fulfilling her promise, Eric said something that made James shiver: "We're coming for you. We're coming for you."

CHAPTER 41

"You're not moving forward in your case," Eric mocked in trance on day two.

Samantha perched on the edge of her chair, holding the notebook and listening to the steady, monotone whir of the tape recorder. "What do you mean?"

"What do I mean? You have no leads, no clues. Your pathetic attempts disgust me to the point of utter hilarity."

"Do you try to sound pompous," she said, "Or does it come naturally to you?"

Sitting on the couch, Eric rocked slowly back and forth like a psychic during a séance, calling up the dead. Ignoring her comment, Eric said, "I would very much like to rape you."

"Stop it. Stop it or I'll end this session right now."

Baring his teeth, Eric let out a growl from deep in his throat, sounding more dog-like than human. Samantha's mouth went dry. The police were right outside. She thought about getting them. Was he really dangerous?

Shifting back and forth, lips curled back from his teeth, Eric stared at her. Or seemed to, anyway.

After catching her breath, Samantha thought, No, I'm not going to bring in the authorities and waste another day when they had so few left. She glanced at the window. A serial killer was out there. He could strike again anytime, anyplace.

Maybe right here.

"I won't play games with you today," Samantha said. "If you're not willing to talk about the case, we're through." She hoped he wouldn't call her bluff.

A moment of silence. Then, "So talk."

Samantha released a pent up breath. "Okay, good. When we started our sessions, you said something in your past was blocking your present memory of what killed Rosalie Parker. Do you know what that is now?"

"Yes."

Samantha glanced at the tape recorder. There was plenty of

tape left. Just in case, she had stacked extra tapes on the table, next to the recorder. "What is blocking you?"

"The past, you stupid slut." A line of spit spilled down his chin. He shook so violently Samantha thought he might tumble off the couch onto the carpet between them.

Unwilling to show her emotions, Samantha swallowed the hard knot in her throat and kept digging. "What about your past, Eric? Be specific."

"My past as a killer. My destiny as a life taker. Imagine blending the two in one moment, then you'll understand."

"What happened the night in the parking garage? Why did you pass out?"

"I met my destiny."

"What? What do you mean?"

"Do I always have to spell it out for you? I met my destiny. It's no fun to just come out and tell you."

"Fun? You think this is—"

Suddenly, Samantha got it. Eureka, she thought. Sherlock Holmes, step aside. "You met your destiny and you weren't ready," she elaborated for him. "When you saw the killer, you saw your future, or what your future had always been in all your other lives. But you weren't ready. It was like sensory overload." The two sides of Eric – past and present – collided, she thought.

Basking in her discovery, overwhelmed with the awe of revelation, she felt as if she had discovered the lost city of Atlantis or deciphered ancient hieroglyphics etched into the decaying walls of a pyramid. Her heart lashed against her ribcage. Her palms sweat.

"Aren't you forgetting something?" Eric said.

In her excitement, she had almost forgotten what she was doing. "Like what?"

"Aren't you going to ask me who the killer is?"

CHAPTER 42

Detective James Wolfe showed up in the middle of a conversation about the afterlife. Eric looked up as he continued to speak: "I've always believed there was something out there, governing everything."

"Wow," Wolfe said, going to the refrigerator, taking out a Mountain Dew. "What's next on the agenda, politics or abortion?"

"Ha, Ha." Samantha elbowed him in the ribs as he passed her to sit at the kitchen table.

In the background, a small radio spilled out tunes from the 80's. Currently, "We Built This City." With the lights on, the kitchen windows became mirrors reflecting ghostly images of the three of them, so Eric drew the blinds.

"You're in a good mood," Eric said, commenting on Wolfe's cheerful disposition.

"Not for any reason. I came up with nothing again. What about you two?"

Samantha cocked her head. "You mean other than solving the mysteries of religion?"

"I didn't know you guys were so hilarious," Eric said.

Wolfe pointed at Samantha with his thumb. "Trust me, she's not."

Samantha slapped him on the shoulder.

"Okay, okay. Really, did you two make any progress?" Eric thought he noticed desperation in the detective's eyes.

"Actually we did," Samantha said, motioning toward the recorder. Wolfe snatched it up greedily, pulled it toward him and turned it on, hovering over it like a wizard peering hopefully into the curved surface of a crystal ball.

Eric drained an entire Coke while Wolfe listened to the tape. Once the recording ended, Wolfe leaned back in his chair, pupils as big and dark as cherries. "I don't believe it. He knows." Eric squirmed in his chair, avoiding the detective's gaze. There was something disheartening in his eyes.

"He *says* he knows," Samantha said. "And he refused to give up a name."

Wolfe rubbed his forehead and stared at the black recorder as if it might reveal the killer's name itself. "We need to find out if he really knows or if he's just jerking our chains."

"How?"

"We can ask him where a body is. That will prove he is telling the truth, and we might find a clue."

"Why can't we just press him for the name?"

Wolfe paused, took a sip of his Mountain Dew. "We need a reason to accuse someone. We can't risk arresting another wrong person. The guy I nabbed hired a few lawyers and they're having a field day suing the police. Come to find out, he's been involved with prior cases for drug trafficking and armed robbery. He even had cocaine on him when he was arrested, but because of the way we handled it, we'll be lucky to get him on anything. We need *proof*."

Eric shifted in his chair and tugged uneasily at the collar of his shirt. Had the temperature risen?

"We might find a clue," Samantha agreed. "And the sooner the better. We should set another session for tomorrow. Early."

Wolfe nodded. "Good. Right now it's the best lead we have."

"You were much more polite today," Samantha said after the session the next day, joining him in the kitchen, where burnished bronze light cascaded through the windows and pooled on the tiled floor.

"Good to know." Eric carried a mug of coffee over to the kitchen table. Early turned out to be 8:00 a.m. He had called in to work and his boss generously offered him extra time to help out the police. "Do you mind if I listen to the tape?"

"Not at all."

Switching on the recorder, he tasted the vanilla-flavored coffee, enjoying it on his tongue before letting it trickle down his throat. He heard Samantha's voice lead him through a set of trance-inducing exercises, some of which he had read about in the library books. Once he was sufficiently under, she started asking him questions; it reminded him a little of the interrogation by Detective Wolfe. Right now, that interrogation seemed like a million years ago.

"Can you tell me where the body is located?" Samantha said on the tape.

"Will you release me to find your serial killer for you?" Eric heard himself reply.

"Maybe. But we definitely won't if you don't prove you know

where he is."

Eric took another sip of his coffee. He liked the way Samantha played hardball, cornering him into confessions.

"You'll never find your serial killer otherwise."

"You're getting off the subject. First things first," Samantha said on the tape. "Where's a body?"

There was a pause on the recording, a brief silence punctuated only by the almost inaudible sound of the tape continuing to record. Finally, the Eric on the tape spoke: "You'll find a body in the woods behind the Hidden View Apartments. Twenty feet north from the second small dam in the stream. On the right side."

After a few more navigational questions to lock in the exact location of the body, Samantha ended the session.

Eric punched the OFF button on the recorder. Samantha sat down in the seat next to him, and he couldn't help but notice how cute she looked with her hair tied back in a ponytail. Sunlight painted her face bronze; her hair into strings of finely cut gold; her eyes into dazzling treasures of the gods.

He faced the sunlight, squinting, hoping it transformed him into something even half as angelic.

"What are you doing?"

"Nothing." He quickly turned away from the windows, rubbing the light out of his eyes.

The doorbell rang.

Samantha jumped up. "That must be James."

Relieved with the distraction, Eric finished his coffee. He would need it for the work ahead.

CHAPTER 43

Detective Wolfe wanted to dig up the body immediately. He argued that since the remains were buried in the woods, they wouldn't have to worry about spectators. And, besides, he'd already stocked up on shovels.

"Are you sure you'll be okay?" Eric asked Samantha on her front porch. A bright morning sky peeked around and between wispy clouds, coloring everything a bold, rusty orange.

"Yes," she said, but she averted her eyes and rubbed at her nose.

For some reason, he recalled the words he'd spoken in trance: *We're coming for you. We're coming for you.*

Samantha pointed to the police cruiser parked next to the curb. "There's police protection. Plus, it's the middle of the day. No one would be that foolish."

Eric thought about the cop with his throat ripped open, but said nothing.

Wolfe seemed convinced; however Eric suspected he really just wanted to get to the body, ASAP. Reluctantly, Eric left Samantha on the porch, trotting over to the passenger's side door of Wolfe's car, a puke-green Subaru redolent with the scent of pine cones courtesy of the tree-shaped air-freshener dangling from the rear-view mirror.

Entering the green canoe gave a new definition to "climbing in" a vehicle. Eric plopped down on the vinyl-wrapped bench seat, gagging at the smell, and noting the clean interior. A drill sergeant would have been proud.

He stretched his feet out. In most people's cars, the floorboard was a graveyard of crumpled wrappers and old receipts; Wolfe's was spotless.

The detective got in on the driver's side and they both closed their doors with two noisy bangs, one right after the other, which sounded a little too much like gunshots for Eric's taste.

We're coming for you. We're coming for you.

Samantha waved from the porch, her image hovering in Eric's

mind like a last goodbye. Wolfe steered the boat out onto the street, switched gears, and floored it past the police car, towards the body.

Wolfe leaned over and turned on the radio. Hip-hop legend L.L. Cool J blared from of the speakers accompanied by a thunderous, addictive beat. The detective bobbed his head along with the music.

For the first half of the song, Eric stared at Wolfe, hardly noticing the scenery blowing by outside the vehicle, as the head-banging police officer steered them through mid-day traffic.

Overcome with disbelief, he said, "You like rap?"

Wolfe peeked at Eric out of the corner of his eye. He raised one eyebrow. "I like a lot of things."

"And I thought I was the strange and twisted one."

Once the song ended, a local DJ trumpeted the glories of a popular fast food chain. Wolfe guided them over the Ohio River on the Sherman Minton bridge, changing lanes to avoid a rear-end collision with a red sports car. He turned off the radio.

"Eric," Wolfe said, "I never got a chance to apologize for treating you like a criminal."

"No problem."

"I mean it." Wolfe twisted in his seat. "I was wrong. I'm not one to apologize easily, but I'm sorry."

Eric believed him. The detective looked depleted already, anxious to move on to another topic. He pretended to stew in silence for a few moments, a not so subtle payback that immediately embarrassed him as a human being. "I graciously accept," Eric said quickly.

They spilled off the bridge into Indiana, headed onto 265 West, rounding a sharp curve before taking Exit 1 into New Albany. Another curve brought them to State Street, where Wolfe turned right, climbing the steep hill that, if followed all the way, would take them to Floyd Knob's. Most people called them simply *The Knobs*. Eric wasn't sure what a *knob* was, but it sounded dirty.

On the drive up the hill, Wolfe said, "Unless we uncover a body, there would be no use calling in crime scene techs – it would only further discredit us with the Chief. At this point proving the realness of your confessions under hypnosis trumps the risk of corrupting evidence."

Rounding yet another curve, the Hidden View Apartment sign appeared. Following the specific directions Eric gave under hypnosis, and Samantha had mapped out for them on a piece of paper, Wolfe guided the Subaru to an apartment building squeezed into the far back corner of the complex.

Wolfe parked on a downward slope. "Looks like they don't keep this baby up like the others."

Eric agreed. Porches sagged from the front of the building, some without any support. A littered yard led up to a set of chipped double doors guarded by the fattest spider Eric had ever seen. He half expected a shriveled crack-addict to stagger out, babbling nonsense, "Mum-Mum, Ye-Mum," strung out and hallucinating.

Wolfe nodded at the back of the building, where a dense forest struggled skyward. Somewhere inside those woods lay a dead body, buried in a shallow, makeshift grave.

Both men circled to the back of the car. Popping open the trunk, Wolfe looked at Eric. "Time to find that body."

CHAPTER 44

What am I doing? Eric thought, taking a shovel from Wolfe. *This is crazy.*

Closing the trunk, slinging his own shovel over his shoulder, Wolfe said, "Let's get going." Around the detective's neck dangled a black camera he would use to snap photos of the dead body. Proof is what they needed and proof is what they'd get.

They trailed behind the apartments, where a small yard separated it from the woods. The back of the building, if possible, looked in worse shape than the front: a few of the porches appeared moments away from collapsing. Eric happily observed that no residents were currently outside smoking legal, or illegal, substances.

Birds chirped warnings in the trees. A fly buzzed relentlessly around his face, apparently unimpressed with his too-slow attempts to swat it.

"Our first objective is to get to the stream," Wolfe said, reading the instructions Samantha made for them.

Walking under a lacework of light and shadow created by the trees, they crunched their way through a mat of dead leaves, Eric following the detective. What was he doing? He wasn't a police officer. He shouldn't be sneaking into the woods to dig up a dead body. He was a twenty-four year old telemarketer. The only corpses he'd seen rested in coffins, dressed up and painted alive with make-up.

As if he'd read Eric's mind, Wolfe said, "If the body's been buried here for a few hours, rigor mortis has already set it, making it as stiff as our shovels." Stomping down a hill, Eric readjusted his shovel on his shoulder.

"If it's been here a few days, the skin is probably deteriorated."

He could see the stream at the bottom of the hill now, not much more than a trickle, winding its way through the forest. "A lot of times the skin will look like black cottage cheese."

Descending behind the detective, Eric said, "I don't remember asking about this stuff."

Wolfe looked over his shoulder as he bounced down the hill. With the shovel, he could pass for a medieval knight hunting the forest for thieves. "I just don't want you to be surprised."

"Good luck with that."

Facing forward, continuing to the bottom of the hill, Wolfe grew silent for a moment, and then said, "The face could be half-eaten away by maggots." Eric scrunched up his face, disgusted. Wolfe howled with laughter. They kept moving.

The stream curved between two up-sloping hills. With sparse cover from the trees here, the sun beat down on them with a fury. Eric had the strange notion that the forest itself would come alive, gnarled roots groping up through mushy earth, beating them to death with rotted knots and Herculean limbs.

"We need to find a small waterfall where the stream pools," Wolfe read from the piece of paper.

"You mean like that one?" Eric pointed downstream toward a rocky area.

"Looks right to me. Could be it."

Zigzagging up the stream on half-submerged stones, Wolfe said, "You know, with the water here, the body could be more preserved."

"I thought we were done with that conversation."

Hurrying toward the mini-waterfall, Wolfe grinned. "I haven't even told you about the eyes yet."

Reaching the pooled water, Wolfe studied the directions, then paced five steps, sneakers drawing sucking sounds from the mud. His face focused fully on the job before him. Eric leaned on his shovel beside the mini-waterfall, watching the detective, waging another battle with a stubborn fly and listening to the almost hypnotic white noise of the water.

He tried not to think about what he was doing here. Images of a hundred dead faces viewed on dark theater screens rushed through his mind. Bloated. Pale. Squishy.

We're coming for you.

The words snuck up on him. Someone was coming not for Samantha, but for him, coming through the cobwebs of shadow, soundlessly moving among the fallen leaves. Eric glanced up at the treetops, unable to breathe, and saw nothing but a canopy of branches. If a horror stalked him, it remained hidden.

Releasing the breath, hearing it in his own ears as too loud, he peeked at Wolfe, hoping the detective hadn't noticed his recent scare.

"Got something," Wolfe said, not even looking up. He stabbed his shovel into the ground. Eric picked up his shovel and joined him. Quickly, they filleted the earth, packing their shovels with clumps of dirt before pitching it behind them. Stab. Lift. Pitch. Stab. Lift. Pitch. The monotonous movement helped Eric not think of death and blood and corpses. In the back of his mind, however, he knew that soon he would be unable to consider anything but those things.

Hair stringy with sweat and plastered to his head, muscles taut and strained, aching already with the burden of use, Eric couldn't help but connect the physical act of digging to his search for answers with Samantha. He had been, in fact, engaged in a life-long search, leading to this very moment.

From the first time he experienced the urge to hurt someone or to damage something, he'd also felt the pang of guilt and the fear that, if left unchecked, those urges would flourish into uncontrollable lusts. In one way or another, he had been digging for an answer ever since.

Lost in his thoughts, at first Eric didn't realize Wolfe had stopped shoveling. He kept plunking the spade of his shovel into the ground until the detective grabbed his arm.

Suddenly back in the moment, Eric found himself eye to eye with Wolfe. His heart stopped beating. "What?" he asked, as if the question elicited unlimited answers and not the single, obvious one.

Instead of giving a verbal response, Wolfe crouched, and wiping away a film of dirt, revealed the bleached cheek of a corpse.

CHAPTER 45

Dusted back by Wolfe's cupped hand, the forest floor unveiled more of the dead face. One glassy eye stared up at them as if out of a swamp – unblinking, a crocodile's eye.

Shuddering, Eric looked away. His insides clenched. This was too much. He couldn't take it.

"Help me uncover the rest of the body," Wolfe said.

"I don't know if I can."

"I'm not jonesing to do this either, but we're running out of time."

Eric's throat felt raw. "Aren't we supposed to call the police?"'

"We will. After we dig up the body."

"I don't know."

Wolfe glared at him. "Look, if we don't, it all ends here. I'll be off the case, the killer will probably remain free and you might never get another chance to find the answers you're looking for. This is our best shot all around. Understand?"

Forcing himself to look again at the pale face in the dirt, at the crocodile eye reflecting both sunlight and truth, he realized it was the most convincing evidence that all the revelations of the past few days were valid. The lifeless eye proved it. How could he know the location of a dead body otherwise?

He really was reincarnated. He really was a serial killer in past lives. And he really would become a murderer if he didn't find a way to stop the cycle.

"Eric, you okay?"

"What?"

"You look sick."

"I'm fine," he lied. He felt dizzy, like he could throw up at any moment.

"Good, I need your help."

Eric hunched down beside him, brushing away dirt, exposing a discolored throat. Silently, they worked the body out of the ground until it stretched naked and white under the sun.

Wolfe tossed his shovel aside. Using his camera, he snapped

twenty-seven photos of the dead body from every angle possible. Eric stood up, gagging at the smell, staggered a few feet and emptied his stomach on the forest floor. The corpse was clearly a young male, left side of his skull tucked into a rotted mask of flesh.

Done with his photo-shoot, Wolfe withdrew his cell phone, dialed a number and spoke urgently into the receiver. "I have one dead body. We need crime scene personnel here *now*."

Huddled around the television in the living room, Eric, Wolfe and Samantha watched the news, celebrating with frozen margaritas. On the television, a bright-eyed female reporter stood outside the woods behind the Hidden View apartments, excitedly recounting the afternoon's events.

"The body of an unidentified Caucasian male was discovered earlier today in New Albany, Indiana. An anonymous caller reported the body to Louisville Metro Police Detective James Wolfe. All we know right now is that the victim died from blunt trauma to the head. A forensic team is currently investigating the homicide. Rumors are circulating that the dead body is connected to the recent string of murders in Louisville, posing the question, 'Is a serial killer on the loose?' Lisa Martin, Wave 3 News."

"There are already rumors," Wolfe said, downing the rest of his margarita. His raised eyebrows made Samantha giggle.

Eric grinned. Three days down and they had a hope, the faint glimmer of a lead. Right now, like a candle in the pitch darkness, even a glimmer blazed brightly. Wolfe had conveniently left him out of the police report, keeping suspicions of his guilt at bay. Who would believe the reincarnation theory anyway? He still didn't know if he believed it.

Next to Samantha on the couch, he inhaled her sweet aroma. He felt the teenage thrill of his arm touching hers.

On the screen, another reporter, this one a black male with a goatee, remarked that Kentuckiana residents were in an uproar over the police department's slow progress in the recent murder cases. Flipping to a video, the news showed an elderly man with liver spotted hands. He stared angrily into the camera. "I've been here for 45 years. Forty-five! And I've never been scared like this before in my life. Watching my back all the time. I never owned a gun, but I bought one today. If you ask me, it's those bee-bop gangsters with their rap music polluting our youth..."

Eric leaned forward so he could see Wolfe on the other side of Samantha. "You're not going to let them talk about your music like that are you?"

Samantha, apparently aware of Wolfe's taste for rap music, burst out in laughter. Wolfe rolled his eyes.

The news hopped from one fear-slanted testimony to another, ending back with the black reporter. "You have to ask yourself," he said, walking in front of a strand of yellow police tape, 'Am I really safe?'"

Wolfe tilted his head back and stared at the ceiling. "If anyone's polluting anything, it's those guys spreading their gospel of fear."

Samantha headed to the kitchen, returning with another round of drinks. As they sampled their margaritas, enjoying the fleeting pleasures of optimism, Eric asked, "What if the body turned up no new evidence, nothing to help us?"

"We could try to draw more information out through hypnotism," Samantha tried.

"But that's no guarantee."

No one else said anything. Wolfe stared at his hands.

Eric thought he understood how the detective felt. Right now, the body might be their last chance for proving his innocence, keeping Wolfe on the case and stopping the killer before he took another innocent life.

CHAPTER 46

The chiming phone startled Detective James Wolfe awake. His eyes popped open as he sprung up in bed, surrounded by the lush furnishings of his bedroom – bamboo furniture from Africa, real palm tree in the corner, entertainment center that any rap artist would envy.

A second ring splintered the predawn silence.

Throwing off silk sheets and Egyptian cotton blankets, James slid out of bed onto the Imported Persian carpet.

His wife had never allowed a phone in the bedroom. She thought it violated the most intimate place in the house. For thirteen years of marriage, glorious years taken too much for granted, no phone passed through the hallowed bedroom door. Now, even after her death, James continued the tradition with religious discipline, like others counted beads and recited Hail Marys, refusing to bring even his cell phone into the room.

He kept it just outside the bedroom door, in the hallway on a shelf.

Across the room, past the vanity desk, where his wife once brushed her hair and worried over her makeup, James hurried to catch the caller before they hung up.

Riiiiing.

Wolfe picked up the cell phone, unlocked the screen, and raised it to his face. "Hello?"

"Detective Wolfe?"

"Yes, who is this?"

"Detective Riley."

"Which department do you work for?"

"Nashville, TN."

Wolfe rubbed his face, his eyes.

"Sorry to call you so early."

Until the self-appointed detective whose name James neither remembered nor recognized mentioned it, he hadn't considered the time. The house was dark. How early was it? "No problem," he mumbled. "What's up?"

After some of his more publicized cases, other detectives frequently called him, wanting to meet him and glean the secrets to stardom. As if stopping a criminal wasn't good enough, when he could not deliver the secrets they craved – he had no secrets beside hard work and uncompromising persistence – they left quickly, never to be heard from again.

"I believe I have some information that relates to your present case."

"Which one would that be?" James wasn't giving an inch.

"The serial killer case."

"Possible serial killer," James clarified. But his pulse jumped. "How do you know about the case?"

"CNN."

James groaned. The case had finally gone national. It wouldn't be long before hordes of vultures descended upon the city, turning the case into a media circus. Making it that much harder to solve.

On the other end of the line, Detective Riley said, "I believe, no I'm convinced, that your serial killer is the same woman who left ten bodies for us to find here."

James paused. Blinked. Did he hear the Detective correctly?

"Woman?"

"Yeah. I'm going to bring up her file tomorrow afternoon, if that's okay?"

After a brief moment of silence: "Detective Wolfe?"

"I'm here. Tomorrow. That's fine."

Having settled on when to meet, James hung up and placed the cell phone back on the shelf. He did this unconsciously. As he sauntered back to bed, bright green numbers on the face of his alarm clock boldly declared 5:00 a.m. "A woman," he whispered to the dark bedroom, shaking his head.

Plopping down on the edge of his bed, James decided that this was the biggest and strangest case of his career. And with the faith of a fanatic, he was convinced that it would only get stranger still.

CHAPTER 47

In the basement of her massive, European-style mansion, Charlize London listened in on the phone call between Detective James Wolfe and Detective Alan Riley.

She knew this day would come; therefore she had prepared for it by bugging Detective Riley's phones – both business and personal. Whenever he called anyone, a computer automatically alerted her and recorded the phone call. As of this date, she had logged three hundred hours of conversations, mostly boring calls between him and his wife or him and one of his three children. Or a routine, brain-numbing police conversation about another dumb criminal too stupid to be out on the streets.

However, as soon as the story of her murders in Louisville broadcasted across the country, she figured Riley would connect them with his cold case. The smart pig. For the past few days, she had done little except listen to his calls. She finally caught him.

After the call ended, Charlize checked her investment accounts online. Her long list of investments trailed back centuries, the vast fortune spread over six continents and counting, which is how she could afford this house with all its cool gadgets. Everything in her portfolio looked good today.

She stood up and walked the length of her basement, stopping in front of a wall-mounted shelf full of blades, power tools and guns. More preparation for the days ahead.

On the floor next to the assortment of weapons lay what at first appeared to be an untidy sack of bones – until it moaned. "Shh," she said. "It'll all be over for you soon enough."

Things would happen fast now. That's how she had orchestrated it. Soon, she would be with Eric.

Choosing a Glock 27 and a dagger purchased in Africa when she had lived there for three years, Charlize left the shelf for the stairs. It was early; but then again, she had much to do.

On the first floor, she strolled through rooms as big as small houses, furnished in leather, expensive paintings and statues of modern art and pagan gods. Retiring to the kitchen, all black and complete with the latest culinary technology, she fixed herself a smoked ham and provolone cheese sandwich. She brought it to the living room and clicked on the theater-sized television.

She wanted to see if any new news reports about the case were being aired. Wolfing down her sandwich, she watched nearly life-sized news journalists regurgitate all the currently known facts about the case. Then the weather. Cloudy day. Thirty percent chance of rain. A weatherman wearing a tweed suit that hadn't been stylish since Reagan was President pointed at a swirling blue mass and followed it across the screen with his finger.

With the push of a few buttons on her remote control, Charlize switched from live television to recorded television. Over the last few weeks, she had reason to record all the news. She froze the screen on a shot of Eric's face.

Warmth flooded her stomach. Overwhelmed with love, she hopped off the couch, padding over to the television, where, with one slender, perfectly manicured hand, she reached out and touched the screen. She closed her eyes. She could almost feel him, feel his energy. They had a connection. Nothing would ever change that.

"My Eric," she whispered. "My destiny."

CHAPTER 48

Unable to sleep, troubled by a quiet paranoia that nothing was what it seemed, James Wolfe dressed, mind replaying the revelation that the serial killer could be a woman. If it were true, it would change everything. He went downstairs to feed Napoleon and Caesar.

Descending the stairs, he heard them chuffing around on the first floor. With the promise of rain last night, he let them sleep inside the house, something his wife would never have tolerated.

This, however, was not like the no-phone-in-the-bedroom rule; he gladly and quickly allowed his pets inside the house after his wife died. The dogs didn't seem to mind, either. They provided the unconditional love and unabated companionship no amount of therapy, however expensive, could reproduce.

Now on the first floor with them, he scratched their heads and necks. Each viewed him with the excited expression only possible with canines and children. On anyone or anything else, the expression appeared fake, even forced. Their big brown eyes, however, radiated sheer innocent devotion. If only people were like that, he thought. *Even halfway.*

After giving each dog a belly rub, he washed their food bowls and filled the bowls with healthy-sized portions of Kibbles 'n Bits. Maybe it wasn't the healthiest of dog foods, but Napoleon and Caesar gobbled it up like starved castaways. For a minute, he watched his boys eat. He took comfort in this simple pleasure. The rest of his life was complicated enough; and, by all signs, it would only get more complicated.

Once the dogs finished their meals, he released them into the backyard to run and play.

While he locked up the house, he called Samantha. She answered on the first ring with a "Hey, you. Eric's here with me."

"Good. I want you both around when I get news about the body." He spoke as he trekked from his front door to his driveway. Neighboring houses lingered like warring battleships on both sides of the street, their shadowed front lawns transformed into moats of semi-darkness.

"You haven't heard anything yet?" Her lackluster tone reduced the question to a depressing statement.

"No. Nothing yet. But the forensic team and the Medical Examiner have strict orders to contact me the very microsecond they discover anything."

"See you soon?"

"On my way. I'm expecting the call anytime now." He reached his car and climbed into the front.

"Better let you go, then."

After he hung up, James studied himself in the rear-view mirror. Lack of sleep showed up in dark purple blotches under his eyes. His had been a long and illustrious career, but age was slowly creeping up on him, and he wasn't sure how much longer his old body could take it. When he started counting wrinkles in double-digits, he switched his attention back to the case at hand. He had at least one more good effort in him.

Fifteen minutes later he pulled into Samantha's driveway.

CHAPTER 49

To the wailing voice of Aerosmith singing, "I don't want to miss
a thing," Charlize London pumped two ten-pound hand-bells. She
watched her bicep muscles flex in the wall length mirror. When
she was finished with those, she worked her triceps, doing three
sets of thirty repetitions before replacing the weights on the
barbell rack. Squats, pull-ups and crunches followed. One after
another, love songs issued from ceiling mounted surround-sound
speakers.

By the time the CD started repeating track 1, Charlize had
completed her daily workout, and stood sweating and sobbing in
front of the mirror. Longing for Eric. How she loved him so.
Hugging herself, she imagined his arms wrapped around her. Her
body shook with desire to embrace him. To make love to him. To
start a family.

Showering, Charlize dressed in low-slung blue jeans, brown
Jesus sandals and a tight-fitting red shirt.

Beside the bed lay a packed Alligator-skin suitcase. Inside it,
between layers of clothes, she stashed a gun, should she need it.
And, she mused, she just might.

She half carried, half dragged it to the hallway, to the top of
the marble staircase. Before lugging it down the stairs, Charlize
backtracked to two doors flanking the end of the hallway.

Entering the room on the left, she checked to make sure
everything was in order. A bookshelf occupied one wall of the room,
lined with volumes about witchcraft, meditation, hypnosis,
firearms, yoga, computers and several medical reference books. On
the other side of the room stood a silver-encrusted table topped
with a recent picture of Eric surrounded by peach-colored candles.
Backed against the far wall, under a window, and bolted to the
floor, was a single padded steel chair, complete with arm and leg
straps. She nodded. Everything looked perfect.

Content with the readiness of that room, Charlize headed to
the room on the right. Much different than the first room, this one
featured a baby's crib, a blue toy-chest and blue and white pastel

furniture. Angel-filled clouds decorated the blue walls.

Crowding the crib and the bed, a riveted audience of button-eyed dolls stared blankly back at her.

Here was the room where Eric's and her baby would sleep. A symbol of their future together. She could hardly wait.

On her way back to her suitcase in the hall, Charlize reflected on the pregnant women she had killed. How they had enjoyed feeling another life bloom inside of them and how she was forced to wait for Eric. It wasn't fair. She was glad she had killed them. She angrily lugged the suitcase down the winding marble staircase to the lobby below. At the bottom, she stopped to catch her breath. One of the few downsides to a million dollar house, she thought and grinned.

One more thing to do before she left.

She headed down to the basement, moving aside an African-designed separator in one of many dark corners, revealing a set of metal shelves. On them set large glass containers filled with formaldehyde. She focused on one of them, inside which floated the bloated face of a severed head.

"You said that I wouldn't amount to anything, that I was a stupid, useless whore-child." She spat at the container. She raised one finger and pointed it at the persevered head. "See, Mother, see what I have become? I am a god. And you... you are nothing."

Smiling wickedly in the dark, trembling with anger and arrogance, Charlize ended her one-sided conversation with her mother. "You'll see when I bring Eric here. When our perfect destiny is fulfilled."

CHAPTER 50

Pumped up on caffeine, Eric, Samantha and Wolfe guzzled mug after mug of coffee, and rallied on the couch in Samantha's living room, hypnotized by the television.

"They just keep repeating the same old information," Eric complained. He glanced over at Wolfe and Samantha. Were they as amazed by all of this as he was? To him, the last week's events had been no less miraculous than the unexplained healing of a malignant tumor.

In the middle of that thought, Wolfe's cell phone jingled.

Samantha turned down the volume of the news as the detective answered the call. "Wolfe," he said, then listened. Eric couldn't hear the voice on the other end of the line so he was left to deduce the conversation from Wolfe's facial expression.

From the detective's stoic appearance, Eric figured Wolfe might either be winning the lottery or finding out that his entire family had been wiped out by a freak military experiment.

"Okay," Wolfe said and hung up.

Both Eric and Samantha watched their friend wilt like a dying flower right in front of them, his face drawn into an uncharacteristic sag.

Speaking to no one in particular, Wolfe said, "They didn't find anything."

"Nothing?" Eric said, dumbfounded.

"No fingerprints, no hair, no nothing."

"How is that possible?"

Wolfe just shook his head. Samantha did too, imitating his stern disapproval of what was now their reality. Eric felt hollowed out inside, empty. How could they have found nothing?

"There's still Detective Riley's information," Wolfe said, but Eric didn't hear even a hint of optimism in his voice. This was bad. Very bad.

Four days down. Two to go. And they still had nothing.

CHAPTER 51

Unwilling to waste the remainder of day four, Wolfe insisted that Eric undergo hypnosis. Find out what he could. It might not be much, but at least it was something.

Eric and Samantha took their usual places in the living room, while Wolfe stood with his back to the wall. Regressed to his past life personality, Eric shuddered on the couch, gaze drifting around the room.

"Detective, what a pleasure it is to speak with you."

Wolfe turned to Samantha. "How does he know I'm here?"

She shook her head, shrugged her shoulders.

"Are you ready to let me find the serial killer for you?" Eric said.

"Not a chance," Wolfe replied.

"Pity, because more people will die."

"Who? When?" He pushed off the wall.

Samantha put a hand on Wolfe's arm. "Don't. He's just trying to get you upset."

Eric smiled, shuddered again. "This all could be avoided if you let me lead you."

"We're not letting you go," Samantha insisted, taking back control of the session. She settled in her chair. Glanced down at her notebook.

"Then you'll never find her," Eric spat.

"Her?" James suddenly felt the same lightheaded confusion as he did on the phone with detective Riley.

"Yes, her. My partner. The partner in all my lives. She's spent more time than you can comprehend mastering the art of killing and getting away with it. You'll never catch her."

Wolfe grunted. "We'll see about that."

"Yes, we will see and very soon."

Eric jerked forward on the couch. Wolfe thought he would topple to the carpet and crawl towards them like an animated corpse; instead, he remained on the couch.

"What does that mean?" asked Samantha.

"You'll see."

CHAPTER 52

Her fully loaded Nissan 350Z spun out of the driveway. Charlize London headed away from Floyd Knobs, driving through Hopkinsville, KY to Clarksville, TN., listening to the latest news about her case, which was, of course, nothing.

No news, as they say, was good news.

Driving into Clarksville at dark fall, she was flooded with memories, memories of tracking Eric down, memories of honing her abilities.

She shook her head, jostling her thoughts back to the present. She wasn't here to relive her past; she was here to step boldly into her future. Into her destiny. Their destiny.

Detective Riley stood in the way of that destiny.

Needing supplies, she stopped at a hardware store. She brought a rope, nails, a box of matches and a red gas canister up to the check out register. After scanning her purchases, the teenager working the register eyed her suspiciously over wire-rimmed glasses. "How will you be paying today?"

"Credit card." She handed her a Visa.

The brunette checked the back of the card. "Can I see your ID?"

With her best smile, Charlize took out a New York driver's license with her picture printed on it and showed it to the girl.

"Ms. Kipfer?"

"That's me."

The cash register attendant nodded and hesitantly completed her purchase. Charlize snatched up her bags and left the store.

Ten minutes later Charlize pulled her car into a BP station. She filled the gas tank until the nozzle clicked to tell her that the car was full. Then she filled up the gas canister and stored it in the truck. Strolling across the parking lot, she noticed a few other drivers refueling, black gas cords plugged into their vehicles like IV lines. In every life, the modes of transportation changed. She wondered about the cars she would see in the future. Would they need gas? Would the station float hundreds of feet in the air by then? No way to tell, really.

A family of three unloaded from a burgundy VW van. A father and mother followed by a little blond-haired girl. Both of the parents stretched. She watched for a moment, then went inside the store to pay for her gas. She asked the skinny, redheaded counter attendant where the bathroom was located. "Round the building," he said, pointing to a rack of Ho-Ho's and Little Debbie Cakes, as if she could just step behind it and squat. She nodded and exited.

Rounding the building per her instructions, she abruptly stopped.

The little girl from the VW van, all blond curls and ruffled white dress, played alone on a long, yellow parking-space speed bump.

Charlize glanced over her shoulder at the van. The parents were gone. Probably in the store. Approaching the girl, she said, "Hello, what're you doing out here by yourself?"

The girl looked up at her with dazzling blue eyes. "My mommy told me not to talk to strangers."

"Smart lady," she said, inching closer. "But I'm no stranger. I'm your mommy's friend. Don't you remember?"

The little girl shook her head.

"That's okay. But your Mommy wanted me to tell you to wait in the bathroom."

Shaking her head again, the little girl said, "My Mommy told me to wait right here on this curb."

"Fine by me if you want to let the spiders and rats get you."

Although it was getting darker, the gas station lights held the shadows at the edge of the parking lot. The area reeked of old gasoline and fresh urine.

Horror streaked across the little girl's face. "Spiders?"

"Big hairy ones."

"Eww." The girl jumped up, blond curls bouncing, examining the ground for creepy crawlers. She edged toward the restroom.

Easing behind her, Charlize pushed open the ladies' restroom door. It gave a piggish squeal. "That's it," she reassured. "Right inside."

"But it's dark."

"Not compared to where you're going."

Charlize kicked the girl in the back, throwing her forward into the restroom. Then she followed her inside. The door swung noisily shut behind them.

With a click, she locked the door and flicked on the lights. Contrary to popular male myth, women's restrooms aren't always clean and better maintained than the men's. Case in point: the walls in this one were stained with yellow, black and green... something. Mold maybe. Alien fungus probably. Toilet cracked and crusted with stains. Scrawled phone numbers and random obscene remarks dotted the mirror. No sofas. No resident masseuse. Sorry guys.

The little girl cowered in the corner, holding herself in a tight ball, whimpering.

Kneeling in front of her, Charlize slipped on thin gloves and wrapped her hands around the girl's neck. She closed her eyes, tightening her grip. She felt the warm flesh against her fingers, heard the weak, gagging begs for mercy. Little hands grabbed at her; little legs kicked.

Charlize thought about Eric, could sense him with her now, and their future child. Their beautiful family.

When the twitching ceased, she opened her eyes. She propped the purple-faced body up against the urine-infested wall, and then, despite the unappealing appearance of the toilet, relieved herself.

As she washed her hands, her body trembled. Compared to killing, sex and drugs and alcohol – and all other gratifying vices – fared a distant second. Really, there were no comparisons.

Staring at herself in the fingerprint smeared mirror, under the jittery bathroom light, the dead child seemed like a purple-faced prophet, convincing her that she was not a demon-possessed freak, but a god with an unstoppable destiny.

CHAPTER 53

Detective Alan Riley awakened early Saturday morning, quietly showering and dressing. He didn't want to disturb his wife's sleep.

In khaki pants, brown loafers and a baby-blue polo shirt – the one with an alligator sewn into the breast, that after nearly three decades had suddenly come back into style – he kissed her forehead. She moaned softly in her dreams.

Twenty-two years of marriage had not dulled her beauty; she stunned him now, in her sleep, as much as she had when he first spotted her at a local café near their college. Everything seemed so perfect back then. So divinely orchestrated.

Outside his house, a one-story with a low-slung roof, Alan locked the front door, pulled out his cell phone and called detective James Wolfe. As he listened to the ring, he admired the sky.

Sunrise painted the horizon in brilliant blues and purples and reds. A breeze provided just enough comfort against the morning heat. According to the forecasts, the day would only get warmer.

Alan accepted the striking beauty as a sign from God, one more sign in a multitude that justice would finally be served. He thought of the ten victims and their countless family members and friends. Ah, justice. He grinned. It was a good day.

"James Wolfe," answered a gruff voice on the other end of the phone.

"This is Detective Riley. I'm just leaving."

"Where do you want to meet?"

"You know the city better than I."

A pause, then: "Howl at the Moon."

"Beg your pardon," Alan said.

"It's a piano bar, not a request. It's part of this place called Fourth Street Live."

"I've heard of it." He had in fact, read about it in The Courier-Journal, Louisville's biggest newspaper. In total, he subscribed to five newspapers, including the Wall Street Journal and USA Today.

"One more thing," Wolfe said. "Be careful. This is the most cunning killer I've ever encountered."

"Sure." Alan thought of the way the killer had taunted him, as if death were a game. As if she weren't toying with peoples' eternities.

Hiking to his car, a green Honda Accord, he ended his brief conversation with the man everyone called *The Wolfe*. Not to his face, of course. Alan couldn't help but feel giddy about their meeting; James Wolfe was a legend in law enforcement, no matter your opinion of his methods.

In his car now, he drove across Clarksville to the police station to pick up the files he needed. By the time he arrived, Alan felt as enthusiastic and hopefully idealistic as he had in years. He just knew something big was about to happen.

Climbing out of his car, humming a church hymn of all things, something about new life and freedom in the blood, he ambled up to the front door of the police station.

Even on a Saturday, a dozen cars lounged in the parking lot. No rest for law enforcement. It was the price they paid for the honor and privilege of administering justice to those who deserved nothing less.

One hand on the door, he looked once again at the sky. It draped everything in curtains of white gold.

Across the street a longhaired blond holding an ice-cream cone leaned against a silver Nissan 350Z. Under the light, backdropped by the new car, she appeared almost angelic. For an instant, emotions more secular than Christian paralyzed him.

The woman waved.

Blushing, he gave an awkward return wave and pushed through the police station doors.

"I don't have a good feeling about this," Wolfe said. "I hate waiting around."

Eric nodded. "Me, too." He sat across from the detective and beside Samantha at Howl at the Moon, which was, as Wolfe described it, a piano bar. Two pianos lounged on a stage directly in front of their table. Currently, no one was playing them.

The bar normally opened later, but the owner made this exception, as Wolfe explained, to win points with the local authorities. Other than the three of them, Howl at the Moon remained nearly vacant, which is exactly the way Wolfe wanted it. The owner stood behind the bar polishing a plate.

"So why wait?" he said, using his straw to swirl the ice in his glass of water. "Why don't we just meet the guy halfway?"

Wolfe wiped crumbs from his lips and mustache with a napkin. "I thought you were only smart under hypnosis."

"Maybe some of it is leaking out."

"Let's hope not."

Wolfe waved the owner over and paid the bill. All three of them got up and hustled out of the bar. Fourth Street was mostly empty, littered only with the occasional shopper wandering in and out of the various businesses – bowling alley, bars, clubs. A Hard Rock Café' sat under a huge replica of a guitar, which lit up at night along with the huge sign designating this area Fourth Street Live.

The perfect weather didn't make Eric feel any better. A lingering dread hung over his soul. He wondered if it was intuition, a physic vibration, or something else.

As the three of them clambered into Wolfe's car – the detective in the driver's seat, Samantha pulling shotgun and Eric in the back – he tried to think only good, positive thoughts.

But he couldn't shake the facts: this was day five and they had nothing to go on except a stranger's unverified claims. Couldn't it be a trick like the false lead the serial killer had given them before? If this was a trap, they were walking right into it.

Or worse, maybe Detective Riley did have information they needed to save Wolfe's job, to save countless innocent lives and to stop him from becoming fate's puppet, but they would never know it. Because maybe Detective Riley was already dead.

CHAPTER 54

As soon as Detective Riley disappeared into the police station, Charlize London dumped the melting, half-eaten ice cream cone in the trash.

She didn't have much time. Maybe five minutes tops. She had to act fast.

The powers that pulled her toward her destiny presented her with a gift: Detective Riley parked his car, not in the station parking lot, but down the street, under the thick, sprawling bough of an oak tree.

Perfect, she thought, walking slowly, just a girl out for a Saturday stroll. Slipping her hand into the pocket of her jeans, she closed her fingers around the pack of nails.

Crossing the empty street, she acted like she accidently dropped something next to the detective's car. She kneeled down. Slipped a nail out of her pocket. With a quick flick of her wrist, she punctured the front right tire; although she couldn't hear it, air was already leaking out, slowly disabling the car.

Charlize stood up and glanced around the street. No witnesses. Good. She walked away, forcing herself to remain slow, pretending to look at the buildings, the flowers blooming along the sidewalk. Just a silly woman who had dropped something, picked it up and was on her way.

Innocent. Unseen. Perfect.

Back in her car, Charlize started the ignition and pulled out into the street. As she sped away, she watched detective Riley in her rear-view mirror hurry out of the police station carrying a thick manila folder.

I'm not going to look. I'm not going to look. Peeking, Detective Alan Riley saw that the blond woman was gone. Frowning, a blade of guilt twisted in his gut. He had a wife at home. Why should he care about that woman?

Alan loaded himself and the file into his car. Praying for a pure mind, one free of lustful thoughts about busty blonds, one focused only on God, he still couldn't shake the image of the woman.

Something about her...

His cell phone vibrated against his hip.

Answering it, he said his name.

"This is Detective Wolfe. Everything okay?"

"Everything's fine. I'm on my way as we speak." Alan clicked his seatbelt into place.

"Good. What kind of car do you have?"

"Honda Accord."

"Color?"

"Green. Why?"

"We're going to meet you half way."

"Why? Everything's fine."

"Just in case it doesn't stay that way."

Ending the call, Alan shook his head. He couldn't understand The Wolfe's lack of faith. No matter. He wasn't going to let anything erode his optimism. "No weapon forged against me shall prosper," he reminded his reflection in the rearview mirror.

Then, he started his car and headed for Louisville.

CHAPTER 55

Just outside the city, just as Eric started to feel hopeful about their proactive decision to track down Detective Riley, just as he leaned back in his seat and rested his head against the car door, he saw the blue truck swerve dangerously into on-coming traffic.

Samantha must have spotted it, too, because she gasped. "James, the truck."

Wolfe jammed on the brakes. The blue truck, a Ford 150, accelerated and tried to get back into the correct lane. Time slowed to a crawl like the visual effects in a movie, forcing Eric to witness every terrifying detail, every resonant color.

Unlike cinema, the world was not sucked up by silence; rather, sound was amplified: engines roaring, tires squealing, horns blaring.

The blue Ford collided with a jeep, which flipped across the highway and landed, roof-first, in a ditch. An arcade of dissonant noises followed, the battle cry of an army of berserkers: shattered glass, twisted metal, broken plastic.

Their car spun wildly in the street – facing forward, then backward and now forward again.

Samantha screamed.

Eric gripped the handle above the window. What was happening? This couldn't be real? It didn't feel real.

A red car skidded passed them, leaving tire marks, coils of black exhaust bleeding out of its muffler.

On the side of the road, next to the metal guardrail, they stopped. All three of them scrambled out of the car. Samantha leaned over the guardrail and barfed. Eric went to help her on numb, shaky legs. He felt dizzy.

I'm not going to pass out, he thought to himself. I'm in control. He held Samantha's hair back as she finished.

When he turned around, Wolfe stood in front of the car, one hand on his head, staring at the carnage. Along with the overturned jeep, two other vehicles – the red car Eric spotted earlier – and another, black mustang, blocked both lanes of traffic, their gutted frames ruined.

"Looks like we're not going to meet Detective Riley anywhere but here," Samantha said, sitting on the guardrail.

Eric nodded. The street smelled of burnt rubber.

Across the highway, a man in a dark, double-breasted suit stood with his arms dangling at his sides, staring at him.

Someone screamed for help. He turned as Wolfe sprinted down the highway towards the jeep, cell phone in hand. When Eric looked back, the man in the suit was gone.

On Interstate 65, Charlize London tailed Detective Riley, keeping back a mile, careful to put other vehicles between them because he might recognize her car from earlier. After all, he was a trained professional.

From her radio flooded the smooth music of Boys to Men singing, *I'll Make Love to You.*

Aware that, sooner or later, Detective Riley's flat tire would force him off the road, she sang along with the music. The words vibrated through her, and she thought of Eric.

Twenty-seven years was too long a time to be separated from your soul mate. The last year spent waiting for him to understand his destiny, to discover their mutual destiny, proved torturous.

A car horn honked, startling her out of her thoughts. Conscious of her surroundings again, she noticed her car sliding outside the yellow lines of the road. Charlize pulled back into her lane and waved at the courteous driver, a bald-headed man with bright red spectacles. He waved back.

She wondered how long before she would see Detective Riley's car on the shoulder. Glancing at the clock in her car, she noted the time: 10:14 a.m. Can't be long now.

She snatched her white gloves off the passenger side seat and slipped her hands into them. Also on the passenger's seat rested the African Dagger. For now, she left it there.

On both sides of the interstate, farmlands blurred by, fields of grazing cows punctuated by bales of hay and old plantation houses.

The song on the radio changed to *Crazy* by KC and Jo-Jo.

Charlize gripped the steering wheel with both white-gloved hands and stared ahead, waiting for Detective Riley's tire to deflate and the next piece of her destiny to be revealed.

CHAPTER 56

Surrounded by ambulances and police cruisers, Eric watched Emergency Technicians and paramedics haul people across the highway in stretchers. Police officers interviewed witnesses, faces awash in flashing Siren lights.

Having emptied her stomach, Samantha sat on the railing that lined the Interstate. Her face pale, her hair tied back in a ponytail, she stared solemnly at the ground.

After helping a woman out of her overturned jeep, Wolfe aided others until the EMTs arrived. Now he stood beside Eric, out of the way, surveying the scene. He dialed a number on his cell phone.

Eric rubbed his neck. It hurt, but the dizziness was gone and strength had returned to his legs. Listening in on Wolfe's phone call, he deduced the person on the other end of the line was Detective Riley. Wolfe told him about the crash. They would meet back at Fourth Street Live as planned.

Wolfe suddenly looked disturbed. He scowled and dropped the phone from his ear.

"What is it?" Eric asked.

"He said something's wrong with his car. Then he hung up."

Between Hopkinsville and Paducah, Charlize spotted a car a quarter of a mile ahead on the side of the road. The car was green.

Her grip on the steering wheel tightened. Switching off the radio, engulfed now in silence, she checked all her mirrors. No other cars in sight.

Perfect.

Knowing that she had little time before another vehicle appeared, she pressed harder on the gas. The needle on her speedometer jumped from 65 to 75 MPH. She kept pressing.

What both excited and terrified her was the window for surprises. Most of the time, she meticulously plotted her murders. This time, however, she was forced to ad-lib. Thankfully, she had bugged his phones long ago. Thankfully, she had centuries of practice in these bloody arts.

Like most things, Charlize discovered that murder blended

both science and art. You had to know the procedures, the anatomy, the gadgetry, how to avoid leaving evidence, how to change your identity. But you also needed pure, raw talent.

As the quarter of a mile of pavement vanished beneath her GT, she watched Detective Riley circle his car and find the deflated tire. He squatted, inspecting it.

Right now, she thought, he was figuring out what had happened. This is no coincidence; this is sabotage. She wondered if he knew how special he was, a thread in the garment of her destiny.

The needle on her speedometer bounced toward 80 MPH.

Still no cars around.

Baring down on him, she saw Riley turn his head and stand up, staring at her, eyes wide with panic. Then he crossed himself.

CHAPTER 57

"Are you thinking foul play?" Eric asked, leaning out of the car window, letting the cool wind splash over his face. Thanks to Wolfe they only had to give a brief account to the cops of what happened. Because no one in their vehicle, or the vehicle itself, was hurt, they were allowed to leave, and now were on their way to find Detective Riley.

"That's exactly what I'm thinking."

Eric couldn't see Wolfe's face, only the back of his head, and in the rearview mirror, his eyes. They told him all he needed to know. Wolfe was nervous.

"Could be bad luck. Look what happened to us."

"It's not bad luck."

"We've certainly had our share lately."

"Detective Riley knew the serial killer. Somehow, she must have figured out he was bringing me information. Booby-trapped his car."

Eric closed his eyes and the bright afternoon faded to gray darkness. Wind whipped over his face and left arm, blowing up the arm of his tee shirt with a pocket of air, like men's swim trunks when they first plop in water.

"Maybe he drives an old car, a real clunker," Eric said.

Samantha, who sat silently in the passenger's seat for the entire ride nursing a headache, turned in her seat to look at him. "No. James is right. Something's wrong."

Over the thunder of the engine, Charlize thought she heard the collective snap of every bone in Detective Riley's body. Her Nissan shuddered at the impact. Detective Riley's body folded over the car, then hurled backwards through the air and into the ditch on the side of the road.

Charlize slammed on her brakes, screeching to a halt ten yards down the road. Snatching the African dagger, she bolted from her car. Down to the ditch.

Behind her, a vehicle washed a wave of humid air over her as it passed. She spun around. An eighteen-wheeler. Had it seen her?

For a moment, she stood and watched it, but it rumbled away, not even slowing down. Maybe the driver was calling the police? Did he get a good look at her?

No, her back was turned. If the driver did see something and if he did call the police, he would only be able to give a general description – height, weight, skin and hair color. All of which could be easily altered, if you knew what you were doing.

The eighteen-wheeler disappeared around a curve.

Returning her attention to the ditch, Charlize moved to where Detective Riley lay crumbled and twitching. She noticed life in his eyes.

Crouching next to him, she said, "Shh. It will all be over soon."

And then she stabbed him in the throat with her dagger.

CHAPTER 58

Thirty minutes after Wolfe called the Kentucky State Police Department and asked if they would check out the area between Hopkinsville and Paducah – where Wolfe thought Detective Riley might be in his trip – for a broken down green Honda Accord, he received a return call.

Once again, Eric deduced nothing from the poker-faced detective. When Wolfe dropped the cell phone to his side, Eric asked what happened.

"They found the car…" He paused, resting his head against the car seat. "And they found Detective Riley. Dead."

"Dead?" Samantha put one hand to her face and shook her head; Eric shook his, too. "What did they say about the information he was carrying?" he asked as Wolfe pulled the car into Samantha's driveway. They had planned on washing up at her house before the meeting with Detective Riley. Now, it seemed, they wouldn't need to.

"Searched the car and his body, but it was gone. She must have taken it."

Eric opened his car door, but didn't step out. Their only lead was gone. And this was day five. Only one more day left. "How'd he die?"

Wolfe killed the engine. "By car."

Once they were inside the house, Samantha took two aspirin, Eric fetched drinks for the three of them – sweet iced tea all around – and Wolfe made a phone call. Ice tinkled into three glasses, followed by the slush of sweet tea.

From what Eric could hear of the conversation, Wolfe contacted Detective Riley's police department and asked if there were any back up files, or electronic files, or anything about the case. After a few minutes Wolfe hung up, took the glass of sweet iced tea and sat down. He placed the cell phone on the table. This time, even through the detective's placid expression, Eric could see the disappointment. Maybe, here at the end, his emotions were getting the best of him.

Samantha covered one of Wolfe's hands with her own and simply waited.

"It's all gone. All the information about the case. No backup copies. No electronic files. All of it. Vanished."

"Her," Eric said.

Wolfe nodded. He hadn't touched his iced tea.

Eric suddenly felt like a car had hit him, snapping not bones, but hope and optimism, flinging him not into a ditch, but into a pit of depression. "What are we going to do?"

Wolfe didn't respond right away. He seemed to be wrestling with something. The only sounds were the whine of the air conditioner, the crackle of ice chips in their cups. Wolfe sighed.

"Something dangerous," he said. "Possibly something stupid."

"No." Samantha clattered her drink down on the table. But she stopped short of arguing. Like Eric, she must have realized it was the only way.

"I'll do it," Eric said, looking at both of them. "I'll do it for all the people I would've killed."

CHAPTER 59

On the sixth day, in the early morning, Eric and Wolfe met Samantha at her house. After three rounds of coffee, which each agreed they didn't need because of nerves, they settled in the living room: Samantha in her chair, Wolfe standing, and Eric on the couch, as usual.

Samantha quickly put Eric into a trance. As always, his eyes glazed. When she led him into a past life, his body contorted — again, as always. Hands bent at the wrists. Skin tight against his face. Eyes seemingly aware.

"Okay," Samantha said, "I'm going to release you."

From Eric's throat came a whispering hiss of a voice: "I thought you'd see it my way."

"But there are some conditions."

"Like?"

"James goes with you and stays with you... the whole time. You're never to be alone."

After a pause, as if this was a negotiation and he was considering the deal, Eric said, "Agreed."

"You have no choice," Samantha said.

"Neither do you."

Samantha looked up at Wolfe, who returned her stare. Between them, the red eye of the recorder promised that the session was being taped. Turning back to Eric, Samantha watched his body twitch. *Was he controllable? Were they making a huge mistake?*

Deciding that it was too late to renege, she said, "Eric, you are released and have full movement of your body until ordered otherwise. You can move freely at will. Right now, you are feeling the control you have over your body. You are released."

On the couch, Eric trembled. A smirk spread over his face as he stood up, as if bemused by some inside joke. His eyes appeared clearer, more focused.

Instinctively, Wolfe reached for the gun on his hip. Something felt wrong. But he left the weapon in its holster because Eric just stood there, grinning. Possibly plotting their demise.

Samantha fixed her eyes on Eric and commanded, "Take James to the serial killer."

CHAPTER 60

James glanced at Samantha before following Eric out of the living room, down the hall, through the front door. Suddenly, he didn't feel so good about this decision. He didn't trust Eric. And he felt unsafe, even with a gun, which is why he refused to take Samantha with him – too dangerous. Besides, she promised that a simple command to wake up would pull Eric out of his trance.

On the front porch, James said, "We're taking my car. Get in the passenger's side."

"What?" Eric said, turning towards him, eyes luminous and haunted. The eyes of the dead. "I don't get to drive?"

"You don't get to do anything."

The blue-orange-hued sky wore a necklace of clouds. August mornings in Louisville were cool, refreshing. This one proved no different. If he judged the day by the weather, it would be perfect. Except he felt a nasty storm brewing.

Behind him, someone touched his arm. He jumped.

"Are you okay?" Samantha asked. "Is this a good idea?"

Without hesitation, James said, "No." He turned halfway toward her, unwilling to let Eric out of his sight. "But he is right. We have no choice. He's the only one who can find her, whether we like it or not."

"Not," Samantha said, leaning against the doorframe.

"Are you going to be alright?"

"I'll be fine."

James remained unconvinced; but again, he had no choice. Eric needed supervision and there was no way in Hades he was going to take Samantha with them. At least there were now two police officers watching her house. Two good officers he trusted.

"I have to go," he said. She nodded and he walked to his car, in which Eric already sat, silent and watching.

When he reached his Subaru, Samantha said, "Be careful." But that's the last thing he would be, or could be – you might as well tell a tornado chaser to be careful. In some reckless pursuits, careful was impossible.

Climbing into his car, he shut the door and shoved the key in the ignition. Every second that ticked past, he waited for Eric to spring an attack. It occurred to him that he was driving a time bomb. Question was: *How much time was left?*

James backed the Subaru out of the driveway, switched gears, and asked Eric, "Which way?"

"Left."

As James directed the car left, he kept a wary eye on Eric, who sat snake-still with his hands in his lap, staring out the windshield. As an avid student of body language, and a regular poker player, James had the overwhelming sense that the man in the passenger seat was overplaying his part, the bluff before the big reveal. James dropped his left hand to his hip holster, ready to drawl his weapon at the slightest provocation.

"Turn right here," Eric said.

He followed Eric's directions, twisting through downtown Louisville. Now they wheeled down Broadway. Few cars passed them this early in the morning. Still, morning workers chugged coffee out of recyclable Starbuck's cups and hurried along the sidewalks to their next destination, some talking animatedly into cell phones, others using Bluetooth. Technology, he thought. These days, it was hard to tell the difference between the crazies talking to themselves and the gadget-friendly career professionals.

His window down, James inhaled the distinct smell of Louisville. Above them, a plane cruised shockingly close to the buildings, preparing to land at the Louisville Airport.

When they reached Bardstown road, Eric said, "Turn right." Then he led them through another series of turns, mostly side streets between enormous, beautiful houses.

"Where are we going?" James asked.

"You'll see."

"Tell me now."

"And ruin the surprise?"

"I hate surprises," he muttered.

"You'll love this one. Promise."

Again, James got the feeling that Eric was playacting. He was being a little too friendly, a little too nonchalant, like a dangerous animal pretending to be docile until you let your guard down.

Three streets later, Eric said, "Here." James slammed on his brakes, screeching to a stop in front of a two-story Georgian style house. "Here?" James asked, raising one eyebrow. The Brady Bunch might live there, but not a serial killer. Eric nodded, looking up at the house, grinning.

Both of them exited the Subaru, which James left idled next to the curb. Eric first, the detective second, they ascended the short stone stairway leading up to the front porch. Rusted iron railing flanked both sides of the staircase.

James held his gun with one hand, retrieved his cell phone with the other. As soon as he verified the serial killer was, in fact, on location, he would call for backup. Producing a valid warrant might get tricky, but he'd done this kind of thing before.

At the top of the stairs, James trained the weapon on Eric. "Open it."

Eric stepped to the side, flashing his open palms. "I'm not an officer of the law; the last I checked it's illegal for me to barge into private residences."

James chewed on that for a moment, rolling it around like a piece of food that didn't quite taste right.

"You're sure she's here?" James said, standing next to him on the front porch. It seemed too easy. Would a professional criminal lounge around waiting to be caught? Probably not. Then again, she didn't know they had Eric's "powers" guiding them to her front door.

Eric moved further to the side. "You woke me up, let me loose and commanded me to bring you here. I'm just following orders, remember. Are you really going to start doubting me now? She's here. But I know her well enough to say that if you don't move fast, she won't be here for long."

That last point pushed James into action. He slipped his cell phone into his pants pocket and reached for the polished doorknob. Locked. Nothing unusual about that: Louisville is a big city, after all. Maybe not exactly the 16th largest in the country, as they so often claimed, but big enough. And, if given the choice, he'd rather live here than anywhere else in the world.

Something, a fist maybe, struck the side of his neck. Pain, alarm, and confusion stampeded to his brain as he lost all control of his muscles. He reeled forward, into the door, before the blackness of unconsciousness took him.

CHAPTER 61

His head hurt.

Opening his eyes, James stared up at the Georgian-styled house, above which the sky shimmered an early morning blue. How long had he been out? Judging by the sky, not too long.

He raised his head and sharp needles of pain stabbed him behind the eyes. Pushing through it, he lifted himself to his feet. Thank God no one had come out of the house, he thought.

Glancing around, he didn't see Eric anywhere. But the car remained at the foot of the stone stairs. Probably left it because he knew James would put out an APB. But why hadn't he killed him? To conserve time?

He patted his pocket and discovered that his cell phone was missing. Panicking, he searched the front porch and both sides of it. His gun was gone, too.

Walking down the stairs, he supported himself with the rusted iron railing, noticing that the car was no longer idling. His head still hurt and the back of his neck was sore. Even so, he moved fast: every second Eric escaped further away.

At the bottom of the stairs, James peered into his Subaru. The keys had been removed from the ignition, which meant Eric probably took them.

Which way had he gone, left or right? If he went left, he could disappear into a jungle of neighborhoods. If he fled to the right, he would run into the park.

Relying on his years as a detective and what he would do in a similar situation and pure gut instinct, James headed right. Hobbling at first, he eased into a jog. He hoped he hadn't been knocked out long. Most of all, he hoped he wasn't too late.

He didn't want to think about what Eric might do if he happened upon someone out this early, with no witnesses.

As he dashed to the end of the street, worry piled on worry. What if he was going the wrong way? What if Eric escaped and they couldn't find him? What if...

He'd lose his job for sure, be lambasted by the media, maybe even serve some time in prison, but that would be the least of his problems. He would be responsible for releasing a savage killer on Louisville. *On the world.*

They might never catch him, which, in effect, meant that they would never track down the other serial killer.

The expanding ramifications filled him with a fear-induced adrenaline. He had never run faster.

Eric darted between houses, now covered by shadows, now revealed under the morning sun. He charged forward with the pistol in hand in case he needed to use it fast. He'd ditched the cell phone through an opening in a sewer grate two streets back.

A primal sense directed him onward, across another street, between two more houses, then along the sidewalk. Memories of other lifetimes flooded his mind, but he resisted the urge to indulge in the past. The future beckoned.

A future full of wonder and excitement and freedom. The woman he searched for, his soul mate, resided in another part of the city. He'd manipulated his way here only to throw Wolfe off the scent and escape.

Near the end of the street, a blue truck whipped by in a rush of wind and noise. The driver didn't even look his way. He hurried onto the next street.

He wondered if Wolfe was following him. By now the detective would have wakened and realized his captive was missing. Had he guessed which direction Eric had run?

It didn't matter. Wolfe couldn't stop him now. No one could.

CHAPTER 62

At her house on Emery Road, Samantha drained a blender full of frozen margarita and switched nervously between the kitchen and the living room. At 4:00 a.m. it was too early for the news, and if it had been any other day, for drinking, too.

In the living room now, she watched an infomercial about weight-loss. A model with less body-fat than an ameba smiled and regurgitated a memorized sales pitch. Something about shedding 160 pounds and a diet designed to boost your metabolism. The product sounded pretty good. And the first month came free.

Buzzing, she walked back into the kitchen. She'd keep a steady watch on the local news. If James and Eric found the serial killer, James would probably call her; but if not, the news was sure to cover the story.

A knock on the door startled her.

She walked hopefully toward the front door, heart beating quicker, and looked through the peek-hole. She half-expected James and Eric to be standing there with the handcuffed serial killer between them. Or just the serial killer.

Through the peek hole, she saw one of the police officer's who had been guarding her house. Dark circles hung below his green eyes. He wore street clothes rather than his police uniform and held his badge in hand, ready to ward off suspicion.

Samantha opened the door.

Holding up his badge for her to see, the officer said, "Everything okay, miss?"

"Everything's fine. It is fine, isn't it?" She was thinking about James and Eric. Had something gone wrong? Her head felt woozy.

"Yes, as far as I can tell," he said, raising one hand to scratch his head. He stared at her for a second. "I just wanted to check. Detective Wolfe told us to take nothing for granted. Even with us out here, it's still not safe for you here."

Releasing a pent up breath, Samantha smiled. "Don't worry about me. Detective Wolfe knows what he is doing."

"I know, but..."

"But nothing. I'm fine. Really."

After the police officer left, Samantha closed the front door and drifted back to the living room. On the television a guy who used to resemble one of the Fat Boys claimed that the weight loss product transformed him into the Schwarzenegger look-alike he was today.

The whine of a floorboard startled her. She jerked up on the couch, heart galloping away in her chest. What was that? As the silence grew long, she laid back down on the couch, her eyelids growing heavy. Probably just an old house noise. Happens all the time. Nothing to worry about. Maybe a quick nap might calm my nerves. James and Eric will be back before she knew it. She closed her eyes, and five minutes later was fast asleep.

CHAPTER 63

Eric hid his gun behind his back as an elderly woman in a pink jogging suit power-walked past him on the sidewalk. She gave him a grandmotherly smile when their eyes met.

He had to find the woman.

What would her name be in this life? He couldn't wait to find out and to discover the pleasures of romance with her all over again. How long had he waited this time? Years? Centuries? A moment without her was too long.

He felt her presence and knew that this was the correct direction. An inner power guided him, pulling him along like a kite on a string.

At the end of the street Cherokee Park spread out before him. He entered it under the drooping boughs of two hickory trees. The park reminded him of so many other parks and places he'd visited – places of beauty, places of peace.

Looking up, he noticed the sky turning colors. The police might already be searching for him. Although that complicated things, he believed that they wouldn't catch him. Even so, he desired to find cover.

Hurrying across a field of grass towards a copse of Bradford Pear trees, he spotted a couple strolling hand-in-hand down the walking path. With their backs facing him, he held the element of surprise.

Slowing his pace, Eric surveyed the park for witnesses. Seeing none, he gripped the gun tighter and slinked after the couple.

CHAPTER 64

Head throbbing with pain, scanning both sides of the street, Detective James Wolfe made his way toward Cherokee Park. He wished he had his cell phone to call Samantha so she could pick him up in her car.

But he couldn't call Samantha.

Samantha!

A thought slammed into him like an unexpected right hook. She could be in trouble. This whole thing could be a grand charade intended to distract him. Had Eric led me here so that he, or someone else, could get to her? Alarm bells broke out in his chest.

He couldn't reach the police, either. It was up to him alone to catch Eric before something terrible happened.

The nearer to the park he progressed, the more he felt Eric had gone the other way and disappeared into a maze of neighborhoods. He chased a ghost into an empty park.

Maybe he should turn around. Go the other way. Or back to Samantha's house. No. He'd already gone too far in this direction. There was no time. Right or wrong, he'd finish the chase in the park or beyond it.

If he were wrong, he'd keep trailing Eric, for the rest of his life if necessary. He hadn't connected with that deep sense of commitment to this case until that very moment. Even if they fired him, which they surely would do, there were ways to stay in the loop, ways to find people.

Galloping along, James felt a moment away from a heart attack. He turned a corner and nearly bulldozed an old lady in a pink jogging outfit. She screamed. Her eyes widened and she flung her hands up in front of her face.

"Sorry, ma'am. I'm so sorry," he said, moving past her. "I didn't mean—"

"To scare me out of my britches? Well, you did." The old lady stood on shaky legs, both hands resting against her chest as if they could slow down her heartbeat.

Walking backwards, James said, "I'm sorry. I really am. But I have to go." With that, he twisted around and jogged forward.

Two minutes later, he spotted Cherokee Park.

James sprinted.

CHAPTER 65

Eric trailed the young couple a hundred yards, passing the cluster of Bradford Pear trees, staying behind them, and silent. He knew he shouldn't be doing this, that it made sense to keep moving and to find the woman.

But the thrill of the chase enticed him, seductive, hypnotic. He felt the comfort anyone feels when they do something they love. Something they were made for.

Just for kicks, he raised his weapon at the couple. He pointed it at the man first, and then the woman beside him. He could easily shoot her. How he would love to watch her fall to the grass in spasms spewing blood; and the man scream over her, powerless to help.

For a few minutes, he followed them with the gun. The power he felt was incredible, undeniable. However, killing at this distance would not do. Close quarters are much better. Contact is best. He liked to watch that last flicker of life in their eyes.

Eric skulked forward, keeping the couple in eyesight, inching across the grass like a stalking lion.

James Wolfe stopped to catch his breath at the entrance to Cherokee Park. Bent over, hands on his knees, his lungs pumped huge swaths of air in and out of his body. He felt fat. And old.

Ten years ago – heck, five years ago – he'd been able to sprint twice the distance and still take down a perp. Shoot strait, the whole deal.

Now he would be lucky to shoot at all.

Lifting his head, he gazed out at the park. Bright green grass; flowerbeds crammed with Lilies; Hickory trees with boughs hung low, as if they, too, were tired. No Eric.

James limped into the park. He'd search the entire area grid by grid and, if he didn't find Eric, he'd continue past it, into the city. Glancing up, he noticed that the sky was even brighter now. Sunrise would soon call the city alive.

He remembered thinking of Eric as a time bomb. Now that bomb was loose in the city. He shook his head. What have I done?

Halfway across the field of grass, he halted; even from behind, he recognized the man a few hundred yards ahead.

Worse, he knew what end Eric pursued: the young couple holding hands.

With no gun, with no weapon at all, and with no idea what he would do when he reached Eric, James gambled against his better judgment and burst across the park.

CHAPTER 66

Samantha bolted upright on the couch in her living room. Blinking, she looked around. She must have fallen asleep, she thought.

She got up, wondering how long she'd been out, when she suddenly stopped and stared at the wall above her couch. All of the plaques that should be hanging there now lay strewn on the living room carpet.

A cold chill washed over her as she knelt to stroke the glassy black surface of one with her finger. Something didn't feel right. She didn't remember taking the plaques down, much less dumping them on the floor. And if they'd fallen while she was asleep, they would have clunked her on the head. Maybe that's what woke her up, she wondered.

She shook her head. No, I must have simply forgotten that I took them down. That's the only logical conclusion. I'm the only one here.

But when she surveyed the dark living room, she had the prickly feeling that she wasn't alone.

Panicking, Samantha darted through the house, checking each room, closet and cupboard. When she finished, she returned to the living room, scooped up the plaques and stacked them on the end table. Something still wasn't quite right. *Why do I feel so terrible? What's going on?*

The memories came to her in a rush, all at once. The young police officer banging on her door. The pained look on his face. The way he averted his eyes when he told her that James was dead. That Eric was dead, too.

She fell to her knees and covered her face with her hands and the weeping came easy. No, she sobbed. *No.* They were dead and there was nothing she could do about it. She should be dead, too. She dropped her hands from her face.

James was dead. Eric was dead. I should be dead, too.

The words sounded strange to her, even as she said them aloud. Although she had found no one else in her house, she felt a presence near, dark and foreboding. She stood up and moved toward the kitchen.

James was dead. Eric was dead. I should be dead, too.

As she walked into the kitchen she noticed a noose hanging from the ceiling. Funny, she didn't remember nailing it up there.

It was just as well. She should be dead.

Below the noose stood a chair carefully positioned for her to easily climb and slip her head through the wicked loop. But that wouldn't be enough, she thought, the ideas flowing fast now like a hungry flood toward an unwary town. I don't want people finding me hanging here in my kitchen. Better to destroy the whole house.

On the kitchen table perched a red canister of gasoline, which seemed an odd location for such an item. The smell was so strong she wondered how she hadn't noticed it earlier. Next to the container was a book of matches. Taking the canister, she opened the lid, releasing the pungent odor into her face. Ugh. She turned her head, waving away the fumes.

Holding the red canister with both hands, she began splashing gasoline on the kitchen table, the chairs and the floor. Then she moved to the living room, dousing her furniture.

The smell was almost unbearable now. She staggered back to the kitchen. Plunked the container on the floor next to the chair and put the cap back on. She smiled at the domestic ritual. Here she was about to kill herself and still she remembered to put the cap back on a can of gasoline. She laughed out loud. The sharp sound startled her, so she continued toward her objective.

James was dead. Eric was dead. I should be dead, too.

Funny how she couldn't remember how they'd died. Just that they were dead. She shrugged her shoulders, took the book of matches from the table, retrieved one match and raked it across the gray striker strip. A red flame immediately erupted on the tip of the match. She watched it for a moment, wondering what it would feel like for the fire to roll up her flesh.

She took the lit match and walked through the living room. Although she wanted the fire to burn her body, she would rather the noose kill her first, so she wanted to set the fire as far away as possibly so that she would have time to die. She silently congratulated herself for such clear thinking. At the end of the living room, where the carpet met the cold tile of the foyer, she flung the match.

A bigger flame burst out on the carpet and raced toward the wall. Not much time now, she thought, as she hurried back into the kitchen. She carefully climbed up onto the chair. Slipped her head through the noose. With one arm, she tightened the rope around her neck. She wondered how she would get the chair out from under her. She had never attempted suicide before. She hadn't realized how much thought must go into it.

CHAPTER 67

Eric lurked closer to the young couple, careful not to make any noise, the silent movement of a predator. Controlling his breathing, he crouched and beelined for his prey.

The couple strolled with their backs to him, fingers entwined like in some stupid chick flick. If they started skipping, he might gag.

They would never see it coming.

He'd have to kill them fast and then be on his way. His plan crystallized with each step: shoot them both – the man first, then the woman. He couldn't touch them because it would leave fingerprints; he'd have to leave them there.

Oh, how he wished he could come back later, when the police arrived, and watch them react to the bodies, to scour for evidence they wouldn't find.

Overhead a blue jay flitted across the park. Eric wondered if some ancient cultures would consider it a sign of danger.

Today, it was.

Eric moved within twenty yards of the couple. The time was now. He raised the gun and trained it at the back of the man's head.

Sprinting across the park, James knew he should slow down and conserve his energy. At this rate, he'd collapse in exhaustion at Eric's feet. Helpless, vulnerable.

But, he didn't have time to slow down. When he saw Eric raise the gun, he knew if he slowed down, someone would die.

So he tore across the park.

His feet clopped loudly over the ground. Eric would have to be deaf to not hear him coming. As he flew past a gaggle of Bradford Pear trees, he pushed his exhausted body to the limit, hoping to reach Eric before he snapped off a shot.

Half a second later, Eric pivoted, registering the detective with wide, angry eyes, and opened fire.

CHAPTER 68

The thunder of gunfire rattled in his ears as Eric stood in the wide stance of a cowboy, waiting to see if the bullet hit. Behind him, he heard the young couple start screaming

How had Wolfe found him so quickly? He watched the bullet tear open Wolfe's shirtsleeve, but the damage was mild at worst. The detective kept up his fast pace towards him.

If he pivoted again, he could take down the young couple. But Wolfe was the bigger threat. Deal with him first.

Eric pulled back on the trigger a second time; the gun jerked in his hand. If this bullet missed, he'd have to fend Wolfe off until he found another chance to shoot.

"Run away," Wolfe roared, probably to the couple. Then the bullet sliced through his arm.

Eric's stomach twisted painfully.

What was this feeling? Did he really need to learn so much about killing in this life?

The detective didn't slow down; he stumbled, regained his balance, and bolted right for him, his face broadcasting a wild mask of anger and fear, two emotions Eric knew well.

No time to shoot again. Wolfe crashed into him, dragging them both down to the grassy floor of the park. His head bounced on the ground. He lost his grip on the gun and it tumbled somewhere beside him.

Lashing at Wolfe with his arms, Eric struck him in the throat and rolled him over. He looked for the weapon but didn't see it. Wolfe kicked his legs out from under him and he landed painfully on his back again.

Wolfe crouched over him, hammering his face. He felt his nose break and blood stream down his cheeks.

Grabbing for Wolfe's wrist, he found it, twisted and applied pressure to it, forcing Wolfe to bend down. With his free fist, he punched Wolfe in the groin.

Throwing him to the side, Eric straddled him and wrapped his hands around the Detective's throat, cutting off the air.

Underneath him, Wolfe thrashed and buffeted his ribs.

Eric squeezed tighter.

CHAPTER 69

As the detective squirmed beneath him, as the sky spilled new, brighter colors on the earth, Eric tightened his grip around Wolfe's neck. He watched life fade from the detective's eyes.

"Eric, Eric," Wolfe said, choking, spitting.

A chill percolated through his body. "Die, die, die."

"Eric, it's me. James."

"Shut up," Eric said, squeezing tighter. Wolfe jabbed at his ribs but his blows were softer now, weaker.

Another chill invaded his body, stronger this time. What was this? Guilt? He felt like someone had turned his gut into a pincushion.

Choking horribly, face a deep, dark red, Wolfe pleaded, "Eric, snap out of it. Wake up. Wake UP!" Eric shook his head. Wolfe repeated his words again, this time louder. First, Eric's arms started to tremble. Then his whole body convulsed, racked by some unseen force.

When Wolfe said the words the sixth time, Eric let go of his neck and toppled backwards. Everything went black. In the darkness, confusion ruled and fear groped with icy, dead fingers.

Someone slapped him. Hard. Blinking twice, Eric looked up into Wolfe's pinkish face. It was packed with worry lines. "Wha— what happened?"

Wolfe grabbed his chin in one hand. "Nothing. Thank God."

"I feel like I did something horrible." His body *did* feel horrible, like he'd slept in a tub full of ice. He watched Wolfe check his arm and noticed the bullet hole.

"Did I?"

"Don't worry about it."

"I'm so sorry."

"I said don't worry."

Eric sat up, dazed, but conscious. "No. I shot you. I could've killed you."

"No way. You were a lousy shot for a serial killer."

Eric shook his head. He couldn't understand how Wolfe could

joke at a time like this. "We've got to go."

"I know," Wolfe said, nodding. "I had the same feeling."

Standing up, brushing grass off his clothes, pain shot through his chest. "I don't know how, but I think maybe Samantha's in trouble. We don't have much time."

CHAPTER 70

Speeding onto Emery Road under an ocean-blue sky dotted with clouds as big and as full of portent as battle ships, Eric stared ahead and saw black smoke coiling up from Samantha's house. *No, it can't be!* As reality shoved its way to his consciousness, it carried with it a terrible, sinking dread.

He stomped on the gas pedal. The car lurched forward and rocketed way above the speed limit for this residential area. He didn't care. Samantha was in trouble. He'd felt it in the park, and like a prophet, now he *knew*.

"Go, go, go!" Wolfe called out beside him, still applying pressure to his bullet wound.

There was no way Eric could go faster; he had the gas pedal shoved against the floorboard. But he leaned forward, over the wheel, as if that might help.

As they barreled closer, Eric noticed more smoke, and flames greedily licking the windows. The whole house seemed to be ablaze. He didn't want to think about what else might be burning inside.

Wolfe made a grab for the steering wheel. "Slow down, you'll miss the house."

"Make up your mind," Eric snapped, keeping Wolfe's hands at bay with his elbow. "We'll *hit* the house if you don't quit." He moved his foot from the gas pedal to the brakes. They screeched into the driveway sideways.

Wolfe bolted out of the car first, before Eric put it in park. Eric lunged out soon after, leaving the door open and the car running. It wasn't the battery he was worried about dying.

Wolfe arrived to the front porch first and ripped open the door. Dozens of movies about fires flashed in Eric's mind, people opening doors and fires blasting them. He half-expected the same thing happen to Wolfe. But it didn't; only a wave of heat washed out.

Ignoring it, they clamored inside, smoke instantly stinging their eyes, filling their nostrils and slathering its burnt taste on their tongues. All around them, fire chewed at the walls.

Many people, when they died, claimed to see a tunnel with a light at one end. If that was the way to heaven, Eric figured this must be the tunnel to hell.

CHAPTER 71

As bright orange flames popped and curled up the walls, Charlize stood in Samantha's kitchen and watched the pathetic woman kill herself. "Who's the master hypnotist now?" she hissed through a wall of black smoke.

On the chair, her face turning purple, Samantha said nothing.

Soon, Charlize thought, soon the slut would die. She surveyed the scene. The fire had made its way hungrily through the living room and was now consuming the kitchen. Gritty smoke needled her eyes, left its bitterness in her mouth, like she had gargled acid.

Click.

The front door pounded open.

Charlize jumped. What now?

"Samantha." "Samantha."

Two voices. Eric and that detective. Damn them.

Charlize shot one last look at Samantha and then kicked the chair out from under her legs. As Charlize disappeared out the back of the house, the last thing she heard was the stunted gag of someone choking to death.

CHAPTER 72

Eric pressed down the flame-riddled hallway behind detective Wolfe, shielding his face with both arms, waving thick, black smoke out of his mouth. His stomach churned at the sooty fumes.

"Do you hear anything?" Eric asked.

"No." Wolfe turned to peer into the living room. Between raised arms, Eric noticed the expression on Wolfe's face change.

The detective lunged into the living room, and Eric followed, not sure yet what was happening. When he entered the living space, he registered the smoldering carpet and burning furniture. The couch where he learned of his past erupted in flames.

Eric looked into the kitchen. *No. Oh no. Oh God no.*

Wolfe cried out as if in pain and hurtled himself through the dark columns of smoke. Eric was vaguely aware of his own body moving forward, though he could not feel his legs. Flames slapped out at him from the floor and the ceiling. Crashing through a wall of heat, they both arrived at the kitchen. Eric's lungs ached for clean air.

"No," Wolfe said. "Samantha."

Eric stared up through the smoke and flames at the body of a woman suspended from the ceiling by a rope. Her legs twitched. *This couldn't be Samantha. Not like this.* The image of the corpse he dug up in the woods popped into his head, but he quickly batted it away.

Heat pressed at him from every direction, smoke threatened to blind them, and sweat was already sluicing down his chest. He moved closer to the body.

Samantha wasn't moving anymore.

As he reached out to touch her, he wondered if she was already dead.

CHAPTER 73

"Grab her legs."

"What?"

"Help me lift her up."

Eric hastily wrapped his arms around Samantha's legs while Detective Wolfe squatted under her and pushed up with his back and shoulders. The taut rope hanging from the ceiling loosened.

Still, the fire raged hotter and closer, spitting bright sparks, grasping at them with dark tendrils of smoke. Eric coughed. He couldn't breathe.

"Get a knife. I got her."

"A knife?"

"Or scissors. Something to cut the rope."

Through the haze of smoke, Eric nodded. He staggered to the drawers in the kitchen. Yanked one out too hard. It crashed to the floor. Bending down, he rifled through old receipts, rusty keys, coupons. Nothing sharp. Next drawer. This one he pulled out slower. No knifes. No scissors. He'd found a knife before, why couldn't he find one now? Sweat laced his brow. He felt more sweat trickling down his sides. He sucked in a deep breath. Mistake. He started coughing and couldn't stop.

"Eric. Knife. Now."

Eric turned once again toward the kitchen cabinets, moved toward a third drawer between the stove and the refrigerator. The smoke was burning his eyes. He tried not to breathe as he jerked the drawer open. Polished silverware gleamed out at him. *Thank God.*

He grabbed the first sharp knife he saw and hurried back to Wolfe and Samantha.

The Detective's face was covered in sweat. Fire swept across the ceiling.

"Up on the chair. Cut her down."

"Me?"

"Eric, she doesn't have time. Do it now."

Eric fumbled onto the chair, reached up and held the rope with one hand while slicing at the thick thread with the knife. He tried not to look at Samantha hanging there motionless. He tried not to think about what that meant.

"How you doing?"

"Slow. It's too slow," Eric said, tears sliding down his cheeks.

"Keep working."

Eric shook his head. The smoke was too thick. The fire too hot. Too close. They were too late. His hand holding the knife trembled, but he continued cutting away at the rope. It might be useless, but he was going to get Samantha down if it killed him.

Eric wasn't sure where he was with the rope when he collapsed. Strangely the fall didn't hurt as much as he'd expected it too. He heard grunting, followed by a string of obscenities. He was vaguely aware of being carried or dragged.

Then everything went black.

CHAPTER 74

The next few hours passed in a blur. Eric woke up as fire trucks and police cars converged on Samantha's house. Two emergency technicians carried James away on a stretcher and loaded him into the back of one of the ambulances.

Police Chief John Baxter appeared through the chaos. "You."

Eric looked up.

"I'm sending you to the hospital to have your burns checked out."

At the hospital, a detective with a lisp sat down next to Eric and took out a notepad. "You are a suspect in an ongoing murder investigation, is that correct?"

Eric nodded vaguely.

The detective scribbled something on the notepad.

"Tell me again what you and Detective Wolfe were up to this morning."

"We were following a lead."

"What kind of lead?"

Eric was silent.

"What about the fire. You say you just happened to show up there with the other two officers knocked out. Very convenient, don't you think?"

Eric scowled. "I don't care what you think."

"You should," the detective said. "All this could get you into big trouble, Eric. Trouble with a capital T."

Eric looked away. Once again, he was under suspicion by the police; all his effort so far felt useless. The serial killer was still loose and Samantha was gone. If anything, things were worse.

Between questions, a nurse fed him medicine, which slowly distracted him from the pain in his head and from the minor burns on his hands and arms. But nothing helped the worst pain of them all, the inside kind for which no medicine had been created.

Eric swung his feet over the side of the hospital bed. "Like I said, I don't care what you or anyone else thinks. I'm done talking. Detective Wolfe was there. He can vouch for me."

The detective sat back and folded his arms. "You're lucky you have him on your side. Damn lucky."

"Lucky? You call watching the woman you lov— a friend – die lucky?"

The detective eyed him strangely.

"What?"

"This 'friend' of yours. You're talking about the quack, right?"

Eric leered at him from the hospital bed. "Careful, detective."

"She's alive. You thought she was dead?"

"Alive." Eric repeated the word as if it were new to him.

"She's right down the hall. Injured and shaken up a bit, but still this side of paradise."

"Can I go see her?" A sweeping relief fluttered in his chest.

He flashed a cheesy, isn't-that-cute smile. "She asked to see you, too. I've already cleared it with the hospital staff."

Eric trailed him down the hallway, the detective silent until they reached the Waiting Room. He leaned in close to Eric and whispered. "I'm not going to drop this. You watch yourself." Then he was gone.

Samantha greeted him in the Waiting Room, in shorts and a New England Patriots sweater. She looked dazzling. Eric had never seen her in shorts and found her legs to be more distracting than the drugs.

Samantha hugged him back. Then pulled away, her eyes cast downward, her head lowered. "Have you heard about James?"

"No, what's going on?"

"The doctor said he suffered severe burns. The bullet didn't hit anything major in his arm, thank God. Right now they've got him knocked out with pain medicine, Oxy-something. He'll be in here for a week or two." She shook her head. "I'm worried about him."

Eric reached out and took hold of her hand. "Me, too."

From the hospital, they headed to James' house, followed by two police cars. Samantha would stay there until Wolfe got out of the hospital, maybe longer. The police chief begged her to enter witness protection, but she refused, insisting that the killer would be insane to try again so soon. To Eric, she seemed to be clinging to last vestiges of normal life she had left.

Napoleon and Caesar wagged their tails excitedly when Samantha visited them in the backyard. Eric watched from the kitchen, through the glass door, not yet ready to make friends with two Pit Bulls. From the way they eyed him, Eric figured they felt the same way.

He moved to the windows in the front of the house and peeked through the blinds. Three undercover police officers in two unmarked cars stared back at him. He should have felt safer knowing they were out there, but police protection hadn't exactly panned out for them in the past. That same itchy feeling he'd felt in the parking lot of Buckhead of someone watching him – someone other than the police – quivered through him and he quickly stepped back from the blinds.

Later that night, after Eric and Samantha showered and ate dinner, Eric called the hospital to check on Wolfe. A friendly operator transferred him to the correct room. Eric was surprised to hear Wolfe answer the phone.

"Don't you telemarketers have a conscience?" Wolfe said.

"Only the lousy ones," Eric shot back. He was glad to know Wolfe was in a playful mood. After all, he could have been burned to death. "I have you on speaker phone. Samantha's right here beside me. We just wanted to see how you were doing."

"I'm good," Wolfe said and Eric heard him moving around on his hospital bed. "But I have bad news."

Eric's heartbeat skipped a beat. Was Wolfe worse off than the doctor told them? He sounded okay. "What is it?"

"I think my chances of a future Mr. Universe title are shot."

Eric breathed a sigh of relief. "I didn't know you ever had a chance."

"Put Samantha on the phone, funny man."

Eric handed the phone to her, and then stretched out in Wolfe's black leather recliner. He couldn't believe it, but he thought he'd found something as comfortable as Samantha's couch.

He closed his eyes and listened to Samantha's one-sided conversation. Her voice was soothing, almost melodic...

When Samantha shook him awake, he rubbed his eyes and yawned. How long had he been out? He felt even more tired than before. "What did Wolfe say?"

She plopped down on one of the wooden bar stools. "He wants us to try to find the serial killer."

CHAPTER 75

In the middle of the night, Eric woke up screaming in a strange, dark bedroom. Realizing that he was in Wolfe's house and no longer running through a burning house chased by a pregnant corpse, he threw his covers off and crawled out of bed.

Nightmares. He hadn't had one in years.

He heard footsteps in the hall, coming fast. Dropping to his belly, he slithered under the bed. It was a stupid move, he knew, but he'd made his choice and, for better or worse, he would have to deal with it.

The bedroom door opened and Samantha stepped inside. "Eric?"

"I'm fine," he said. "Leave the lights off."

She flipped them on. Then almost fell over laughing as he wriggled his way from under the bed.

"What's so funny?"

Bent over, holding her gut, she tried to talk but lapsed into another fit of laughter. When she finished, she stood up straight. "A killer comes after you and that's what you do? Hide under the bed? Haven't you ever watched a horror movie? That's the first place they look."

Eric shrugged, face hot with shame. "I'd like to see you do better."

Dancing over to him in her blue pajamas with a stupid grin on her face, she poked him in the side. "I'm sure plenty of middle-school girls would have done the same."

"That's it," he said, lunging for one of his goose-feather pillows, "You're dead." His first swing caught her in the chest, catching her of guard. But the next one missed completely as she scrambled onto the bed.

Eric whirled after her and received a face full of pillow for his effort. Thank God for the pain medicine. Blinking his eyes, he slung his pillow madly back and forth. He couldn't see. A plump pillow smacked him in the side of the head. Then the knees, forcing him to the floor.

Another blow knocked his pillow out of his hand.

Samantha stood in front of him, pillow raised. "Say it" she said.

He paused. "Uncle."

She hit him in the face with her pillow.

"Hey, what was that? I said uncle."

Raising one eyebrow, she said, "Do I look like an uncle to you?"

"Who *are* you?" Eric massaged his neck.

"Pillow-Fight Champion, three weeks in a row when I was ten."

"I had no idea."

"Humph." Flipping her hair, she turned and walked out of the room. With the pillow.

CHAPTER 76

"The Chief took me off the case," Wolfe said over the phone late the next day.

"You're kidding me?" Samantha carried the cordless phone to James' living room, where Eric sat watching coverage of the fire on CNN. He looked up at her and then turned his attention back to the television.

"Afraid not. Looks like it's up to the two of you. Everything okay there?"

Samantha massaged one of her hands with the other. "Yeah, everything's fine. I've been taking care of Napoleon and Caesar all day. I gave them both a much needed bath." She paused. "Well, I guess there is something. Eric keeps feeling like someone's watching us."

"Have you told the police officers?"

"Yes, but they haven't seen anything. It's probably nothing."

"Probably, but after what's happened before, you keep them informed, no matter what. Okay?"

"Okay."

"Good." He sounded satisfied. "And, Samantha?"

"Yeah?"

"Let's catch this killer."

Thirty minutes later, Samantha quickly placed Eric in a trance, leading him backward through time until she reached The Other Eric, whom, it seemed, was the only one that could help them. "Am I talking to the reincarnated Eric?"

Grunting, Eric said, "I think you know who you're talking to. Why don't you just get on with it?"

"I guess that answers my question." Samantha glanced at the tape recorder in her lap. It was turned ON.

"I told you we would come for you."

Samantha stared at him, so smug looking sitting on the black leather couch in James' living room. The entire furniture set was made out of the same material. Silk curtains hung in front of line windows. A huge stone fireplace, bordered by family portraits, swallowed the back wall.

"Well, aren't you going to say something? You contacted me."

Samantha snapped out of her own trance. "How did you know she was coming? How could you know?"

"I wish she would have killed you. I wish you would have burned to death." Eric flashed a grin, a type of which only This Eric could produce. "But then again, I would have missed tonight."

"What's tonight?" Samantha said.

In response, he only grinned.

CHAPTER 77

Charlize crouched in the dark kitchen, listening to Samantha and Eric talk, dreaming of all the things she wanted to do with both of them. And soon would do.

Who was going to stop her? She patted the Pit Bull's stomach and thought, *good boy, Napoleon, good boy*. Running her fingers up the dog's mane, she stopped at its throat, which yawned in a wide gap of blood and bone. *If you had been upstairs sleeping like Caesar, it might not have come to this.*

She moved through the kitchen one silent step at a time, careful not to arouse suspicion. The element of surprise was with her and she wouldn't lose it. Not after all she'd done to make this night possible.

Tonight she would show Eric his true identity, help him reach his full potential as an immortal like herself.

Charlize entered the hallway, slowly working her way behind Samantha. She wasn't worried about Eric; he wouldn't say anything even if he noticed her. Why would he? They were soul mates.

At the end of the hallway, she turned and crouched again, sliding into the living room behind the black leather couch, hearing Eric taunt Samantha, and loving it.

Yes, something would happen tonight. She would happen.

CHAPTER 78

Someone was choking her.

Two arms wrapped around her neck, Samantha fought to keep herself on Wolfe's black leather sofa, clutching the attacker's arms, trying to tear them away from her throat.

She couldn't breathe. Whoever was behind her – and she thought she knew who it was – pulled her backwards, over the top of the couch. As her body bowed in the shape of an upside down horseshoe, Samantha planted her feet on the couch, frantically struggling to remain conscious.

Confusion gave way to fear and fear to all out panic. What was happening to her? Was she going to die?

Her back stretched halfway over the couch. Pain stabbed at her spine. At first, she felt dizzy, lightheaded; then, as her butt slipped over the top of the couch, darkness flooded in from the corners of her eyes.

She could hear, but she couldn't see. "Sleep now. Relax now and float off to sleep." It was a voice she'd heard before, a woman's voice. She didn't have to look at her face to know it was the serial killer. In James' house!

Having practiced it for six years, five years as a professional business, she knew that the serial killer was trying to hypnotize her.

Not again. What sick drama would the killer have her play out this time? Even in those last moments of consciousness, she battled to hold on. Because if she let go, she knew she would die.

The killer's arms squeezed tighter, constricting her airway, forcing her body to pass out. As the soothing voice faded, and with it an unsettling reality, she suddenly understood. The killer wasn't trying to hypnotize her at all.

She was hypnotizing Eric.

CHAPTER 79

Charlize dragged Samantha's body off the couch, onto the floor, across the imported Persian rug, around the crystal coffee table on which Wolfe centered a gigantic tomb entitled, *The History of Warfare: Killing through the Centuries.*

Fascinating. Perhaps she would take the book with her when she left. But now she would kill Samantha – or more precisely, have Eric kill her.

So far everything had worked out perfectly. She took care of one of the Pit Bulls – the other one was apparently still sleeping – and knocked out Samantha. The guards outside were dead. Foolish bureaucrats. They think that they can overcome anything with sheer size and number.

Her heart fluttered in her chest. She couldn't wait to awaken Eric to the pleasure of taking a life. How much sweeter that his first murder in this life should be the woman who was falling in love with him.

As a woman, the innate intuition of her gender allowed Charlize to spot attraction easily, and she definitely sensed it within Samantha. Of course, who could blame her? Eric was stunningly beautiful, charming, almost vampire-like in his seduction. Many a poor girl had fallen prey to his powers.

Charlize dropped Samantha at Eric's feet, her head lolling over his tennis shoe. "Here, my love. A gift."

Eric said nothing, only stared in the glassy-eyed way of someone in a trance. She leaned over and kissed his forehead. His skin felt warm against her lips. On a whim, she pulled back the collar of his shirt, revealing the mole by which he was marked in all his lives. Stroking his cheek, she whispered into his ear: "I am your destiny and you are mine. Tonight, I will show you the truth, set you free."

Overwhelmed with emotion, she looked away from Eric, unable to stand his very appearance. She couldn't wait to hold him in her arms as they made love; couldn't wait for him to understand her devotion and for them to start a family together.

"Oh, Eric," she said, "If only we had more time tonight." Reaching down, she slipped her hands under Samantha's armpits and pulled her up against the black love seat.

Wiping tears from her face, she hurried into the kitchen, retrieved a steak knife, one with a wicked blade. Carrying it back into the living room, she handed it to Eric. "Take this in your hand," she commanded.

Eric curled his fingers around the handle of the knife. The image of him, seen so many times in her past lives, forced her to look away again, barely holding in another outburst of tears.

Light from two polished chrome lamps glinted off the blade. In her mind, she saw Eric in Berlin, sneaking up on a young man in a military uniform; in Belo Horizonte, Brazil stabbing a girl in the throat over and over again, blood spraying everywhere like a sprinkler; in Detroit, Michigan crouching in the darkness outside the MSU football stadium.

Memories. Her heart swelled with them – all beautifully lucid, like a film in her head.

Here she stood in Wolfe's living room, commanding Eric: "Grab her by the hair." He did and it pulled her head taut.

"Good. Now hold it up higher. That's good."

The air conditioner clicked on, startling her, rushing cool air through the house. It must be set to turn on when the temperature reaches a certain degree. The only other sound was her heavy breathing.

"Put your knife to her neck."

At this command, Eric hesitated, but slowly moved his hand down, over Samantha's face, to her exposed throat.

"Now listen very carefully, Eric, to what I want you to do next."

CHAPTER 80

James Wolfe lifted his head off the pillow and stared around the dark hospital room. On both sides of him, computerized machines blinked different color lights – red, yellow, blue. What had wakened him?

Then he heard it. Ringing. Painfully, he reached for the phone next to his hospital bed, in which he had spent day and night, for at least four days now. Holding the phone up against his head: "This is James Wolfe."

"Wolfe, long time, no see, guy." His informant. What did he want? And at this hour. "I heard about the fire. Man, I'm sorry to hear it."

James struggled to sit up in bed, something the nurses strictly forbid him to do. He needed rest, they said. To relax and recover, they said. But they knew nothing about how it felt to track down killers, and nobody had murdered their spouses.

"You better have something good," James said through the red rotary phone. Holding the ancient piece of technology, to him, felt like switching from an iPad to a typewriter.

"I do. Man, you're not even going to believe what I got. This guy I know told me yesterday that he seen the guy who killed your wife down in Hopkinsville, KY."

James sat up even more. If the nurses caught him, he'd be in big trouble. But right now he didn't care if the whole hospital staff walked in on him. He wasn't lying back down after news like that.

"In Hopkinsville. He's sure?" James asked.

"Absotively, positutley sure."

"He saw his face?"

On the other end of the line, his informant cleared his throat, pausing as if what he would say next rivaled the Gettysburg Address. To James, it did. "Man, he saw the guy's nose hairs. It was him, all right. Head to toes."

James figured he might never understand his informant, but right now he loved the man to death.

"Address?" James glanced around for the notepad and pencil –

another dip back into the pre-computer past – which he kept by his bed at all times in the off chance that he stumbled upon a lead in the case.

His job now was thinking, analyzing, prying back folds of mystery with his mind. For once in his life, he had all the time in the world to do it.

"923 Creekside drive. Funny thing is, man, there's no creek around there. Closest thing is the Little River and, man, you don't want to go fishing or swimming in there."

James wrote down the address. "Yeah, sure. Thanks." Then he added, "Really."

"You know it."

His informant gave him the account number at which he would receive payment. James scribbled the number down next to the address.

"I'll send half now and the rest after I see the murderer with my own eyes."

"Sure man, I know how it goes."

"These doctors probably won't release me for another couple days. In the meantime, I'll send a couple boys in blue to check things out for me."

His informant paused, then: "Either way, it doesn't matter. The guy is staying put for now."

James ended the call and immediately dialed one of his many associates on the force, quickly running through what he wanted to happen, then hung up.

Propping himself up in bed, lights blinking all around him, sheets ruffling every time he moved, James stared at the notepad with the simple set of numbers and couldn't sleep. How could he?

In any other condition, he would have already left, might even already be in Hopkinsville busting through the door where that scumbag was holed up.

A zigzagging line on one of the machines showed his heart beat jump. Lying down, holding the notepad on his chest, he tried to slow his breathing. The last thing he wanted right now was a nurse to run in here and think he was dying.

He closed his eyes. He hoped his informant was right and the man who killed his wife and kid would still be there.

CHAPTER 81

Growling, lips pulled back from fanged teeth, nails clanking like dropped change on the polished wood floors, then silent on the Persian rug, the pit bull rounded the corner and charged at her.

Charlize shrieked in surprise. She had heard nothing of the dog's approach until now. So caught up in helping Eric, she had forgotten all about other safety concerns.

In front of her, Eric sat on the leather love seat holding Samantha's head up by her hair with one hand and a knife to her throat with the other. He appeared calm, unruffled by the turn of events.

Charlize considered yanking the blade out of Eric's hand and using it as a weapon. But that wouldn't do against an alert and angry pit bull. She needed something a little stronger. Like a rocket launcher.

The other pit bull had been eating when she snuck up on him, slashing his jugular. Blood spewed everywhere as if the opened vein were an untamed hose. She had used similar tactics in many of her murders.

Caesar leaped through the air, mouth open and ready to tear her apart. Charlize ducked to the right, snatched a glance over her shoulder as the pit bull snapped eagerly at her legs.

She staggered across the living room towards the back deck. Perhaps out there she would find an answer to this problem. Her destiny hadn't brought her this far to let her be mauled by a dog.

Slamming against the glass back door, she fumbled for the lock, opened it, slid it along its groove, stepped halfway onto the lacquered back porch.

Then Caesar pounced on her back.

CHAPTER 82

Knocked onto her side, Charlize rolled across the dark cherry-colored planks, grazing a lacquered bench with her right shoulder, smacking against a table in the center of the porch. Grasping the leg of one of the chairs, she jerked the chair between her and Caesar.

The pit bull chomped angrily at the chair, trying to get at her, its powerful jaws snapping over the wood. Caesar growled and barked and shook his head back and forth. In his eyes, Charlize saw hatred, instinct and bloodlust. She didn't see fear.

How had she let it get this far? She wanted so badly to go back inside and help Eric realize the truth. But lights went on in houses across from Wolfe's. Dark silhouettes stood at windows.

As Caesar chomped halfway through the chair, Charlize twisted onto her stomach, scrambling under the table. She heard Caesar following her, breathing heavy, a deep guttural growl caught in his throat. Kicking another chair at him, she grabbed two of the tables' legs and flipped the table on its side.

The fear that flooded her body minutes ago when the pit bull lunged out of the darkness of the house was now replaced by adrenaline. She felt alive, electric, completely in tune with her destiny. She felt new.

Charlize didn't even care that the neighbors watched. They couldn't stop her; and if they tried, she would kill them, too.

Hoisting up one of the chairs, this one with an intricate lacework designed into the back, she watched as Caesar clawed around the table, strings of spit flapping out of his mouth. Hissing sounds issued from him, as if a legion of demons infested his canine body.

This was her destiny: to be in control, dominating all others. She was the killer, not the killed; the hunter not the hunted. This is how it had been forever into the past, as she remembered it, and would be, forever into the future.

Swinging the chair in an arc over her head, staring into the dog's black eyes, Charlize mashed Caesar in the skull. He whined and retreated a step. She lifted the chair and hit him again, this time in the ribs. Something cracked. Over and over again, as Caesar whined, she crashed the chair down on his head, legs, and hip. One of the chair legs snapped off when she slammed it into the pit bull's neck.

When Caesar lay bruised and twitching on the wooden planks, she bent down, took him by the baggy skin of his throat, and stared into his face. With her other hand, she plunged a broken chair leg into his belly.

CHAPTER 83

When Eric woke up, he was still on the black leather couch. Samantha sat next to him, shaking, with the recorder in her hand. He noticed the terror on her face and wrapped his arms around her.

"Eric, something terrible happened."

Still holding her, suddenly feeling cold, he said, "What is it?"

"Listen."

Samantha played the recorder and Eric heard the entire session, everything they said to each other. Then he heard Samantha gasp, struggling and finally silence. The cold spread through him like a fast-growing cancer, twisting its malignant tendrils up his spine.

He heard another voice. A woman. Somehow he knew it was the serial killer, the one bent of tracking him down and destroying his life. That is, if his fate didn't kill him first.

No, I am in control, I am in control, he thought.

"Pull her up by her hair..." Eric heard the voice say on the recording. Whose hair? Samantha's? What had he done? "Now put the knife to her throat."

"No." He must have said it audibly because Samantha hugged him tighter. On the recorder, the voice said, "Listen closely to what I say next."

When he heard the following command, Eric pulled away from Samantha, his body trembling with fear and anger. Who was this woman? Why did she want me to cut Samantha's throat?

Tears formed in his eyes. "I'm... so... sorry," he said.

Samantha nodded, then buried her head in his chest. He didn't understand how she couldn't be mad at him. He was mad. Mad at himself. Mad at the serial killer. Mad at life and God for putting him in this situation. Why? He wanted to scream. Why?

For awhile, they sat there, holding each other, crying — Samantha into his chest, Eric into her hair.

When she raised her head, Eric kissed her. He didn't know if she would push him away or slap him. She did neither. She kissed him back.

CHAPTER 84

Police arrived fifteen minutes later, three men and one woman who checked the entire house with guns drawn. They found the three dead officers outside and the two pit bulls inside, also dead.

Samantha and Eric clung to each other, both in a paralytic shock, unable to cry anymore. They barely heard the ambulances arrive. Someone tapped Eric on the shoulder. He looked up and saw the Chief, who regarded them with a somber expression. "How you two get into so much trouble, I'll never know. Come on, I'm taking you to the hospital."

At the hospital, Eric and Samantha refused to separate and were finally allowed to remain together for their exams. While waiting in the examination room, someone knocked on the door. Eric stood up to see who it was when Detective Lisp strolled in, notebook in hand.

"You've got to be kidding me," Eric mumbled under his breath.

Detective Lisp made a shooting gesture with his hand. "Hey, Shooter. Good to see you, too." He dropped his hand when he noticed Samantha. "Dr. Jones."

"Ben."

The detective made a show of taking a seat in a corner chair. He smoothed his shoulder-length black hair and raised his notebook. "Just a few questions for the two of you and then I'll be gone. All routine, I assure you."

"We're not answering any of your questions, Ben," Samantha said. "Not without legal counsel. And I'm not so sure the Chief would want you badgering us like a couple of suspects."

Ben's eyes widened and he angrily closed his notebook. "I'm not badgering anyone. And I'm tired of the two of you getting special treatment just because you know Wolfe. It's insane. You two have more blood on your hands than O.J. Simpson." He stood up and paced back and forth. Stabbing the notebook at Eric, he said, "I expect this attitude from him, but not you, Samantha."

"That's Dr. Jones to you."

The detective stopped pacing and glowered at Samantha and

Eric. "This isn't over," he said and then exited the room.

After they gave a brief statement to another officer and met with the Chief, Eric and Samantha asked to see Wolfe. Surprisingly, they were ushered into his hospital room immediately, at a quarter to two in the morning.

"You two just can't stay out of trouble, can you?" Wolfe said, sitting up in bed. Eric closed the door behind them as Samantha gave Wolfe a hug and then a kiss on the cheek.

Eric took the one chair in the room. Samantha sat on his lap.

Raising both bushy eyebrows, Wolfe said, "Isn't there some rule against client-therapist fraternization?"

"I don't think there are any rules in this situation," Samantha responded, smiling.

"Well, I suppose I condone it."

"You *suppose?*" Eric asked.

"Don't push your luck, kid."

They laughed. Eric couldn't believe how composed Wolfe was, even after being in the hospital, suffering from burns, and learning both his family pets were murdered.

Wolfe filled them in on the latest about his wife's case. "If I'm lucky, I'm going to take down the murderer myself in a few days. It's something I just have to do."

Samantha held Wolfe's hand. "I understand, James. I'm just worried about you in your condition."

"It's not ideal, I know," Wolfe said, "But I could never live with myself if I let him get away. Not when he's so close."

They discussed his plans further, which included calling for more back up if anything felt suspicious. He wasn't stupid enough to walk into a trap, Wolfe said, no matter how much he wanted to catch the person who killed his family. He wouldn't take any additional officers with him, however, because it might tip off the guy and ruin the best chance he's had in three years.

Turning the conversation back to the present serial killer case, Eric said, "Chief Baxter is putting us into the Witness Protection Program. Splitting us up. He's taking over the case himself."

"He'll never catch her," Wolfe said.

Samantha nodded. "We know, James. But what can we do?"

Wolfe lay back down in his hospital bed and it creaked under his weight. Next to him, on a steel table, rested a food tray filled with red Jell-O, beans and catfish. All of it untouched.

The only other decorations in the room were several machines, a sink, a small television hooked to the wall and two paintings of colored squiggly lines that Eric thought he could do in the dark, with his eyes closed, holding the paint brush between his teeth.

"I know some people," Wolfe finally said, staring at the ceiling. "They'll help you."

CHAPTER 85

Eric was shocked by how quickly the police changed his identity – new clothes, new address, new driver's license. It seemed like it should be harder than that to become a completely different person.

He arrived at the Galt House, an historic hotel that squatted on the Ohio River, on Wednesday morning. His undercover police protection, a scrawny guy named Leo, helped him carry his bags up to room 644 in the West Tower, which connected to the East Tower by a third-floor walkway.

"I'm going down the hall to get a coke," Eric said, walking toward the door.

Leo lifted his head from the James Patterson mystery novel he was devouring. After one day at the hotel, he'd already gone through one paperback. Now, hunched over in a blue chair next to the door, he worked on a second. He stood up.

"It's okay. I'll go alone."

"You know the rules." It was the first thing he had said in three hours.

"If you're going to go, why don't you just get me one and I'll wait here. That way I don't commit a deadly sin and step outside of the cell." That's what Eric called the room – The Cell – as in the prison type. No one was allowed access to the room, not even room service, and he wasn't allowed to leave unsupervised.

Dog-earing one of the pages of his book to keep his place, Leo shook his skinny face. He had blond hair and yellow-blue eyes. "You know I can't do that."

"What if I made a run for it?"

"Then I'd have to shoot you." Most people would smile after saying something like that. Not Leo.

"Okay, whatever," Eric said, "Then I'm taking a shower." He had already taken two today, but it was something to do, better than lying in bed watching Leo read.

Chief Baxter had the television and phone removed from the room. There was to be no contact, whatsoever, with the outside world until the case was solved or enough time passed to ensure his safety.

In the shower, Eric closed his eyes and let the hot water stream over his body. He thought about Samantha, which, naturally, led him back to the case.

Wolfe's words ambled through his mind, as they had hundreds of times since being locked in The Cell. "I know some people. They'll help you."

Eric wasn't so sure.

CHAPTER 86

Across town at The Brown hotel, Samantha lounged against the balcony rail with other hotel guests, who oohed and aahed as one of the well-dressed staff name-dropped celebrities who had occupied the historical Louisville landmark. Muhammad Ali, Bo Derek, Elizabeth Taylor and the Duke of Windsor were among them.

Beside her, her police escort, Benni, sipped hot tea and prattled endlessly about his years on the force. He was so into a story about two Mexican thieves, she wondered if he even knew she was there.

"And you won't believe what those two jokers did then... oh, look at the time."

Glancing at his watch, he shook his head and flared his nostrils like a bull about to charge. "I can't believe it. Time's flying." He led Samantha back to the suite where they played dominoes until Benni's cell phone jingled, conjuring Yoda's voice: "Hmmm. An Incoming call you have. Answer it quickly you should."

Benni blushed. "Star Wars Episode Three," he said.

Samantha laughed.

Answering the call, he said, "Benni speaking, how may I assist you?" He sounded like an English butler. Blushing, he grinned and slipped into the adjoining bedroom. Samantha heard him whisper, "Honey you know I love to talk to you but I'm working right now..."

An hour later, he reappeared, blushing even more than earlier. "Sorry about that. My girlfriend, Tallulah, always calls me at work, no matter how many times I ask her not to. One time..."

And he was off on another story. Samantha listened, enjoying Benni's dramatic portrayal of mundane events. If he ever left the force, she thought he'd make an excellent actor.

The night passed with more stories, more dominoes and a few more calls from Benni's girlfriend, who Samantha perceived as straddling the wobbly fence between affection and obsession.

When she closed her eyes in bed that night, Samantha couldn't have known how much her life was going to change.

CHAPTER 87

Waking from another nightmare, Eric blinked open his eyes and saw a man's face looming out of the dark. He tried to scream, but the stranger covered his mouth with one hand, yanking him out of the bed with the other.

Am I still dreaming? The face now took on a form — a man dressed in black clothes. His eyes looked gray in the dark hotel room. He put one finger to his lips in the American sign for "silence."

Marching him across the hotel room, the man in black did not stop to let him gather his clothes or bathroom supplies. He walked straight for the door, which was cracked open. Halfway across the room, Eric noticed that Leo was missing. What had happened to him? Is he dead?

As he passed the open bathroom door, Eric found his answer. Leo rested in the bathroom, head slumped against the white tile wall, hands and feet bound with plastic straps. Poor guy, Eric thought, stepping out into the hotel hallway. At least now he's living one of those James Patterson novels.

In the light of the hallway, Eric could see the man better. He stood six foot, at least, but probably only weighed as much as Eric did himself. "This way," the man in black said, an English accent filtering through his voice.

Eric closed the hotel room door and followed his rescuer down the hallway, onto the elevator. In silence, they dropped four floors, stopping on the second. When the elevator doors slid open, they stepped out, headed to the end of another hallway, past an ice and coke machine, past a room where Eric heard at least six different voices, male and female, and smelled pot.

The man in black stopped at room 224, pulled a keycard out of his pants pocket, and opened the door. Nerves no longer numbed by sleep, now fully awake, Eric hurried into the hotel room.

As the door closed behind him, he stared into the muzzle of a handgun. He didn't have to ask the identity of the woman holding it. On the bed, hands tied behind her back and mouth gagged,

Samantha slouched, staring at him with wide eyes. The man in black plopped down on the bed beside her. He smiled at Eric. "Pretty isn't she."

"Don't touch her," Eric said.

"She's good company. I can tell why you dig her."

"Shut up."

The man in black shook his head. "Tsk. Tsk. I don't think she finds anger attractive. She liked my stories, though, especially the ones about my made-up girlfriend."

Holding the gun, the blonde smiled, too. "Eric, I've waited so long to meet you. My name is Charlize. I'm your wife."

CHAPTER 88

"Untie her," Eric said, stepping toward Samantha, hearing the gun click. He thought the sound indicated the safety being released.

If the safety was on, that meant they expected him not to resist. They were wrong.

"Eric," Charlize said, holding the gun on him, "Don't."

The man in black clothes stood up, no longer smiling. From his pocket, he withdrew a switchblade, flipped the blade out and slid the flat side across Samantha's cheek.

In the small hotel room the four of them appeared an army about to do battle, with all the tension of a cataclysmic struggle. Eric halted where he was, unsure of whether to continue resisting or call their bluff.

"Don't be a hero," the man said. "I'd hate to start removing body parts from your girlfriend."

"She's not his girlfriend," Charlize snapped and the man in black flinched as if he knew he'd made a huge mistake. His gray eyes suddenly looked troubled.

Eric met Charlize's eyes. Lowering his voice, trying to squeeze the tension out of the atmosphere, he said, "Just let her go. She has nothing to do with this."

Tilting her head to one side, Charlize's expression morphed to one of concern. "I know it's hard to understand now, but you will. You'll see."

Eric hated the tone in her voice, like the worried parent of a small child. She seemed to care about him, to really care. Perhaps he could use that to his advantage. Would she shoot him? Someone she claimed to love?

He had to stall her. "What do you want?"

"Don't turn this into a script from a bad movie," the man in black said, obviously recuperated from the back lash of Charlize's verbal attack. His eyes returned to normal – steady, cold, the eyes of a killer.

"Shut up," Eric said.

"Maybe I should cut off her tongue." He grabbed Samantha's throat and touched the tip of the knife to her lip.

Before he knew what he was doing, Eric lunged at the man, crashed into him; together, they tumbled in between the two twin beds.

He waited to hear a gunshot. To feel an instant of excruciating pain as the bullet entered the back of his head, burrowed through his skull like a ferret, and burst out of his forehead. Then, he would slump to the floor, dead.

But he didn't hear the gun fire or feel the bullet. Instead, the man in black, after the first few seconds of shock, punched him in the teeth. His head snapped backwards. Blood sprayed down his shirt.

How could he have been so stupid? This guy was bigger and stronger than him and had the look of a trained fighter.

Lashing his fist out, he made contact with the man's cheek, but his blow bounced off without doing much damage. Another swing landed across the man's face, one of his knuckles digging into an eye socket.

Whimpering, holding his eye, the man struck him in the middle of his chest. Eric doubled over, unable to breath, still bleeding from his mouth.

He heard a muffled crack and he knew it was over.

CHAPTER 89

Eric did not realize he had closed his eyes until he opened them. He was alive, or at least he thought he was alive. His mouth ached. Looking down, he noticed the blood on his shirt.

The other man laid in front of him, still between the twin beds, gray eyes lifeless. A hole decorated the side of his head. In his hand, the man clutched his switchblade. He was probably about to use it, and that made Eric shiver. He could have been gutted like a fish.

Behind him somewhere he heard the muffled voice of someone trying to speak. Turning, he saw Samantha, still tied up and gagged. Her eyes were wide. He thought she looked frightened, or maybe shocked. Or both.

He forced a smile, wanting to reassure her, but she fainted. He jumped up, heart racing, wanting to help. Then he realized that his teeth must be bloody and his mouth a mess from the man's punch. "Samantha," he said gently slapping her face. "Wake up. Samantha."

"Eric."

He had almost forgotten about the woman. She still pointed the gun at him, but now it was fitted with a silencer. She won't use it on me, he decided. But on Samantha?

Tears filled her eyes. "I'm so sorry you have to go through this every time. It was hard for me, too, at first. But it gets easier. I promise."

He couldn't believe what he was hearing. This woman really thought he was going to become a serial killer with her. She's nuts.

"I know you feel it," she continued. "The thirst to kill is in your blood, in your genes, just like it's in mine. It's our destiny." Her eyes became distant, like she was imagining some future, or past, scene where everything was ideal. It reminded Eric of the look in the eyes of a religious fanatic.

Eric did feel something, a slight stirring from deep within, but he refused to admit it. "The only thing I feel is disgust."

Charlize's face hardened. Her grip on the handgun tightened. "I didn't want to do this, but it appears to be my only choice."

CHAPTER 90

The phone rang.

It was the middle of the afternoon and twenty people had already called to check up on him. Sometimes James Wolfe wanted to rip the phone cord out of the wall.

But when he answered it, his heart pounded in his chest. Because his room included a television, he watched the news constantly, following the serial killer story. He worried over Samantha and Eric. Everyone he contacted to help get them out of the Witness Protection Program said they were too busy.

His informant immediately started talking. "Wolfe, you need to get down here, man. Your guy is packing up his things and shipping out, if you know what I mean."

"I get the point."

"If you don't get down here soon, man, he will be gone. Thought you want to know. Plus, I want the other half of that money."

"Thanks," James said and hung up. The phone rang again. Snatching it up, he said, "What?"

A pause, then a girl's voice said, "This is Robin Green calling from The Courier-Journal Newspaper, where we add color to your life..."

James slammed down the phone. This time he did yank the phone cord out of the socket, slinging it like a whip across the tiled hospital floor. No big deal. He wouldn't be here to take any more calls.

He was going after his wife's killer.

CHAPTER 91

Eric drove, while Charlize held a gun to Samantha's temple in the backseat of the Yellow Jeep, and issued him directions. "Left here," she said, as they merged into downtown traffic. Even this early, commuters flocked to work in sleep-deprived trances.

Winding toward the Ohio River, Eric found it hard to concentrate; his hands trembled on the yellow-leather steering wheel; sweat beaded on his face. *How could this have happened? How could the serial killer kidnap them from police custody?*

Eric glanced in the rearview mirror and met Samantha's fear-strained eyes. If he said anything to comfort her, he feared Charlize might shoot her in the face. Gagged, Samantha couldn't say anything even if she wanted to.

"Keep driving," Charlize said. "Across the bridge."

She sounded angry, like a rejected girlfriend. Is that what she thought we were – boyfriend and girlfriend? She had introduced herself earlier as his wife, but there is no way he would ever marry her. Not in this life, anyway.

"To Indiana? Somewhere in Indiana?" he asked.

"I wish I could tell you now, Eric, but you're just not ready. Soon. Soon you will know everything and we'll get on with our lives like before."

"Before *when*?" In the rearview mirror, he watched her expression change to the one in the hotel room, a concerned lover, not a psychotic killer. He thought he glimpsed genuine love in her eyes.

"When you're ready," Charlize said from the backseat, still holding his gaze in the rearview mirror, "Only then can I explain everything."

"I'm ready now."

"Take 265 West," she said and he took it. Then Exit One and a right on State Street, up Floyd Knobs towards the apartment complex where Wolfe and he dug up the dead body.

"We've always been honest," she said, her expression flipping in the rearview mirror, "Why would you start lying to me now?" She pressed the gun harder against Samantha's temple. Samantha leaned away from the gun, making muffled groans of protest.

Panicking, he said, "I'm sorry. I didn't mean it." He almost hit the railing running along the edge of the narrow, curvy road. They passed the apartment complex. Two cars squeezed around him and darted up the small mountain.

"Drive faster," Charlize ordered. Looking over the side of the railing, down the hundred or so feet drop, he gulped and accelerated. He drove fifty miles per hour for a few minutes before she told him to go even faster. At sixty, he strained to keep the Jeep away from the railing, as they zipped up Floyds Knobs, past huge houses, running a red light, leaving drivers honking their horns and cursing out their windows.

"Faster."

"You're crazy. We'll wreck."

"Our destiny won't allow it." Once again, she pressed the gun against Samantha's temple, this time eliciting a louder groan of pain. "I can't say anything for her destiny, however."

The scenery whipped past at eighty miles per hour. He barely missed a truck driving down the mountain; he saw the terrified faces of three small children in the back seat.

Maybe a cop will spot us and pull us over for speeding.

"Take the next right," Charlize said from the backseat. "We're here."

CHAPTER 92

Wheeling the Jeep into the dirt driveway off the main road, Eric felt hope dwindle down to nothing. Alone, up here on this small mountain, who would find them? The only chance they had was to use the crazy woman's love for him against her. If he could somehow convince her that he was on her side and believed all that destiny crap, maybe she would let Samantha go. Maybe they could survive.

On both sides of the dirt driveway, Oak trees loomed over them like sentries watching POWs march into a death camp. The yellow jeep bounced up the road, and more than once, Eric had to slam his foot down on the gas to dig one of the tires out of a hole.

Ten minutes later, Eric rounded a bend in the trail and saw the house. Mansion was the more accurate term – a massive complex that might be featured on MTV Cribs. Layered, tan roof arching high into the horizon. Wide, paved circular driveway looping around a fountain complete with angelic statues spouting crystal blue water from their stone mouths. Colossal iron front door that looked like it was transferred here from a medieval castle.

"Slow down," Charlize said.

Eric braked hard. Distracted by the house, which was easily twice as large as any he'd seen in person, he raced along, headed straight for the sweeping structure. The jeep jerked to a halt twenty feet from the front door.

"Give me the keys," she said and Eric handed them over. Then she jumped out of the Jeep, trotted around the back of it and opened the door closest to Samantha. After letting her out, Charlize led her to the front of the Jeep at gunpoint. Eric watched all of this from the driver's seat. If he still had the keys, he would have mowed Charlize over with the Jeep, grabbed Samantha and drove them to safety.

Angling her head towards Eric, Charlize spoke in a cool, even tone. "I'm trusting you won't try anything foolish. I have no qualms about blowing her brains out, if you make me. I'm sorry that I have to do this."

Eric responded with a tight nod. He stepped out of the Jeep, sweating in the usual places. Strangely, he wasn't scared. Maybe after awhile, terror, like hope, shrank. Maybe after a while, you could get used to almost anything.

The question was: what else would he be able to get used to?

While the thought disturbed him, something else nagged at the back of his mind, something evasive and hard to pin down at first, but as he stared up at the white mansion, it became clearer.

A feeling of comfort, of homecoming.

CHAPTER 93

Entering through the wide steel double doors of Charlize' mansion in the woods, Eric felt like an unwary knight, crossing into a dragon's lair. Instead of flickering torches, bright crystal chandeliers guided them into the foyer.

Other than the heavy slabs of dread punishing his nerves, the mansion was nothing like he expected. There were no piles of dead, rotting corpses, no racks filled with sharp, pointed objects useful for butchering small children, no smell of cooked flesh, no glass jars packed with eyeballs, organs or other disturbing contents. Not within eyesight, anyway.

If their host wasn't a savage killer, Eric might be inclined to admire this house, to enjoy his stay here and to even feel giddy about being on the inside of such an enormous, richly decorated structure.

"This is my house," Charlize said, behind him, as if she didn't have a gun to his back. "I do hope you like it?"

"I feel like an honored guest on the Titanic."

Samantha looked over her shoulder at him. Her mouth was still gagged, so she couldn't say anything, but she didn't have to because the look in her eyes told him everything he needed to know.

"I'll take that as a compliment," Charlize said, leading them deeper into the house. Now they walked down a hallway, flanked on both sides by murals of ancient Greece, Rome and Jerusalem. At the end of the hallway, Eric noticed a gigantic portrait of The Last Supper, by Leonardo daVinci. It seemed strangely prophetic.

He had seen the picture only in textbooks and slides, never in person. But he'd always wondered how Jesus could eat knowing what was going to happen the following day – the brutal beating, the abandonment and, of course, his crucifixion. Eric didn't think he would ever eat anything again.

Charlize stepped up beside him. All three of them were crowded around the painting like admiring art critics or college students on their first foray into culture. "You like it, don't you?

You've always like that piece."

Her words sent a shudder through him. Turning his eyes away from the mural, he stared at the floor, covered in brilliantly woven red carpet. A river of blood.

"Do you know why you've always felt drawn to it? There is a very good reason," she continued. "Because you were there."

CHAPTER 94

Gawking at the portrait of the Last Supper, reeling inside with confusion, anger and disgust – a triple threat of emotions he had become all too familiar with in the last few weeks – Eric wondered how her words could possibly be true.

You were there.

There? What did that mean? I was in the room? I was sitting around that table with Jesus of Nazareth? If so, which one was I – John, Peter, Mark, *Judas*?

His stomach knotted, twisted, churned. Suddenly, he felt like he could puke at any moment, like he was caught in a perpetual fun house ride spinning forever around and around and around.

Looking to Samantha for support, he saw that she, too, stood wide-eyed and amazed by the revelation. Who wouldn't be? Although it must be a lie. How could it be anything but one?

"What do you mean?" he croaked, but she said nothing.

He wasn't going to let this go so easily. As Charlize swiveled to lead them further into her mansion, he repeated, "What do you mean?"

Charlize stopped and spun around. "You are not ready to know."

"Tell me."

Their captor remained silent on the subject, chewing her bottom lip.

"Was I one of the…"

"No, not one of the disciples, but you were there nevertheless. We both were among the crowd that followed him. I keep the mural as a reminder of the power of surrendering to one's destiny, as Jesus surely did. You could learn something from him."

"Learn what?"

"Who you are."

"Who am I?"

"You know who you are."'

"The Messiah?" he said sarcastically.

Spinning the other way again, she motioned for him to follow her and, reluctantly, he did. Deeper into the house. Deeper into the mystery. Deeper into trouble.

After traipsing through a few rooms large enough to fit both Eric's apartment and Samantha's house into several times, Charlize halted in front of another large iron door. Opening it revealed a set of descending stairs.

Samantha stepped through the doorway first, nervously trying to keep her balance, as if it were a tight rope stretched across the Grand Canyon and not a simple flight of stairs.

Eric went next, then Charlize behind him. Against the concrete steps, his shoes made a plopping sound that echoed down into a stygian darkness. Even just inside the doorway, a pungent stench of rotten meat flooded his nostrils, torturing his sense of smell, making him feel queasy.

He pinched his nose with a forefinger and thumb. He kept taking steps, sinking into the gloomy abyss with the sullen slowness of a funeral procession.

"I bet that smell brings you back," Charlize said behind him, but he refused to turn around. Besides, he might lose his balance and tumble into... into wherever this staircase led to. Hell, probably. If he was lucky.

"We used to make love to that smell," she continued, "Now it reminds me of us. I know that sounds sentimental, but what can I say, I'm a girl in love."

Love? Did she say love? Yes, and it reminded him of his only hope for escape: to twist her devotion into something useable, some way of escape for him and Samantha. It would have to be deception because he didn't think that he could take her one-on-one.

"You're probably overwhelmed... I understand that, I really do. It takes time, these things. At least now we're together."

The further they descended, the less light penetrated the heavy shroud of shadows, turning everything, even Samantha's back, gray. Gray walls, gray skin, gray hands, gray air.

He must do something. Anything. *But what?*

"Why are we going down here?" he asked, but really didn't want to know. Gooseflesh rolled in bumpy waves across his arms and the back of his neck; it was ten degrees cooler here than upstairs.

"You need rapid training to accept your destiny. This is the only way."

Taking another step, Eric said, "What way? Why can't we stay upstairs?" He didn't know what he was going to say until he said it. The words tumbled out like verbal gymnasts performing an impromptu routine for a panel of sadistic judges demanding perfection. One wrong move could mean elimination.

"Upstairs there is too much distraction. You need focus. And there is lots of solitude down here. It's where I come to relieve stress. Block out the rest of the world." She sounded happy, almost chirpy. This was her comfort zone.

Finally, stepping onto the basement floor, also made of poured concrete, Eric locked his eyes on Samantha. Was she making it okay? Would Charlize kill her? How much time did they have left? Would this be the end, death down here in this dark dungeon?

Everything in the basement was gray. Mostly empty space, there were shelves in one corner and an assortment of tables, chairs and storage boxes crammed in another. In the stairway, the smell of rotten meat assaulted his sense of smell; down here it *raped* it.

"Nice," Eric said, shivering, trying to will his teeth from chattering. "Reminds me of my college dorm room. Only this is a more welcoming atmosphere."

As soon as the words left his lips, he regretted them. One of the verbal gymnasts slipped, fumbled the recovery and struck the mat headfirst. In his mind, Eric heard the audible snap of a neck breaking.

Circling them, Charlize covered them with the gun as she spoke. "I always loved your sense of humor, Eric. It's the first thing that attracted me to you, but we'll get into that later. Right now," she flashed a twilight-gray smile. "It's time for someone to die."

CHAPTER 95

Screws popped off the demon-operated carnival ride Eric rode in his mind, flinging his seat off in a dizzy rush of fear. He wobbled where he stood, thought he might fall, shuffled to the right, but caught his weight and regained his balance.

Who had to die? Him? Samantha? Please God let it be him.

Directing the handgun between the two of them, Charlize offered few answers to his questions. It was as if she was toying with them, a little game of mental torture before she got down to the real reason the three of them were down in the basement – good old fashioned killing.

"Eric, you always liked to draw out your murders, nice and slow, letting your victims fight back, even run away," she said, looking at Eric and ignoring Samantha. "I, on the other hand, like it quick."

Speaking in a low whisper, he said, "I don't know what you're talking about. You must have the wrong person."

"I guess I should just kill you two, then." She said it with the cool, sharp tone of a nun in an all-girl's catholic school. Her eyes never blinked or turned away, her face remained stoic and unaffected.

She said it as if she would kill both of them, but her gun shifted to Samantha now. He readied himself to charge her if she so much as flexed her trigger finger.

When her hand holding the pistol twitched, Eric stepped forward, ready to throw himself at her in a desperate attempt to escape. Maybe it would give Samantha enough time to flee back up the stairs and lock Charlize in the basement. But his legs wobbled and he felt drunk.

Charlize didn't fire the gun. Eric halted and the sudden blocked movement made him keel over and vomit. Wiping chunks of puke from his lips, he watched her pad over to him.

"You are further away than I thought," Charlize said. "I'm glad I brought you here where you could remember."

"I'll never remember."

She slapped him hard across the face. The shock of her action took away most of the pain, but his cheek throbbed with the force of her blow. He quickly questioned his former belief that she wouldn't hurt him.

Charlize reversed and trolled away into the dark grayness of the cellar.

They were alone. Eric pulled himself to his feet, still teetering from side to side, stomach churning, head fuzzy. "Let's go." The words were just off his tongue, Samantha already edging in his direction when the sharp, clanking rattle of chains froze him where he stood.

Charlize reappeared dragging what at first appeared to be a skeleton. In the graveyard light of the cellar, the man did look undead; something dug up in the middle of the night by witches and reanimated to fulfill their wicked appetites.

Stooping under the weight of heavy chains clasped to his ankles and wrists, the skeleton shuffled along as Charlize jerked him forward by one arm.

She kissed the barrel of the gun against his head. To Eric and Samantha, she said: "You two weren't thinking about leaving were you? I didn't think so. I said it was time to kill someone. Meet Kyle. He's about to die."

CHAPTER 96

James struggled out of bed, wincing from the bursts of pain caused by his scars. Because the bed creaked each time he moved, he was sure that a nurse would come barging into his hospital room at any moment.

Standing barefoot beside the bed, he shivered; the coldness of the floor seeped into the bottoms of his feet. He walked to the edge of the bed. Paused. Listened. Heard nothing.

If he didn't hurry up, his toes were going to harden into ice cubes. Still trying not to make any noise, watching the door, James hurried across the hospital room to the cabinets. Over the last few days, he'd seen towels and supplies in the cabinets, but also a pair of scrubs.

He heard a flurry of footsteps out in the hall. Keeping himself as still as a body in a casket, he listened to the footsteps grow louder and louder, until they reached his door...

The footsteps passed by his room, disappearing down the hallway.

He released a tight breath as he opened the cabinet door. It creaked, of course, so he froze again until enough time had elapsed that someone who heard the noise might decide not to check into it. Humans were such funny, crazy, sometimes outright loony creatures. He wondered if God put up with them only because of how often they made Him laugh.

The cabinet he opened held only white hospital towels, latex gloves and a box of Kleenex tissues. In the next two, he found more towels, another box of tissues and enough toilet paper to outlast a diarrhea epidemic.

Only when he opened the last cabinet on the left did he realize that the scrubs were no longer there. One of the nurses must have removed it. Or stolen it. They were always complaining about the prices of those ugly things.

James shook his head. He'd just have to go like this. He could find clothes later. Right now he needed to get out of the hospital without anyone seeing him.

Tiptoeing through the bluish glow of moonlight flooding through the window, he pressed his ear up against the wooden surface of the door. He heard only silence so he risked turning the steel doorknob. Slowly, he pulled it open and peeked through the crack. No one out there.

This was it. Time to go. James widened the gap enough for him to squeeze through and slipped into the hallway.

There would be cameras mounted on the walls, so the best way to escape would be to act naturally, like he was supposed to be up walking around. If a security guard spotted him on one of his television screens, got to questioning why a patient was wandering the halls in the middle of the night, his plans of finding his family's murderer would be ended.

Moving quickly, he glanced from side to side, hoping the nurses were all preoccupied at the front desk. Just like the security guard, if they saw him fleeing the hospital room, he'd have a much more difficult time getting out.

His feet bristled with cold, as if he was walking across a frozen lake, the temperature dropping ten degrees in the hallway from his hospital room.

When he reached the bank of elevators at the end of the hallway, James kept going. Elevators drew attention with their squeaky descents and noisy arrival bells. Traveling the staircase was a much safer idea. No one would see him and he wouldn't be trapped in a small metal box.

Above the door to the stairs a neon sign displayed the word EXIT in tall, plastic letters. James had his hand on the doorknob when someone behind him called out, "Hey, what are you doing?"

CHAPTER 97

"Over behind those shelves, you'll find a rack of knifes. Go get one." Charlize dug the barrel of the Glock into the skeleton's skull to reinforce her words. She was not making a request; she was issuing a command.

Eric hesitated. If he went, she might kill the skeleton and Samantha, maybe even shoot him in the back. But if he refused to go, someone would surely die.

His heart pumped huge swaths of blood through his veins as he started towards the shelves in the corner of the basement. Out of the corner of his eye, he watched Charlize and the gun. With its clawed hands, paranoia scratched the chalkboard of his mind.

Like in a dream, everything moved in ultra slow motion. Each step required a forced degree of focus and energy.

"What's taking you so long?" Charlize yelled at him and then fired her gun.

Eric whirled around, expecting to see Samantha flat on her back, a bullet hole in her forehead just like the black man in the hotel. Either that or the skeleton lying on his side, the thin layer of skin on his face peeled back, his mouth caved in by the sheer force of the bullet.

Both Samantha and the skeleton remained alive and standing close to Charlize, who flashed a sinister grin. "Next time," she said with a flourish, "I won't miss. Now get a knife."

Frightened, he did an about-face, scrambling to the shelves. As he approached them, a deepening horror swept through his body as he recognized the contents of the many glass jars, the kind his grandmother horded in her Pennsylvania cellar – one more habit left over from the depression. Instead of jams, these glass jars preserved a cannibal's buffet of body parts.

Here an eye, there a nose, here a fungi-infested tongue. On the end the severed head of a woman swam in pinkish fluid. Every shelf packed with glass jars, each offering a fresh surprise. Jeffrey Dahmer's idea of a full refrigerator.

The sight alone made him retch again. Pushing through the

nausea, thinking of the poor captive in chains who obviously hadn't eaten in days, he finished his hike between the shelves to a previously blocked part of the cellar.

Fastened to the wall by a series of hooks, a sweeping barrage of knifes gleamed like jagged mirrors. He must pick one. For what? Or more precisely: for whom?

He had lots of choices. Knifes with pointed blades, convex and curved blades, toothed blades or hooked blades – all ready to be plucked like steel flowers from a butcher's garden.

No time to be picky. He grabbed the closest knife to him, one with a wicked, toothed blade, and turned back toward the others.

CHAPTER 98

James resisted a glance behind him; instead, he flung open the stairwell door and left his pursuer in the hallway. There was no lock on the door, and anyways, he didn't have a key, so closing the door would be a useless waste of time.

He leaped down the first flight of stairs, fear of being caught before he escaped overwhelming the fear of broken bones. Pain shot up his body as he landed on bare feet, already hotfooting it for the next flight of stairs.

If the person following him alerted security, the main doorways would be blocked, an alarm sounded and security guards waiting for him on the bottom level.

Revising his plan, James stopped his rapid descent. Above him, a gangly teenager with black hair and long arms dashed into the stairwell. "Stop, stop."

The teenager sported a doctor's white coat, which immediately struck James as strange. He exploded back up the stairs, towards the young doctor.

Yelping in surprise, the teenager backpedaled out of the stairwell, but it was too late. James was already on him, wrapping his huge arms around his head, pulling him to the floor of the hallway. In his arms, the teenage doctor struggled. He flapped his long arms against James' thick, expansive shoulders.

James squeezed his bicep until the flapping ended and the teenager's body went limp with unconsciousness. Lying on the floor, still holding the young doctor in his arms, he looked up into the glassy black eye of a video camera.

CHAPTER 99

Eric shuffled back through the shelves of bottled body parts, the smell almost worse than the sight of torn-off lips, fleshy fragments of ear and eel-like pink organs. His stomach revolted, but he kept going, clutching the knife in one hand, and covering his mouth with his other.

Rounding the shelves, he glimpsed Charlize poke the skeleton in the ribs with her Glock. How long had he been here? Why had she kept him so long?

Seeing him with the knife, she said, "Good. Now we can get on with it. You're probably wondering what I want you to do with the knife, right. I think you know, already."

"I'm not killing anyone," Eric said flatly.

"You've done it so many times before. You're really good at it, and besides, it feels wonderful. Remember how much pleasure you got out of it?"

Inside, he was screaming, *YES*, but he said, "No. You're wrong."

"Am I?" Charlize poked the skeleton in his bony ribs again. "You can't tell me you didn't want to finish off that police officer I left for you outside Samantha's house. I saw the look on your face when you opened the car door. Admit it, you were giddy with delight. You wanted to hurt him."

"No." It was all he could think to say. He was afraid if he started talking, all the confused emotions inside would gush out in the form of real words; those words would create real sentences which would communicate real ideas, ideas he'd been running from and repressing all his life.

He held the knife away from his body. It was the only weapon he had at his disposal, but he didn't want it. Not now. Not ever.

"Well, you forced me, Eric," she said, shoving the skeleton towards him. The links of the chains attached to his wrists and ankles rattled against each other. She turned the gun on Samantha. "Cut him or she dies. Your choice."

"No... I can't." He looked back and forth between the skeleton and Samantha. How could he choose?

"I'm not asking you to kill him, just cut him a little. One little cut, that's all."

"No," he said again, more firmly. "I won't do it."

In the skeleton's eyes, Eric thought he saw the slightest sliver of life and that was enough for him to defend. Maybe others would just cut him because he looked like walking death, like a de-robed grim reaper, but he just couldn't do it.

"You'll enjoy it. All your life, you've felt it within you, the craving. I felt it, too. At first, I hid it away from everyone, even from myself. I was terrified of what it might mean, of who I was. You can be free of all that, like I am, but only if you let yourself be free."

Muffled by her gag, Samantha shook her head and moaned. Her eyes were wide as if she, too, felt what he felt — that there was another presence in the room. No, not a presence. A force.

All I have to do is cut him. Just a little bit. And Samantha will live. Maybe it won't be so bad. Maybe...

Eric pitched the knife across the basement floor, its blade flashing in the gray darkness.

CHAPTER 100

Charlize swung the gun towards the skeleton again.

Samantha cried out through her gag. Eric watched the gun, heard it pop as a bullet whipped out of its steel chamber.

The muscles in Charlize's arms shook. The skeleton opened his mouth as if to swallow the bullet, but it struck his hip and flipped him on his back, chains jingling.

The skeleton didn't scream or even whimper, lending to the belief that he was, after all, nonhuman.

When the zombie-man hit the cellar floor, when the chains fastened to his body went silent, Eric still stood in the same position. The only difference between a moment ago and now, for him at least, was the tremor of fear along his spine. He thought fear had given way to blank numbness; but fear returned, like an old friend, not as kind as one remembered.

"Now he's going to die anyway, whether you cut him or not. He's suffering, can't you see? I'll give you one last chance to save your friend. Use the knife or I'll place my next bullet in Samantha's head."

Clutching the air with his hands, he said, "Why? Why are you doing this?"

"Help him, Eric, he's suffering. Help him die and help Samantha live."

Scampering across the basement, Eric scooped up the knife. He still didn't intend to use it on the skeleton – how could he? But he needed time to think, time to come up with another option, some way of getting out of here.

Slowly, he padded back towards the skeleton.

"Where should I cut him?" he asked, stalling for time.

"Anywhere you wish. It doesn't matter where you cut him, only that you do."

Samantha shook her head, voicing muffled protests through her gag. Sweat plastered her forehead, her cheeks, her neck. She trembled and Eric thought that she looked as afraid as the skeleton should be.

But the skeleton remained on his back, groping his bullet wound with one bony hand, blood oozing out between his twig-fingers.

Eric's mind, his heart, his soul felt split. One side urging him to surrender to base desires, those sickly delicious yearnings he'd felt all his life. Just cut him, that part of him whispered. It's not murder. Cut him and save Samantha. That's why you'd be doing it. You're still in control. You won't give up power – you will save the life of someone you care deeply about.

How could I let Samantha die? Isn't cutting the dying man the right thing to do? Wouldn't anyone in their right mind do the same thing?

Yet, the other part of him, the part which had defended against those other urges over and over again, warned him: Think of how far you have come, what you have suffered to resist so long. You'd be giving it all up. And for what? Is your soul worth the trade? You are not killing Samantha; Charlize is killing her. You can't cause pain to one person to save someone else from pain.

Now he stood over the skeleton, as emotion and logic battled it out inside him, threatening to tear him apart.

"Do it," Charlize nudged, "Save Samantha."

Eric glanced at Samantha, who furiously shook her head. How could he let her die? And within, as it so often did, emotion overpowered logic.

Kneeling beside the skeleton, he whispered, "Forgive me." The skeleton showed no response – not anger, confusion or even fear. To Eric, the man appeared dead already.

Scanning the skeleton's body, he decided upon the arm. Somehow it seemed the best place to cut. He hoped it would cause the least amount of pain. Closing his eyes, because he dared not watch, Eric placed the teeth of the blade against the soft bulge of the skeleton's bicep.

The skeleton moved faster than Eric could ever have predicted. Eric snapped open his eyes to see the shriveled man seize the handle of the knife with both hands and drive it deep into his own chest. Gasping, dry sandpaper sounds issued from his throat. The skeleton twisted the knife. Out of his chest, like a deep well of oil, blackish blood gushed, forming a dark charcoal pool around his body.

Behind him, Eric heard a scream. His first thought: the prisoner's bold move had caught Charlize by surprise. When he spun towards the noise, however, he saw Samantha ram Charlize with her shoulder, causing the serial killer to stumble across the basement, losing her grip on the Glock.

As it tumbled out of her hand, as it clattered on the basement floor, one thought dominated Eric's mind: *The gun is freedom.*

He dove for it.

CHAPTER 101

Panicked, James wrestled the passed-out teenage doctor off his body, got to his feet and headed for the stairs. The security guards would have to be blind to not have seen him through the camera lens.

The stairwell door stood open. James bounded through it, as if it were a magical doorway that might transport him to safety. But James didn't believe in fairytales. He did believe in the thunder caused by his rush down the stairs. He did believe the pain in his feet and ankles.

Flight after flight of stairs, he flew down, trying to work out a plan in his mind. And a backup plan when that first plan inevitably failed. It was a rule of life James accepted.

If, by some divine intervention, security hadn't spotted him through the camera, someone would surely hear him pounding down the stairs. The authorities would be contacted and police would be waiting for him, guns drawn, on the first floor.

His feet throbbed. His breath came in sharp spurts, which made him sound like an asthmatic patient without the benefit of an oxygen mask.

To keep the pain from overwhelming him, James focused on a mental image of his wife and unborn child, whose lives were cut short because, even with all his experience and fame, he wasn't good enough. He couldn't protect everyone.

By the time he reached the last set of stairs, he was sobbing. He burst through the first floor door, no longer concerned with a quiet escape. If he had to, he would fight his way out.

As expected, four police officers, all faces James at once recognized, but at the moment couldn't put a name to, rushed at him. Surrounding him, they latched on to his arms and legs until he quit struggling. Then they pulled him to the lobby floor.

On his back, staring up at the lobby's ceiling, with the four officers still pinning him down, James released a few years worth of pent up tears.

As the brunt of those tears subsided, Police Chief Baxter

appeared over him. "Wolfe, we bugged your phone. We had your informant's story checked by local police and there is no hotel by that name he gave you. It was a set up."

Bugged my phone? Of course they did. He had lifted his head when the Chief walked up, now he let it fall back to the carpeted lobby floor. How could he have been so stupid?

"We traced the call. We know where the guy is."

Wiping tears from his face, James said, "Have you sent officers to the location?"

"Yes, along with the Indiana police. I persuaded them to hold off until we arrived."

James perked up at the use of a certain pronoun.

The Chief nodded. "Thought you would want to be there."

Shrugging off the other officers, James raised himself to his feet. "What are we waiting for? Let's go get him."

CHAPTER 102

Eric snatched up the Glock and pointed it at Charlize. "Don't move. I'll shoot." Charlize stood, having found her balance, face twisted in a scowl of rage. She followed his orders, probably because she figured, even with all his hesitation, he would pull the trigger.

Samantha scuttled toward the cellar stairs, bobbing her head as if to say, "Come on, let's get out of here."

Keeping the gun on Charlize, Eric chased Samantha toward the stairs. A sliver of hope cracked the dark concrete slab of despair.

Somehow dragging himself to his feet, the skeleton yanked the knife out of his own chest, raised it high over his head, and leaving a trail of his own blood, limped toward Charlize.

Another distraction. It was just what they needed to reach the stairs and climb them to the first floor of the house.

Eric tromped behind Samantha up the dark, loud staircase. Samantha crashed into the door with her shoulder, flinging it open. Both of them fumbled into the hallway, where Jesus dined with his twelve disciples on the wall.

Eric heard a horrible hiss from the basement, as if a disturbed teenager had clamped hot jumper cables to a cat.

Down the hallway they ran – Samantha first and Eric second, still gripping the Glock in a tight fist. Dizzy, confused, sick with the smell of rotting body parts, he felt as if he sprinted through a nightmarish landscape where reality and fantasy blended into an indistinguishable one.

He half-expected something worse than Charlize to fly up out of the basement, covered in leathery skin and gnashing gleaming rows of razor-sharp teeth.

He stayed right on Samantha's heels, glancing around her. *Come on, Come on,* he urged with his thoughts. *Move!*

Samantha mumbled something through her gag. Eric peeked over her shoulder and saw the front door. It was just through the entrance. Maybe they would make it, after all.

As they spilled into the massive entranceway, easily the size of a room in any other house, Eric heard the cough of gunfire. He looked down at his own weapon. Had he accidentally fired it?

Samantha went down, almost tripped him. Swiveling his head left and right, Eric spotted the man in the doorway of another room, dressed exquisitely in a suit and tie, holding a gun. The man from the highway. The one wearing the suit.

Dropping to his knees, Eric turned Samantha onto her back. Ripped off the gag that had silenced her up until now. She was balled up, blood weeping out of wounds on both sides of her body. The bullet had drilled a clean hole straight through her.

He held her face, which was now tightened by pain. "Eric," she croaked, eyes bulging in their sockets. She reached up, grabbed his shoulder, and pulled him close. He felt her hot breath against his face.

"Nooo!" he screamed, trying to pick her up, but she was too heavy. The man in the doorway hadn't moved. He was probably waiting for their reaction.

Anger he had never known surged through his body like a squalling hurricane. "No!" Pouncing to his feet, Eric raised his gun and loosed round after round after round of bullets. Two hit the walls, one the floor.

Across the entrance, the well-dressed man shook with each impact. Eric didn't stop, even when the chamber clicked empty. Click-click-click, he kept squeezing the trigger.

CHAPTER 103

Bounding through Louisville, the officer transporting the Chief and James drove with sirens blaring and lights flashing. He disregarded street lights, speed limits and traffic signs. *A normal cop.*

"We traced him to Indiana," Chief Baxter explained, nervously wringing his hands. He looked more like a rookie officer than a seasoned pro.

James studied him. He knew it was the consequence of too many years sequestered behind a desk. "Good. I want to take him down myself."

No hotel by that name. No green van. A set up.

"In your condition? I don't think so. And the Indiana police are taking charge of the scene."

"You can't stop me, and neither can they. This guy is mine."

"I can and I will. You're hurt. Badly. Me bringing you in on this is a privilege."

The officer driving switched lanes, zoomed past an eighteen wheeler and laid on his horn through a four-way light.

James grunted, tugged at his moustache. "I'm not going to waste this opportunity."

"Don't do anything you'll regret."

James grinned. "Don't worry. I won't."

What had he done? Eric stared across the entrance way at the man sprawled on his back. Guilt twisted through him like barbwire, slicing his veins, splitting open his heart, shredding his sanity.

"Eric."

Samantha! Kneeling down, he rolled her onto her stomach, shuddering at the sight of so much blood. By the time he slung one of her arms over his shoulder, his hands and shirt were covered with dark red blotches.

"Here we go. On your feet. Ready?"

She nodded. Planted both feet firmly on the floor. Arms around each other's shoulder, Samantha leaning heavily on him, they inched toward the doorway.

Nothing mattered but getting Samantha to a hospital. The closest one was Floyd Memorial, a small, but effective one, right down State Street.

"Eric," she whispered, her voice muffled now by something more insidious than a cloth gag. "I love you."

In another time and place, those words would tackle him with joy. But behind them, creeping like a lunatic with a chainsaw was a belief dark as the cellar in this house. As much as he wanted to return her affection, he knew to say those words meant accepting that the battle was over. And he just couldn't do that.

At the door, Eric turned the knob, pulled, but the door didn't budge. Locked. Examining the door, he found that there were four locks, all of which had to be unlatched before they could escape.

He heard something behind them. Peeking over his shoulder, he watched Charlize ascend from the basement, brandishing the knife he himself had chosen.

CHAPTER 104

Four locks.

Two People.

One killer.

Eric aimed the Glock at Charlize. It was empty, but she didn't know it. Perhaps it would grant him and Samantha enough time to unlock the door.

He heard Samantha fumble with the locks; she worked slowly, weak with loss of blood.

Charlize continued toward them at a brisk pace. "Why can't you see the truth?" she said, her voice hollow. Almost lifeless. In her fist, the toothed blade swung like a deadly pendulum.

Every second that ticked by, Samantha grew heavier; and therefore, him weaker. Remembering the way he had fired the gun earlier at the man in the dark suit, Eric knew that even if the gun had still contained bullets, he'd probably miss Charlize anyway.

He felt Samantha grow more panicky. Her nervous hands working on the locks sounded like scuttling beetles, their many legs tick-ticking the floor.

"Don't you know I love you?" As she walked, she didn't appear concerned that he trained a lethal weapon at her.

Another lock clicked open. Charlize was too close. They didn't have time open the other two. If Samantha was in better shape, they could fight Charlize off, but in her condition, Samantha was a weakness, not a strength. If the serial killer reached them now, she could butcher them easily.

The gun was empty. How could he have been so stupid? Why didn't he save a few bullets? He strained his mind, as if he could push bullets into the Glock with only his thoughts.

"Stay where you are?" he said, hoping to bluff her. Time. They needed time.

"No, I think I'll come."

"I swear I'll shoot. Don't be foolish." He hoped his acting didn't sound as fake to her as it did to his own ears. Tick, tick, tick, Samantha kept working on the locks. Her breath was a low, shallow wheeze. Was she working slower now than before? Letting his eyes drop to the floor, he saw the puddle of blood. How much had she lost?

"No you won't," Charlize said, striding down the hall. "If there's one thing I know, it's guns. Especially my own. You're out of bullets."

CHAPTER 105

At first Samantha resisted, perhaps not understanding what he was doing, perhaps not knowing a killer stalked so close with a wicked blade in her tight fist; then relaxing, her muscles loose, she let Eric jerk her away from the door with only one lock to go.

Samantha felt heavier. As he half-drug her across the entranceway, under the snowflake light of the chandelier, he wondered if the weight he felt was her body mass only or also the responsibility to keep her alive.

He focused straight ahead because he didn't want to know how close Charlize was to them. At any moment, he expected her to suddenly appear, stabbing one of them in the back. A knowing chill rippled through him.

How close? How close? Instead of answering his own question, he hobbled with Samantha toward the dead body in the other room. Other than the hallway and front door, which weren't options anymore, this room offered the only way out of the foyer.

When they made it to the body, Eric risked a look back.

Charlize had vanished.

Where had she gone? Another path through the house? Was she playing with them, like a hunter waiting for a wounded animal to die?

"Eric," Samantha said, pain apparent in her voice. "The gun."

The gun? He had forgotten about the other man's gun until now. Lowering both himself and Samantha, he snagged the firearm. It was heavier than the Glock and he hoped that meant it was a more powerful weapon.

Before struggling from a squat to a standing position, Eric viewed the corpse, who, in his black suit, was coffin-ready. Three bullet holes peppered the man's chest. Bloodstains, like a psychotic's version of tie-die, soaked through his white undershirt.

Eric shook his head and blinked his eyes. He had killed another human being. Although he knew it was in self-defense, and that no jury in the world would convict him of murder, he still felt like a cold-blooded killer.

He lifted himself and Samantha to their feet. Where to now? They could try the door again, maybe make it outside now that he had a gun. But what if Charlize waited in the hallway? Would he have time to shoot? One of his hands had to help Samantha along; the other held the gun. Samantha would have to unbolt the last lock by herself. Did she have the strength left in her?

As if the loss of blood pushed her into a realm between life and death, where reading minds was common practice, Samantha said, "Not the front door. We don't have a car key. I can't walk very far."

They *didn't* have a car key, which meant, even if they did manage to unlock the front door, they would have to walk to safety. From the long drive up to her house, Eric realized that Samantha would bleed out long before they reached help.

They had to stay in the house.

CHAPTER 106

Wielding the bigger, bulkier gun, with his arm around Samantha's shoulder, with her blood dribbling on his pants and sneakers, Eric staggered through the room just outside the entranceway.

Stepping into this room was like crossing the threshold between past and present: antique bookshelves, chairs, and pewter lamps left him with the impression of a scene out of *Gone With the Wind*.

"You're doing good," he encouraged her, struggling across an intricately designed red carpet. In truth, she seemed less able to walk now than a few minutes ago. He wondered how long before her legs gave out completely.

Worry tightened his face. Watching her out of the corner of his eye, pushing forward to an unknown destination, he saw her eyelids droop.

He shook her lightly. "Stay awake. I know it's hard. But you've got to keep your eyes open."

He thought she nodded.

Exiting this room, entering another, Eric detected a sound. A creaking that seemed to come from somewhere close. He swept his gaze in every direction, following with the gun, as if it were a metal detector for serial killers.

His first thought was Charlize: somewhere in the house, slipping from room to room like a wraith, undetectable, translucent.

Listening, he heard no more movement. No floorboards creaking under heavy footsteps. No clothes scratching whisper-quiet against the walls. No breathing. If Charlize were close, Eric had no way of knowing it.

Samantha groaned. Her eyelids had slipped closed. How much blood had she lost? His hand trembled as he brushed it against her cheek.

"Samantha... Samantha."

Her eyes snapped open wide then closed just as quickly. In a thick, grainy voice, she said, "I can walk."

They continued into the room, this one as modern as the last one was antique. Everything was made of steel and glass. Tall, skinny lamps hooked over bright red and yellow couches.

Halfway through what Eric labeled "The Jetson's" room, Samantha collapsed.

Strength sapped from constant exertion over the last half-hour, muscles burning, neck tight, Eric struggled under her weight, wavered and then fell. He hit the carpet first, Samantha landing on top of him.

He reached around her waist and placed his hand on her belly. When her stomach rose and fell under his palm, he sighed. *At least she was alive.*

Then all the lights in the house went out.

CHAPTER 107

Charlize stood in her Mud Room, flipping the gray switches in her breaker box to the OFF position. Throughout the house, rooms went dark. No reason to make it easy on them to escape.

She still held out hope that she could influence Eric. Opening up to truth required time. She had given him 16 months, waiting patiently for him to discover what she already knew about their past together, while making contacts and building alliances, preparing for this moment. Certainly, she could allow him a few more hours.

Once she turned all the lights off, Charlize crept into the kitchen, where she tossed the toothed, blood-crusted knife into the trash in favor of a Chef's knife.

Ten inches long, its curved blade perfect for mincing and chopping. She gripped it by the handle, admiring its perfection, adjusting to its weight. It was by far her weapon of choice.

Moving stealthily out of the kitchen into a short hallway, she listened for movement. She had heard the loud crash a few minutes before, but nothing since. Had they fallen and not gotten back up? Or were they being quiet, realizing their vulnerability in the now shadowed house?

From the noise earlier, she knew their general direction. But her house was huge. That could be an advantage or a disadvantage.

Lucky for her, she knew the design of her house so well she could picture each room in her mind. Even if she were blind, she would be able to easily navigate around sharp edges and blunt objects.

The hall branched off into a number of other rooms. She chose the second one on the right, angling her way toward Eric and Samantha.

Even with her patience, remaining optimistic proved difficult for Charlize. She couldn't shake the idea that Eric cared deeply for the other woman. He protected Samantha when he should be protecting her – his true love.

Loving her was his destiny. Loving him was hers.

Charlize heard movement deeper in the house. She hurried toward it.

CHAPTER 108

"We're here." Chief Baxter slapped James on the leg.

The driver veered off the main road onto a bumpy, dirt path clogged with stones. He slowed down and turned off the headlights so the roar of the engine or the lights wouldn't alert anyone of their arrival.

"Remember, no problems okay?" the Chief said.

Stretching his neck to peer down the dirt road, James answered without looking in the Chief's direction. "Yeah. No problems."

"I'm serious."

"I'm sure you are."

The police car struck two head-pounding bumps as the Chief put the walkie-talkie to his ear and asked for a description of the scene. Most importantly, had anything changed? New information sometimes altered the plan. Other times, it demolished it.

Dropping the walkie-talkie to his lap, Chief Baxter turned to his best detective, who was still searching the darkness for people to hurt. Possibly kill.

"There are two cars instead of only one," the Chief said, repeating the information the other officers already at the location just fed him. "Gunshots were heard and the lights in the house just went out."

James raised his eyebrows. "Clever." A bump in the road vibrated through the car. "Clever?"

"Whoever is in the house," he explained, "knows they are better off with no lights. It puts them in the advantage."

"What are you saying?"

Sitting back in his seat, Wolfe said, "Whoever is in the house either knows we are here or thinks someone is here. And my informant isn't pulling the strings."

"You got all that from a few gunshots in a dark house?"

James ignored him, talking mostly to himself. "My informant isn't that smart. But I can think of one person who is."

Back seat squishing under him, Chief Baxter stared dumbly

out the window at the passing shrubbery. "Who?" he asked, his bottom lip quivering.

"Have you checked on Samantha and Eric?"

"They're safe. I've separated them and put them under 24-hour police protection." He avoided James' gaze, his hesitant tone revealing doubt.

"Have you checked on them lately?"

"No. Why?"

The last few puzzle pieces clicked into place.

James sat up and locked eyes with him. "Our serial killer is in the house."

CHAPTER 109

After gently sliding out from beneath Samantha, after waiting for sounds of approaching footsteps in the dark house, Eric leaned close, whispering in her ear.

"I'm going to pick you up. We've got to keep going."

Her response was a weak nod, but when he put his arms under her arms, she helped him stand up. Once they were vertical, Eric tugged on her as if to say, "Let's go this way."

Through the room, where corners of furniture jutted out dangerously in the dark, they maneuvered slowly, Eric searching for...

What was he searching for? He needed a way out of here. Keys, maybe. But how would he know what the keys went to? He could find a set of keys, make it outside to the vehicles, only to discover that none of them worked.

Besides, Charlize hunted them. He couldn't risk the noise and time it would take to find keys, slog through the house, go outside, get Samantha in a vehicle and try to start it. They needed something faster.

A phone.

If he found a phone, they could call 911. Then, they'd just have to survive until the police arrived.

But Charlize knew what she was doing. She'd probably cut the phone lines already. However, she was also cocky, perhaps *too* cocky. Maybe she never thought it would come to this. Maybe she wasn't prepared.

He did have a gun. After they contacted the police, he could find a room, lock the door and hunker down.

Approaching the doorway into the next room, every shadow seemed to hide something sinister: gray-haired hags crawling across the floor, chittering goblin-like from tongue-less mouths.

Eric bit his bottom lip and, carrying Samantha, stepped into the room. Smaller than the other rooms, and obscured in a deeper darkness, only the outlines of furniture were visible; he tried his best to follow a narrow path around them.

Straining his eyes, peering at every piece of furniture, Eric looked for a phone, or something that resembled a phone. When he didn't see one, he kept moving toward what he thought was another doorway into yet another room.

When they reached the doorway, he found out that he was wrong. It didn't lead to another room at all; instead, a narrow staircase rose in a steep incline into blacker darkness.

Samantha moaned, as if rejecting the idea of a climb in her condition. She could barely walk. How could she make it up the stairs?

Behind them, somewhere in the house, somewhere close, Eric heard a floorboard creak.

CHAPTER 110

His nerves rattled like ice cubes in an empty glass. Not daring to retrace their path through the house, the only options were to stay here and defend themselves or attempt the stairs.

Although Eric's eyes adjusted to the dark, he didn't think a gunfight in this small space would be to his advantage – even if he had good aim. And there were no disillusions there.

The prospect of heaving Samantha up the staircase seemed just as ludicrous. Even if they reached the top of the stairs, which Eric strongly doubted they could do, there was no guarantee that they would be in any better situation than down here. Yet, he must decide. Quickly.

Placing his lips next to her ear, he said, "We have to take the stairs. I'll need your help. As much as you can give me."

At least in the narrow confines of the staircase, his chances of shooting Charlize improved. Surely, even he could hit a close target. After all, he had killed the guy in the suit.

Standing at the foot of the staircase, Eric decided on the best way to get up the stairs while protecting themselves. He faced Samantha, kissed her lips softly to let her know everything would be all right, and then hooked his arms under hers.

Stepping backwards, he rose to the first step, pulling Samantha toward him, up the stairs. If Charlize appeared, he could easily move his arm and fire the gun.

He would only pull the trigger if he saw Charlize. He didn't know how many bullets were left in the chamber and he couldn't risk running out again. It was their only protection.

When he took another step backwards, Samantha lifted her foot, struggling to help him. Eric pulled her as she shifted her weight forward. This might work, he thought, already raising his foot to the next step.

Two more steps up and Eric was convinced: they would reach the top, find a room with a phone, lock themselves in, call 911 and wait. They would survive

About to step backwards again, he felt Samantha droop in his arms. She almost tipped away from him, down the stairs, but he caught her. Clenching his teeth, straining his back, he kept her from falling.

He jerked her toward him, plopping down on a stair. Her head rested against his chest, her body between his legs. To an outsider, they might look like two lovers in a passionate embrace.

Breathing hard, Eric clung tightly to Samantha. They were halfway up the narrow staircase, lost in the dark maze that was this house. He knew now that they couldn't make it up the stairs. Or back down them.

Flipping her over, Eric placed the gun in both her hands. She grasped it as if it were a magical artifact that would heal her bullet wounds and return her lost blood.

She now lay on her back, on the stairs, the gun aimed at the foot of the staircase. He bent down once again to whisper in her ear. "I love you. If you see anyone, anyone at all, shoot."

CHAPTER 111

Hesitating, Eric stared down the staircase into the room below, which was now robed in shadows. At any moment, Charlize could appear, swinging her blade in mad arcs. How could he leave Samantha here?

Here to die, completed the unspoken end of the question. If he left to search the second floor for a phone, even for a moment, he felt as if he were abandoning her. Logic demanded that he go and search; but, next to emotion, logic is a stumbling, weak-kneed master.

And so he hesitated, kneeling on the staircase above Samantha. She had drawn up her knees and on them rested her hands, which held the gun.

The musty smell of blood filled the stairwell. Inhaling it, paranoia suddenly rippled through Eric, flooding him with the irrational fear that the stench would attract Charlize, as if she were not human at all, but like the skeleton-man in the basement, a malevolent entity sprung from hell.

Yet, she did not appear, melting from the shadows or stepping into view via the room below.

Samantha twisted her neck and craned her head back to look up at Eric. He met her eyes, now twin gray mirrors in which his reflection wavered and swam and shifted.

"Go," she said, the one word released from her mouth with a tremor of effort.

Eric shook his head. He thought she was going to say something again, but her voice cracked and dissolved, restraining her to silence. In her eyes, below his reflection, he saw something else – courage and a deep resolve to survive.

Abruptly he realized that his fear of abandoning Samantha masked his real cowardice of being alone in this house. He was not worried about her, but about himself. Unable to move, stuck on the staircase, bleeding to death, she exhibited more bravery than him.

Leaning down to kiss her brow, Eric thought about saying, "I won't be long," but no words or phrases of assurance felt right. So he said nothing. As he turned from her, Samantha let go of the gun with one hand, moved it to her side, slid it into her pants pocket and retrieved a small, black box. The tape recorder.

Not understanding why she kept it in her pocket, or why she pulled it out now, Eric watched her wobbly hand transport it to his own. He took it because the ritual seemed important to her.

Samantha returned her hand to the gun.

Eric stared at the device, a visual reminder of everything they've been through in the past week, before continuing on his task. On his hands and knees, with no weapon, he crawled up the stairs to find a phone.

CHAPTER 112

Out of the pitch-blackness of the night ran a white-faced police officer waving his hands above his head. The driver braked to a halt. In the backseat, Chief Baxter rolled down his window.

"What   it   is?" The officer outside lowered his face to the open window. "Someone spotted a woman with a gun. In the house."

"When?" James leaned close to the Chief to hear the answer. Since hearing about the gunshots earlier, he feared that meant there was gun fighting. His mind followed its natural detective's path, as conclusion after conclusion collided in a domino effect of trouble.

"Just a moment ago or I would've called you." The officer's face twitched and his fingers held the car door in a death grip.

James said, "We've got to get into the house as fast as possible."

Peering through the open window, the police officer eyed him and then said. "Aren't you James Wolfe?"

"Yeah, so?"

"I heard about the fire. Aren't you supposed to be in the hospital?" His vise grip on the door eased a little, but his face continued to twitch.

Chief Baxter rolled his eyes. "Let's go," he barked to the driver. A moment later, they rolled forward, the police officer outside keeping pace until they braked to a halt again three hundred yards later.

First out of the vehicle, James took off toward the house, which was now partly visible. He heard car doors creak open.

"Where are you going?" The Chief stuttered out behind him.

Not looking back, James said, "To break my promise to you."

CHAPTER 113

An antique grandfather clock clamored through her house with one loud, reverberating *Gong.*

Charlize froze, listening, thinking she heard movement from a few rooms over, near the small staircase. The thrill of the chase ran along her arms, her spine, her neck. Oh, how she loved this part.

And yet, her stomach twisted with anxiety because of Eric. He was not coming around. She had been sure, that by now, he would have realized his true identity. But this false Eric somehow hung on, stifling her precious lover, smothering his impulses.

She clung to the image of him poised over her plaything in the cellar, ready to cut him. It was just a start, but from his willingness she glimpsed his true nature – if she ever doubted who he was, she would never doubt again.

More noise. It did originate from the direction of the staircase. Were they trying to escape out a window? Or hide upstairs? Intrigued, she proceeded toward the noise.

Through one room after another, she continued to listen. She heard more movement and... breathing, yes breathing.

As she drew closer, a mutiny of memories long imprisoned in the vaults of her mind escaped into the open field of her conscious thought. Hurrying through dark streets in London; picking a lock on a church door; meticulously removing the toes of a small child who lay screaming on a bedroom floor; tearing open a man's chest and scooping out organs, one by one, with her bare hands.

She was used to these occasions, when memories of past lives lit upon her. They occurred frequently since she first, with the help of a pagan friend, opened her mind to receive all past life experiences. Her friend was loath to keep the door open, but Charlize wanted to know everything, every last detail because knowledge brought her closer to her destiny.

Mind alive with flashes of death scenes, she followed the breathing sounds into the small room with the stairs.

CHAPTER 114

Reaching the second floor, feeling for a door in the dark, jumping at the noise from the clock, Eric found a door handle. Twisting and opening it, he peered into a bathroom, fashioned from floor to ceiling in white marble. The toilet looked like a throne.

Because there was no phone in the bathroom, Eric proceeded to the next door, only a few feet down the short, narrow hallway. It was on the left also and opened to an office with a desk, bookshelves, a computer, and a phone. A phone!

He ignored the panoramic view of forests provided by a large window behind the desk. Grabbing the phone, a white cordless one, Eric punched in 911. He put it to his ear and heard silence. No dial tone. He tried the number again. Same result. He checked to see if the phone was plugged up and turned on properly. Maybe the computer hogged the only phone line.

After discovering that everything was plugged in properly, he replaced the phone on its plastic receiver. His heart sank. If this phone didn't work, most likely, none in the house functioned.

He leaned against the desk. What other options did he have? He could throw the computer chair through the window, or just open it, jump off the roof and get help or find a match, set the books on fire and try his hand at Morris Code.

Thinking about the books, Eric looked at them. Three titles on reincarnation; two on hypnosis, which reminded him of Samantha's gift of the tape recorder; one on anatomy.

The computer. How had he missed that idea? The computer put the world within reach – he could contact anyone, even the FBI or CIA.

Right now, anyone would do.

Standing behind the desk, he moved the mouse slightly. Nothing. Like the phone, it too was dead, leaving only one conclusion: all the power in the house must be out.

Next to the monitor leaned a framed picture of him in which he wore dark shades, a blue denim jacket, and a checkered button-down shirt. He was grinning at something outside the picture. Behind him, New York's Twin Towers touched an azure blue sky.

Twin Towers. The picture was taken before 9/11, on his trip to New York. What was that, two year ago?

The revelation swung like a clock's pendulum in his chest. Charlize had followed him for years, not months or weeks. How many more pictures of him existed in this house, in her demented possession?

What was he going to do anyway, e-mail the police? It might be hours before anyone checked for new emails. And he couldn't remember any of his family's e-mail addresses.

Eric stared at the black screen as if it were one of those pictures in which, after a considerable amount of time focusing, a hidden design suddenly appeared. No image leapt from the computer screen, however, and he turned to leave the room.

Then he heard the gunshot.

CHAPTER 115

Boom.

Eric reacted as if he'd trained all his life to move at the sound of gunshots. Whipping around the computer desk, he flew out of the room with its reincarnation textbooks and panoramic view of Indiana, and into the second floor hallway.

Unconcerned about creating noise, he thumped towards the top of the stairs. His temples throbbed. Both eyes hurt from constant strain. His mouth felt dry and hot.

At the top of the stairs, looking down, he witnessed his worst nightmare: Charlize bent over Samantha, driving a long knife into her belly, now into her chest, now into her face. Blood painted the walls a dark crimson.

Another gunshot rang up the stairwell. Eric blinked, wanting to force the image from his mind, as if, like Dorothy tapping her slippers together in *The Wizard of Oz*, the physical act would make everything better.

The bullet, if it was meant for Charlize, missed horribly. She continued stabbing-thrusting-plunging her knife. Underneath, unable to free herself and yet unable to resist her human instinct to fight, Samantha wriggled, causing the blade to twist and tug against her skin.

A scream burst through his fear-chapped lips. Eric flung himself down the stairs — anger, hate, shock, pain, fear and confusion blended together into a delirious concoction mixed by a bartender in Hell. And, tackling Charlize, he chugged it, tumbling to the small room below.

As they crashed at the foot of the stairs, Eric landed on his side. Something in his pocket pinched his leg, but the hard fall knocked the air out of his lungs cutting off a cry of pain.

Flipping him over, Charlize straddled his body, pressing down on his chest. She could easily strangle him, but she hesitated. The crazy woman was still trying to save him.

"She'll never have your baby now," she said between deep breaths.

"What baby?" He asked between clenched teeth, reaching into his pocket, feeling the hard, rectangular shape. *What was it?*

"Our baby."

The tape recorder.

Wrapping his hand around it, he yanked the tape recorder out and swung it like a brick at the side of her skull.

CHAPTER 116

James gripped the front door doorknob when he heard the first gunshot. In a chain, link after link of logic rattled through his mind: gunshot, conflict, opposing sides, Samantha and Eric, Charlize and the informant. The two vehicles in the driveway, jeep and blue impala, supported his mental argument.

Turning the knob and shoving the door, he found it locked. He cursed under his breath. If the front door wasn't made like the drawbridge of a castle, James might have kicked it open. Obviously, the builders designed the door to keep people out.

A second gunshot erupted from the west side of the house, rifled through the air, echoing even through the manufactured rock siding.

James took off in that direction, trampling over the flowerbed which hugged the perimeter of the residence, looking into windows, seeing nothing but closed blinds and dark curtains.

Behind him, from the edge of the woods, Chief Baxter whisper-yelled, "Wolfe, get back here. You need backup. You don't have a weapon."

He did need backup. And he didn't have a weapon. Unless you considered his hands and feet lethal weapons. If he beat some poor sucker to death, that's what the court would label them. When he discovered a way into the house, a jury may just have to make that distinction.

Tape recorder meets skull. The sound was a peculiar *clack*, like two stones thrust together.

Charlize fell to the side, screaming, hands scrubbing at her head as if she could somehow grasp the pain and tear it away. Rolling, reaching back for him, her fingers groped along his left arm.

Eric thought about using the tape recorder as a weapon again, but then glanced around for the knife, a tool more useful for causing damage than the recorder.

He spotted it a few feet away, crawled the distance, and curled two fingers around the handle before Charlize kicked him. Both the knife and the tape recorder flew out of his hands.

Most people in this situation would chase after the knife. Eric watched the tape recorder bounce across the carpeted room still intact and hit the wall. To him it was no longer a tape recorder, but the last gift from Samantha. As he scrambled to retrieve it, the thought of her swept him up in the only emotion stronger than hate: love.

Snatching it up, it occurred to him that her voice, her life, her hopes and dreams remained in the device. Their interaction, hours of it, and therefore a significant part of their relationship, immortalized. He clutched it against his chest, this symbol of their intimacy, this child.

Turning, he noticed Charlize rise to her feet, no longer scrubbing the pain from her head. "Strange. You hold the truth so dearly in your hands, yet you won't let it into your heart."

Still drunk with anger, he blurted out, "I know about the devil, but I don't let him in either."

"What devil? The only devils here are you and I."

"Speak for yourself."

Flipping her hair, as if this were an expensive dinner party, as if her golden tresses weren't caked in dried blood, Charlize said, "Doesn't matter. It is your destiny. You will become what you are, whether you resist or not."

"I'm in control." He breathed quickly and averted his eyes.

"You're a mess. But don't worry; we'll get you cleaned up." She stepped towards him.

"Stay away."

She froze, tilted her head to the side. "You are weak now, but I see power brewing inside you. You fight but you feel it, too."

"I don't feel a thing," he said, shaking his head. Yet he did feel it, he always had and it scared him to death. He pressed the tape recorder tighter against his chest.

"Why are you so afraid? Don't you want power?"

He did want power. He wanted the power to kill her, power to avenge Samantha, power to free himself from the shackles of his destiny.

Charlize stepped forward. In another place, in different clothes, blood cleaned off her face and throat, she would be beautiful, seductive, enthralling. Eric twitched, grasped the tape recorder tighter. The pressure against his chest must have pushed one of the buttons, because the tape recorder squealed like an angry, dying pig.

"Yes, I want power," he said, and for the first time in his life, he knew how to get it.

CHAPTER 117

"You're a terrible liar," Charlize said, her head still tilted to the side, taking another step closer to him. He pressed the STOP button, silencing the nasty squeal from the tape recorder.

Across the curtain-shrouded window moved a shadow. No, not a shadow. The silhouette of a person. *Who is that? Another one of Charlize's goons?*

"Look, the police," he said.

Charlize spun towards the window, through which neither she nor the trespasser outside could see. "What the—"

The silhouette disappeared beyond the window frame.

Eric ran toward the stairway in her moment of distraction, but she whipped around and grabbed his wrist before his feet touched even the first step. For her size, she was unusually strong.

"Where are you going?" she asked, yanking him backwards, away from the staircase. "Back to your lover? She's dead."

The words stung him as if huge wasps were latched to his back, digging their stingers into his spine. He smashed the tape recorder into her face. Blood sprayed his hand. Charlize's head jerked backwards, her hands flying instinctively to her face.

Eric wanted to continue beating her, but he knew she would eventually snap out of the spell that stopped her from hurting him. And when she did, he had no chance of winning. His only hope lay in the recorder.

Dashing up the stairs, he turned his eyes away from Samantha, stumbling the final few steps to the top. He resisted the urge to go back to Samantha, to see if by some divine miracle she survived the savage knifing. He knew the truth: she was dead. Days from now, if he got out of this house alive, he would grieve. Right now, however, grief remained a luxury he could not afford.

As he hurried down the hallway, Eric opened and slammed the door to the office with the unhelpful computer and dead phone, hoping to distract Charlize and give him the necessary time to complete what he needed to do.

Quiet as he could manage, he followed the hallway to the end.

He opened the door on the right only enough for him to squeeze through the crack. Inside, he shut the door behind him and punched the privacy lock on the doorknob. It was no security lock because anyone stronger than a flea could kick the door open. The lock, however, provided another ticket with which he hoped to purchase time.

CHAPTER 118

As night tarried on, as Chief Baxter and the other officers huddled in the woods, James trudged around the house, past the window he was certain connected to the room where the gunshots originated.

He passed by the window. Knowledge is power and he didn't want whoever was inside the house to know that he knew they were in that room. Therefore, he continued along the house for ten yards, until he was reasonably sure no one inside the room could peek out and see him standing there.

He heard people moving around inside the house, then a voice – a woman – but the windows and thick walls muffled her words into meaningless garble. More movement. Someone smacked someone else with something hard. Footsteps running up stairs.

All this information processed through his mind in an instant. An escape. Samantha or Eric, if they were in there, and he strongly clung to that hope, was fighting back. One of them fled up the stairs.

James lunged back toward the window, banging on the glass with both fists. If he could distract the enemy, probably Charlize, even for a moment, maybe then Eric and Samantha could survive.

Halfway up the stairs, nose burning from pain and bleeding from impact with the tape recorder, Charlize heard the windows rattle and froze. Someone was pounding on the window. Why? Who?

She had the terrifying feeling of an animal wandering through the forest about to step in a hunter's trap. Glancing up the stairs, she heard a door open and slam shut. Somewhere close. Her office?

Downstairs, the fool outside, who had already caused her to lose an opportune moment with Eric, still punched away at the glass. The windows were not inexpensive. Neither was her time with Eric.

Heading back down the stairs, Charlize scooped up the gun from Samantha's bloody lap. Now in the small room, she spread her feet in a shooter's stance and aimed the gun at the shadow on the other side of the window.

CHAPTER 119

With the door locked behind him, Eric carried the black tape recorder now smeared with Charlize's blood to the middle of the room decorated in different shades of blue. Baby blue carpet and wall paint broken by angles and clouds, a darker blue-maybe navy-coated the baby crib and two dressers. Dolls peered lifelessly from every surface in the room. Above the crib, secured to the ceiling by a blue cable, pictures of him dangled like a dream catcher.

On closer inspection, he noticed the pictures were of different places, of different times, spanning two years or more. One portrayed him standing in front of the multi-colored fountains in Nashville's famous Opryland Hotel.

If he had time, he would have checked each photograph, searching for the exact date and destination. He didn't have enough time, however, so he sat cross-legged in the middle of the room and placed the tape recorder on the baby blue carpet in front of him. Please still work, he prayed.

Turning it on, he heard Samantha's voice: "Go back, further and further, past your birth, further back before you were born." Thank God. He shuddered as he heard her smooth, hypnotic speech. With no time to grieve, he struggled to hold back tears.

Using the fast-forward button, he jumped ahead on the tape. The recorder purred in his hands. Again he punched the play button. Again, he heard Samantha's voice: "Tell me where you are?"

"Germany, 1814," he heard his voice answer.

Fast-forwarding again, because this wasn't the place on the tape he required to accomplish his task, Eric heard himself hiss, "Are you afraid of me?" He pressed the fast forward button. The tape whined.

When he played the tape again, he found his spot, although he had to rewind a few seconds. As he touched the record button with his finger, he noticed his pulse quicken. His hand froze, for a moment unable to go through with the necessary action.

Taking a slow, deep breath, Eric did his best to quiet his mind, pushing out all the troubling thoughts: Samantha, his past, and the consequences of what he was about to do. He had no idea if this would help or destroy him.

With one eye, he glanced at the pictures dangling over the baby's crib, expecting to see not himself anymore, but many faces of Charlize, somehow alive on the film and watching him.

The pictures had not changed and neither Charlize's nor his own photographed faces seemed to notice he was there.

Another deep sigh, then he pushed the button. Buzzing indicated the recording mechanism worked. He spoke quietly into the recorder: "Release all the skills and knowledge, but not the full personality." When he finished, he stopped the tape and rewound to the right spot. This was it, then.

He played the recorder and from its electronic brain Samantha said, "You are relaxed, more relaxed than you've ever been in any of our other sessions, so relaxed..."

Sitting cross-legged on the floor, Eric closed his eyes and listened as Samantha hypnotized him from the grave.

She heard silence from upstairs. Standing in her preferred shooter's position, with legs spread, weight shifted slightly forward toward the balls of her feet, Charlize aimed at the shadow outside her house. The shadow continued to beat her window, rattling it in its frame.

She could think of only one person who would be out there: James Wolfe, the persistent detective who should be three hundred miles away right now, hunting his wife's killer.

Somehow he must have figured out that it was a set up. But how had he traced her here, to her own house? Perhaps a homing device had been attached to Samantha or Eric. She didn't think that made sense because both of them were supposed to be hidden in police protection.

The only rational conclusion was that someone, the police most likely, had spotted her leaving the hotels with Samantha and Eric. They, in turn, alerted James before he fled the hospital. After going through the scenario again in her head, Charlize was certain that is what happened. But, she reminded herself, destiny is destiny, no matter how hard we fight against it.

If the detective was outside, then other law enforcement would also be on her premises. How many? How soon would they rush the house? It was locked, but that wouldn't keep the police out forever. She must save Eric quickly.

Training the gun at the shadow's head, Charlize pulled the trigger.

CHAPTER 120

"You have complete control of your body..."

Through the hidden chambers of his mind, Samantha's words echoed like God's own voice, direct and powerful. His body sat in the baby's room on the second floor of Charlize's house, but Eric's essence – what truly made him more than flesh and bones – had floated backwards through time to some other realm far removed from Indiana.

"Control of your limbs, complete control of yourself..."

Coldness washed over him as if he lay in the push and retreat of an ocean tide, white bubbles of foam popping all around.

"You are released..."

With a shudder, his eyelids fluttered open. His essence connected to his body once more, Eric pressed the stop button on the tape recorder, silencing Samantha's ghostly voice. He stood up in the blue room, surrounded by baby furniture.

Like the tide, two opposing forces pulled at him. One, the past; the other, the present. Love and hate. Forgiveness and revenge.

"I am in control," he said aloud to himself, even as another voice, loaded with rage contradicted him, *No, destiny is in control. Only destiny.* Ignoring the voice, he approached the bedroom door and unlocked it.

The round struck the bullet-resistant window with a sharp *clack*, leaving a small opening roughly its own size. Outside, the shadow slumped beneath the view of the window frame.

Charlize thought about releasing a few more rounds. She loved the feel and sound of shooting a gun, and right now she needed to relieve her stress. However, she didn't want to waste any bullets she might need later. Therefore, she waited to see if the shadow reappeared in the window.

When it didn't, she listened for sounds in the rest of her house. Although her residence offered up too many hiding places for her to be absolutely certain, she heard no one moving through the rooms. Certainly, she would hear someone breaking through a window or picking her door locks.

Then, she did hear something. A soft click. A door opening. Upstairs.

CHAPTER 121

Gunshot.

Downstairs.

Who had fired a gun? Charlize? Or the person outside?

His hand on the doorknob, Eric paused because, as if opening the door to the bedroom opened another door in his mind, knowledge tumbled into his head. Knowledge of guns, knives, hunting, identity theft, anatomy, forensics, police, torture and killing.

He pushed the door open wide enough for him to step through it into the hallway. Craned his neck. Listened. Nothing.

In the hallway now, he moved slowly, methodically. A hunter. Noise would arouse the suspicion of his prey, and that just wouldn't be helpful in the present circumstances. A funny tingle worked its way up his spine as he inched toward the top of the stairs.

If Charlize had fired the gun – and she remained the most promising candidate – that meant she was armed. He was not. Attacking an armed and trained killer would spice up the game, but he couldn't risk being shot and possibly dying before he got his hands on Charlize.

Eric controlled his breathing. The creepy voice inside his head whispered, *Release yourself to your destiny*. It was something Charlize would say, and for that reason alone he resisted the words.

He thought about entering the other rooms in the hallway in search of a weapon. Deciding, however, that such an action would create too much noise, he slid closer to the top of the stairs.

You can't have my knowledge without me, the voice, which he attributed to his past lives, said. I'm taking over, little by little, but I'm taking over. Soon, there'll be none of you left. Only me. Only me.

Eric hoped the voice was bluffing, but there was no way to be sure. He had tempted fate with his bold move to hypnotize himself and, good or bad, he must deal with the consequences.

Placing his back to the wall, he listened. Breathing. Downstairs.

He waited, because that's what good hunters did. They waited, waited until the opportune time; and then they struck hard and fast and with no regrets. Unlike most hunters, Eric didn't have all morning to wait for the perfect shot at the perfect animal. He had minutes. Maybe.

He heard footsteps on the stairs.

CHAPTER 122

Listening to the footsteps climb the stairs and the breathing grow louder, his back against the wall, what was once a tingle up his spine became a throb. Eric grasped his pants with both hands, then released the bunched up jeans. He needed free hands for what might happen next.

More footsteps. More breathing. Both closer, closer... until they were almost at the top of the stairs with him.

Soon, the voice within him whispered. *It'll just be me very soon.* Forcing the voice back, hoping he could act before the Other Eric took control of his limbs, Eric spun into the stairwell, startling Charlize, who raised but didn't fire her gun. He took advantage of her hesitancy.

Striking at her throat, his knuckles pressed deep into her larynx. She choked and gaped at him, wide-eyed with shock.

He stabbed at her solar plexus with one hand flat, fingers strait and bunched together, a move culled from his recently gained reservoir of hand-to-hand combat. A spear-hand strike, used mostly in martial arts, but effective in any close encounter with an opponent.

Holding her throat with one hand, Charlize blocked his attack with her gun-wielding hand. Still, she didn't use the weapon. Instead, she shoved the muzzle into his gut.

"Downstairs, now."

"No."

Digging the gun into his stomach, she said, "What did you say?"

"I said, 'No.' I won't go downstairs."

"I'll shoot you." Her voice was still shaky from his punch.

"No you won't"

"How do you know for sure? I've done it many times before?"

Grimacing from the pain in his gut, he said, "Not to me." Eric kicked her in the shin, throwing himself against the side of the stairwell as she squeezed off a round into the upstairs wall. The bullet would have torn a hole straight through his small intestines.

An instinctive action on her part, not a willing defiance of her love for him.

Grabbing her wrist with one hand, her shoulder with the other, he shoved her backwards, down the stairs. He went with her, tumbling over Samantha to the room below. Before they hit the bottom of the stairs, Charlize fired two more rounds, both of which missed Eric and sank into the stairway walls.

He managed to remain on top of her even as they hit the carpet. Charlize still held the gun, so he twisted her wrist, wrenching the weapon from her grip. She let out a catlike screech as her hand bent at an unnatural angle.

When he reached for the gun, she kneed him between his legs. Eric buckled over, sharp needles of pain making a pincushion of his groin.

She pushed him to the side, slithering from beneath him, probably going for the gun. With on hand, he latched on to her ankle and tried to pull her back towards him. For a moment, his vision blurred. When it cleared, he was looking into Charlize's eyes. He felt the cold muzzle of a gun against his temple.

He released her ankle.

"Get up and come with me."

He stood up.

"Something's changed about you. I don't know what, but something..." she said, catching her breath and leading him out of this small room into another larger one.

Eric glanced at the window now decorated with a bullet hole. He wondered if the bullet also hit someone outside.

"Keep moving," she prodded

The house remained dark, but Eric's eyes had adjusted and he could see to avoid furniture. They walked through a few more rooms before Charlize spoke again.

"Through the kitchen, out onto the deck. We don't have much time."

Eric was thinking the same thing, because the voice inside his head repeated the two words, *Only me,* over and over again, like a yogi's mantra. *Only me. Only me.*

As they passed through the kitchen, Eric noticed the array of weapons available: knives, heavy pots and pans, marble vases, China plates fastened to the wall. Each item, plucked from its position, could be turned into a lethal tool.

Only me. Only me.

He must turn the tables and gain the upper hand. But how?

Charlize held a gun to the back of his head. This time, if he tried anything, he feared she would shoot him.

Spilling onto the wooden deck, he said, "I understand."

"What?"

"That's what's different about me. I understand now."

She pressed the muzzle of the gun harder against the back of his skull, as to say, *keep walking*. Obeying, he continued forward, stopping between two wooden tables, both encircled with wooden chairs and topped with umbrellas. She hit the back of his head again with the gun. He walked to the edge of the deck, which appeared to span the entire width of the house, and placed both hands on the railing, also wooden.

From the deck, Eric looked out on the Indiana countryside – hills, forests, and in the distance, a smattering of houses lit up in lights. Peering over the railing, Eric gulped at the long drop.

"Turn around."

He did.

Staring into his eyes, still holding the gun at his head, she said, "Yes, something has changed."

"I told you. I understand now." For clarity, he added, "About us."

Charlize seemed to consider this for a moment; then shook her head, slowly, back and forth. "No. You don't. Not completely. This is your last chance. Accept your destiny or die."

CHAPTER 123

Only me. Here I come.

The throb along his spine became a tremor. An icy finger with the flesh peeled back from the bone gently rubbed the back of his neck. The finger of death. Shuddering, Eric leaned against the wooden railing and found it sturdy.

No time. If he didn't act now, the Other Eric would take control and he would lose his chance to avenge Samantha forever.

"So what's it going to be?" Charlize asked again. "Death or destiny?"

"Destiny," he said. As the word left his lips, he flipped one hand toward her face, blinding and distracting her while his other hand ripped the gun from her grasp before she had time to pull the trigger. Turning the weapon on her, he smirked. "Just not the destiny you want."

"I love you," she pleaded. "Why don't you remember?"

"I do remember. I just don't want it to happen again." He gripped the gun tighter.

"But we're so great together. Our family is great."

Here I come.

No time. "Sorry, there's not going to be any family."

If you kill her, you are giving in to me. You'll become me.

Was that true? Would he become what he hated? "No I won't," he answered out loud.

Charlize regarded him strangely. "You won't what?" She appeared more sad then afraid.

"I won't become my past." He spoke this out loud, too, but he said it to both Charlize and the Other Eric.

"You have no choice."

"This is my choice." He pulled the trigger.

CHAPTER 124

The gun cylinder clicked empty.

His smirk faded from his face. A pitchfork of fear stabbed through his lungs, gouging his heart. Dropping the gun, hearing it clatter on the deck, he leaned back against the wooden railing for support.

Dizzy, as if on a spinning-wheeling-whirling carnival ride, Eric heard the maniac voice in his head laughing at him.

So close. All he needed to do was pull the trigger, shoot Charlize, kill her. And then he would be free from his past lives forever. Free to be himself, from becoming a serial killer. At least, that was his theory. He had no idea if that was what would have happened. Or if, by murdering her he would become the killer, as the voice in his head promised. It wouldn't have mattered to him as long as he had killed Charlize.

He felt her grab one of his arms and twist it as she shoved her shoulder into his ribs. Suddenly, his feet no longer touched the deck. Balanced on Charlize's back, he rolling forward, over her shoulder, over the wooden railing.

She let go of his arm.

Flailing his arms, he grasped the bottom of the deck with one hand. But the weight of his body jerked him downward and he couldn't hold on. His fingers felt like they were ripped from his hand as he let go of the deck. He hurtled backwards, down the sloping tube of the night.

As he fell, wind whipping his body, the dark sky seemed malignant with tumor-filled black clouds.

The voice inside his head no longer laughed, as if it, too, realized the approaching doom.

Instead, his mind overflowed with thoughts about Samantha, about their first meeting, the experiences they shared, the love they developed. At least he would be with her. Whatever mysterious realm existed beyond the thin fabric of this life, and he thought he had a pretty good idea of what it was – a place of hope and peace, devoid of serial killers and pain – at least they would be together.

As he hit the ground, he had one final thought before a darkness blacker than anything he'd ever known erased even his mind.

Together, in death, they would outrun destiny.

CHAPTER 125

Nine months later, in Johnstown, Pennsylvania, Charlize laid on her back on a hospital bed, dressed in nothing but a white bare-backed hospital gown, surrounded by three nurses and one doctor, who cheered her on as she groaned, clenched her teeth and pushed out a baby.

When they said her name, it was not Charlize, but Jasmine. In the past nine months she had changed her identity. It was not the first time and probably would not be the last.

As Jasmine, she moved from Indiana to Pennsylvania, slipping out of the wild police search continued even now by detective James Wolfe. Her bullet scraped his head, but had not killed him.

The only time she risked returning to Indiana was for Eric's funeral, although she disguised herself as just another mourner in a black dress.

That night, she returned to the cemetery. Alone, she knelt beside Eric's grave and spoke at length about their future together, how much she loved and missed him and how wonderful it will be when they see each other again. She wept bitterly.

"Push, Jasmine push," the doctor said in the present. "I see a head."

A month or two after arriving in Johnstown, she started throwing up in the morning. When she also gained ten pounds even on her strict diet and exercise regimen, she reluctantly bought a pregnancy test from Wal-Mart. She had slept with so many men in the past year that it was not surprising when the test proved positive. She was having a child.

If it were a girl, her name would be Destiny; a boy, his name would be Fate. Refusing to know the gender before birth, Charlize trusted fortune to decide.

"Keep pushing. You're doing great," one of the nurses encouraged.

She clearly remembered giving birth in many of her other lives, but the memory of pain, like any emotion, faded quickly. And she never remembered experiencing pain like this.

"Almost out," the doctor said. Charlize wondered if he meant the Toyota-sized object that must be squeezing out of her or an actual child. She dug her fingers into the hospital bed.

"Come on, come on," one of the blond-haired nurses repeated. The soon-to-be-mother thought the nurse might break out a pair of pom-poms and do a cheer.

In a burst of pain that felt like a track full of racing horses galloping over her stomach – with spiked hoofs – the doctor lifted a baby into her view. "Congratulations. It's a boy!" he said, cleaning the newborn.

Once the nurses checked her son's health, the doctor snipped its umbilical cord and handed him to Charlize wrapped in a warm blue towel. Exhaustion settling through her bones, she took him in her arms, wondering what would become of her child.

For some reason her mind went back to the death of the pregnant woman in the parking lot. The woman's desperate plea rang in her head: *Please God, save my baby.* She had hoped that event would have lead to a new life with Eric, but here she was, starting a new life on her own. Emotion welled up inside Charlize as she looked on her newborn.

"Fate," she whispered, letting the word play on her tongue. Looking him over, her breath caught in her throat. Clearly visible between his neck and shoulder blade was a familiar brown mole.

Just like the one on Eric.

CHAPTER 126

Darkness.

Pain.

She felt the blow against her face, light but painful. Her head lolled to the right.

Another slap. What's going on? Where am I?

"Hey, you awake? You awake?"

Charlize lifted her head, tried to open her eyes. Blinked. Some of the darkness receded. The blurred image of a man stood over her.

"You awake?"

"Ungh."

Someone slapped her twice again. Her head lolled back and forth.

"You awake?"

She blinked and more of the darkness receded. "What happened?"

A stocky man with a moustache bent over her. "I'm Detective James Wolfe. You're in the hospital. And now you're under arrest."

"What? How the—" She jerked up on the hospital bed, but the detective pulled a gun out of nowhere and pointed it at her chest while a handcuff clicked over her left wrist.

Charlize whirled in that direction, meeting the dead stare of another cop. Where had he come from? How could this be happening? My baby? Her gaze quickly snapped from one person to the next. The unknown cop to Detective Wolfe to... Oh my God...

The third person in the room waved. "Hi, Charlize."

"How?" she stuttered out. "You... you're supposed to be dead."

Eric smiled. "Oh, I'm very much alive actually."

"I went to your funeral."

"A funeral," Wolfe corrected. "You went to a funeral. It was staged." He grinned. "It's kind of ironic because we got the idea from you."

Charlize moved her gaze from the Detective to Eric, then back to Wolfe. Her chest and neck tightened and her cheeks burned with anger.

"When we remembered all the identities you and Eric had shared in other lives, the plan basically fell in our lap. After Eric's fall, we rushed him to the nearest hospital. We convinced the doctors to release a report that he had died and had the ME confirm it after a fake autopsy. Meanwhile, we hid Eric the best we could. We knew you had bought it when you showed up at the funeral. It was simply a matter of keeping tabs on you after that."

She turned to Eric, who she suddenly noticed had been reclining in a chair the whole time. "But the fall. You should have died."

Eric nodded. "You're right. In fact, the drop would have killed me if a paramedic team wasn't already in place nearby. Somebody had thought ahead. I don't remember who." His eyes looked far away for a moment, but then he shook his head. "Anyway, I broke four ribs, my left arm and both my legs in the fall. It's a miracle I can still walk."

"I don't believe in miracles."

"You don't have to," Wolfe said. "Not where you're going."

The unknown cop dragged her out of the hospital bed. "It's time to go now, Charlize," he said with a lisp.

She struggled but rose to her feet. "I'll tell you when it's my time to go, Lisp Boy."

"Shut up," the cop muttered, but then hung his head. Black hair fell over his face.

"Where's my child?"

"We'll take care of him," Wolfe said. "Don't you worry. We'll make sure he never knows what his mother was."

As he and Detective Wolfe led her from the room, Eric stood up and slowly limped behind them. He winced every few steps.

In the doorway of the bedroom, Charlize stopped, thinking of something.

"Samantha."

Wolfe's eyes narrowed. "What?"

"Samantha." She turned and spoke at Wolfe and Eric. "She's dead and she'll always be dead. I may have to live in prison, but you both have live with *that*." She was about to turn back around when she caught James shaking his head.

Her gut felt hollow. "What? Don't tell me she survived, too. That's impossible."

"That as it may be," Wolfe said, "She's alive. So you get no satisfaction from her death, either." He glanced back at Eric.

"You're not telling me something." Charlize studied Eric's face, now covered in a thick, brown beard. He was still as stunning as ever and she inwardly groaned.

Eric shifted his weight from foot to foot and then said, "She's on life support. I don't know why I'm telling you that, but she is. She's been on life support since your attack. But I'm hopeful."

"Ah," she said. "So there is some satisfaction left for me after all."

"I'm hopeful," Eric repeated.

"So are the people in hell, but that doesn't mean they're getting out."

"Enough!" Wolfe said. The cop with the lisp shoved their prisoner into the hallway. Detective Wolfe followed with the gun. "You coming, Eric?"

"No. There's something I need to do."

Later that night, Eric sat in a private room in Baptist East hospital in Louisville, KY, gently stroking the hand of the patient who lay motionless in the hospital bed beside him, a feeding tube jutting unnaturally out of her beautiful mouth. Every few minutes he had to look away. The sight was too painful.

As he massaged her knuckles, he whispered to her the story of catching Charlize in Pennsylvania, hoping that somehow she could understand. When he finished, he brought her hand up to his mouth and softly kissed her fingers. "It's over," he said. "It's over."

About the Author

Christopher Kokoski lives in Southern Indiana with his beautiful wife, daughter, and their dog. He is currently working on his next novel.

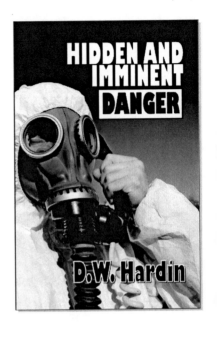

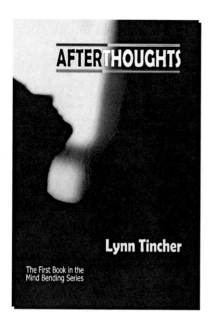

AFTERTHOUGHTS
by Lynn Tincher

Detective Paige Aldridge was found beaten and without any memories of the previous few months. When her nephew is found dead a year later, she begins to have terrifying flashbacks, plus visions of the murders of her own family! As her loved ones begin falling prey to a serial killer, Paige believes that she must be going mad. With her family dying around her and dark suspicions forming in her mind, Paige has to pull the pieces together before it's too late. [Psychic Crime Thriller, ages 14+]

LEFT IN THE DARK
by Lynn Tincher

Paige's adventures continue as she learns more of her developing powers, while she deepens her relationships with her partner and her sister. Can she regain control of her own mind before the powers that threaten to tear her apart claim her sanity and the life of a ten year old girl? Past, present, and future all collide with fear in this chilling sequel. [Psychic Crime Thriller, ages 14+]

CIRCLE OF PREY

by Marlene Mitchell

Ambition. Wealth. Greed. Power.
Truths turning to lies, father
against son, friends becoming
enemies, predator turning into
prey and the circle continues.
Pitting man against the largest
and one of the smartest animals
on the planet makes for an
interesting turn of events as you
follow the journey of Jakuta, a
bull elephant who is the ultimate
prey.
[Modern Thriller, ages 14+]

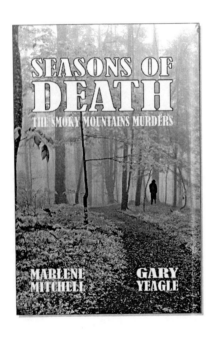

SEASONS OF DEATH

THE SMOKY MOUNTAINS MURDERS

by Marlene Mitchell, Gary Yeagle

In the fall of 1969 in the
mountains of eastern Tennessee, a
poor backwoods farmer and his
wife were brutally shot and killed
by four drunken hunters, along
with their three dogs, horse and
two fawns. The farmer's two young
sons managed to escape but were
unable to identify the killers. Now
decades later, someone has decided
to take revenge.
[Murder Mystery, ages 14+]

\ information can be obtained
ICGtesting.com
the USA
'244070414

9 781613 181091